Christopher Healy

Memoir of Christopher Healy

Principally taken from his own Memoranda

Christopher Healy

Memoir of Christopher Healy
Principally taken from his own Memoranda

ISBN/EAN: 9783337167431

Printed in Europe, USA, Canada, Australia, Japan

Cover: Foto ©Raphael Reischuk / pixelio.de

More available books at **www.hansebooks.com**

OF

CHRISTOPHER HEALY.

PRINCIPALLY TAKEN

FROM HIS OWN MEMORANDA.

PHILADELPHIA.
AT FRIENDS' BOOK STORE, 304 ARCH STREET.
1886.

THE following Memoirs of our beloved Friend Christopher Healy, it will be observed, are principally taken from his own memoranda and letters. His fervent zeal for the cause of Truth, so near his heart, is shown throughout the volume, and his memory is warmly cherished by those who still recall his loving council and gospel labors.

TABLE OF CONTENTS.

CHAPTER V.—1810 to 1812.

CHAPTER VI.—1812 to 1813.

CHAPTER VII.—1813 to 1814.

CHAPTER VIII.—1814 to 1824.

CHAPTER IX.—1824 to 1828.

JOURNAL

OF

CHRISTOPHER HEALY.

CHAPTER I.

BIRTH AND PARENTAGE. EARLY RELIGIOUS IMPRESSIONS. ATTENDS A MEETING OF FRIENDS FOR THE FIRST TIME IN HIS FIFTEENTH YEAR: OBSERVATIONS THEREON. SUCCESSFULLY OPPOSES THE DOCTRINE OF PREDESTINATION. CALLED UPON TO ADOPT THE PLAIN LANGUAGE AND A PLAIN DRESS. RECEIVED INTO MEMBERSHIP WITH FRIENDS.

HAVING for some time believed it required to leave behind me a relation of the dealings and tender mercies of the Lord my God with me from my young years, for the encouragement of the sons and daughters of men who may set their faces Zionward; and also to bear my testimony, that the Lord will bless and favor all those who are obedient unto Him, with the reward of peace which this world cannot give nor take away, I commence this account.

I was born, according to records obtained, on the eighth day of the Tenth Month, one thousand seven hundred and seventy-three, at East Greenwich, in the State of Rhode Island. My parents were Joseph and Rachel Healy, who were accounted honest people; and who, when I was about a year old, removed to the State of Connecticut into a town since called Montville: where we lived about fourteen years. Before I was eleven years of age, I often felt, when alone, the judgment of the Lord upon me for my disobedience—the secret stirrings of the grace and truth of the Lord Jesus manifested in my heart. Which light did teach me what I should do, and what I should leave undone ; and when this judgment of God in my heart for sin and disobedience was felt, I promised amendment of life.

My parents not yet being so much concerned for our spiritual welfare as they ought, gave us too much liberty ; so that I, with some of my older brothers, went at times to places of diversion, where were music and dancing.— Oh! the mournful case of those that spend their precious time in this way. I have since believed there is no amusement more destructive to the precious seed sown in the heart, than this kind of diversion. Dear youth, remember these words. Oh, you parents, guard your tender offspring. Watch over their inclinations. Much may you do towards bringing them into an early acquaintance with God, by carefully watching the tender impressions on their minds, and faithfully discharging your duty, by instilling therein the great first principles of religion ; and that there is a God before whom all must give an account at the close of life. How many children there are whose minds call for good instruction; such as may be compared to bread to their state; if parents are careful to give in the Lord's fear, when openings may be made on their susceptible hearts, they will not be charged with giving them a stone ; but will be clear of their blood. I have mourned for the dear children, since I have come to riper years, in consideration of the neglect of parents and masters in not making the training of their children in the law of the Lord their constant care; and have remembered the inspired language, "Hear, O Israel: the Lord our God is one Lord: and thou shalt love the Lord with all thine heart, and with all thy soul, and with all thy might. And these words which I command thee this day shall be in thy heart: and thou shalt teach them diligently unto thy children, and shalt talk of them when thou sittest in thine house, and when thou walkest by the way, and when thou liest down, and when thou risest up."— Oh! dear parents, leave not your tender offspring exposed to the dangers that are in the world, lest you be cruel as the ostrich in the wilderness, that leaves her young exposed to the foot of every passer by.

After I was twelve years old my father hired me out to work at farming by the month; and being often alone and having many serious thoughts upon another world, I was well convinced that, if I died in sin, I could not be happy. And I well remember in a severe tempest accompanied with thunder and lightning, in the night season, when I was alone in bed, I had to examine into my state and situation by the light which did clearly shine, to show me how the case stood between me and my God. And finding myself not fit to leave the world, oh! how faithfully did I promise, if the Lord would be pleased to spare me to see the light of another day, that I would follow Him with all my heart. Sometimes these good resolutions lasted many days; though at other times when the morning came, and things looked pleasant as to the outward, I too often forgot my solemn promise made to my God. Dear youth, be careful to keep to your covenants made at such seasons; for the Lord is well pleased with an early sacrifice that is without reserve.

When I was between thirteen and fourteen years of

age, my parents first made profession of religion; my
father being convinced of the principles of truth—the
light of Christ shining in the heart of man—as held to,
and maintained by the people called Quakers: which
people, till then I had never remembered to have heard
of. But my mother inclined towards those called the
New-light Baptists; and was zealous that way. This last
named people were numerous where we then lived; but
there were none of the Society of Friends in that part of
the country. And I, with the rest of my father's children, who were all older than myself, except two brothers,
very often attended the Baptist meeting. Our father seldom went to these meetings; but I well remember many
times in evenings, after reading the Holy Scriptures and
other good books, he imparted much good counsel, which
has been remembered since to my benefit. I also recollect
a valuable book which my father borrowed and brought
home, called Sewel's History of Friends, which he set me
to reading in. This book gave an account of Friends'
sufferings in early times, and how patiently they gave up
their lives for Christ Jesus' sake, their ever living Redeemer. These affecting circumstances which I read,
made great impression on my mind in those days; for I
was convinced it was the power of God that upheld and
supported these early Friends; and I desired to be like
unto them. And oh! that we who profess to be led by
the same holy principle of divine light and life, may be
faithful and obedient thereunto.

I very well remember, though I was then quite a child,
the day my father brought Sewel's History home with
him. If I was but a little fellow, yet I was quite a good
reader, and my father set me to read the book to him,
whilst he sat upon his bench making shoes; for he was

by trade a shoemaker. I recollect distinctly, as though it was but yesterday, how much I was affected in reading some parts of that book; especially where it told of the constancy which so many of those poor people, both young and old, showed under suffering and cruel persecution. I often had to stop reading, for I could not go on for weeping; and my sister Hannah, who was older than I, would take the book and read till I was composed enough to go on again. My childish sympathies were indeed very much stirred up on account of these poor, innocent sufferers of whom we read; and I thought that if there ever were any really good people in the world, these surely were some of them. And I said in my heart, if the Lord should ever make me a Quaker, like he did the people of whom we read, and give me his testimonies to bear for the Truth, that I also would be willing to suffer for His sake; and that I would rather lay down my life, and die for him, than draw back and give up my religion because of persecution. And I now gratefully remember that the Lord did, in his own appointed time, visit my soul; and reveal his dear Son in me; and as I was made willing to bear his yoke, and become obedient to the word of Life, that He gave me from season to season, as I was able to bear them, one after another of his precious doctrines to believe, and more and more of his noble testimonies to uphold and declare before the people, for his great name's sake.

And now I feel bound in gratitude to say, that He has graciously enabled me to continue faithful to him, my good Lord and Master, for nearly sixty years. It will be sixty years this coming summer since I first attended a Friends' meeting. My brother John and I thought we would like to go to a Quaker meeting, and as the nearest one to us we heard was at Hopkinton, Rhode Island, we concluded one First-day morning that we would go to it. I was not then quite fifteen years old. So after our very long walk we went into the meeting; and when I saw Friends sitting around me in solemn silence, I was much struck with it, and with the very great difference there was between what I now saw, and all that I had ever before seen in religious meetings. In every meeting that I previously had been at, there had been no silence, no waiting on the Lord, and no preparation for the solemn duty of worshipping Almighty God; but they went right away to singing, or praying, or preaching; and when they were done, they hurried off without ceremony, and without taking any time for solemn reflection, that they might profit by what they had heard. But here all was changed.

When I looked over the meeting, and saw many people sitting quietly around me, I asked myself this question: What are these people doing? for they have not yet heard preaching, or any good advice for them to be thinking about. And I said, can this be worship? are these people really worshipping their Heavenly Father? I looked very attentively at the Friends in the gallery; and when I saw the solid gravity with which they sat, and especially after I had observed that tears were trickling down some of their cheeks, although there had not been a word spoken, I said in my heart, surely these people have something in them which I know nothing about. And I felt an earnest desire in my heart, to know what that something was; and where they got it from; and how it was to be obtained; that if it were possible I might get some too, and come to know what it was, that made the tears run down their faces, without any of the common means having been employed to produce such effects.— Thus the Lord began to open my spiritual eyes, by first kindling holy desires in my heart to know and understand the mysteries of godliness; and blessed be his holy name, He not only raised these desires in my heart, but by the inshining of his Holy Spirit. He gave me an understanding of one mystery after another, as I was able to receive it, until I was brought, through Divine Grace and by the revelation of his light and love and power in my soul, to set my seal to all the doctrines and testimonies which He raised up Friends in the beginning to uphold before the nations of the earth. No doubt the reading of Sewel's History and other now forgotten incidents, prepared, in a measure, my heart for the reception of their truth; but on this day I was first made sensible of a true convincement; and saw the dawn of the true gospel day arise in my soul; and thus those principles and doctrines of life and salvation began to be recognized by me; and blessed be my Stay and Holy Helper who has preserved me from departing from them, from that day to the present time.

After meeting, Friends showed great kindness to us poor lads, and we had many invitations to dinner. We went home with one, which would not take us out of our way, and this Friend was indeed truly kind to us. He told us that he would be glad to see us at meeting when we should feel inclined to come, and pressed us to make his house our home when we did come. His truly friendly conduct to us made a deep and lasting impression on my mind. This man was doctor Thomas Wilbur, the father of my dear friend John Wilbur.

The following anecdote, though not in the memoranda, is deemed sufficiently interesting to insert here:

" When Christopher Healy was between thirteen and fourteen years of age, he attended a school in New Eng-

land, taught by a Presbyterian master, who heard them
every Seventh-day morning say their catechism. This had
for some time been very irksome to the lad, the secret
witness testifying against it. In looking at the answer
that fell to his lot in the lesson one day, he found that to
the question, ' What are the decrees of God?' he must
reply, ' That God's decrees are the wise, free and holy acts
of the counsel of his will, whereby from all eternity, he
hath, for his own glory, unchangeably *foreordained* whatsoever comes to pass in time,' &c. This doctrine of predestination, in subversion of man's free agency, was what
his Bible had not taught him; and he found that he must
decline these lessons; but how to break his determination
to the master was the question; yet, as his peace consisted in it, he made the request. In surprise, the teacher
desired to know why he wished to be excused from saying
his catechism, which he looked upon as next to the Bible,
if not equally sacred. The straitened boy could only
reply, that he did not feel easy to learn it. ' But,' said
the master, ' I cannot excuse you unless you give me a
reason.' At length Christopher had fairly to tell him he
could not learn his catechism because it was *not true*.—
' Not true!' said the astonished master, who, although he
set great store by the lad, seemed almost horror-struck at
his declaration. However, finding him firm, he told him
that if he would make his word good by proving the
catechism to be false, he would excuse him hereafter from
these lessons; and a time was appointed for the proof.

A time of deep trial the little fellow had till the hour
came, to which nearly all his school-fellows staid. But
Christopher, though so young, had read his Bible with
care, and had a retentive memory; and the good Remem-
brancer brought to his recollection this passage of the

prophet Jeremiah, where, speaking in the name of the Most High, it is said 'They have built the high places of Tophet, which is in the valley of the son of Hinnom, to burn their sons and their daughters in the fire, *which I commanded them not, neither came it into my heart.*' Showing that these things were not preordained of God, but were of man's own wickedness. The astonished schoolmaster could only say, he 'did not think there had been anything like it in the Bible.' However, he released the lad from saying his catechism any more.

"Twenty-five years afterwards, when Christopher had been recommended as a minister of the Society of Friends about seven months, a concern came upon his mind to visit the scenes of his childhood; and having procured the requisite credentials from his Monthly Meeting, he came to this very spot, and appointed a meeting, to which his old schoolmaster, and former schoolfellows were invited and came. In this meeting he was led to relate this anecdote, saying, 'and ye are my witnesses,' as he appealed to them, and detailed some of the dealings of the Lord with him in drawing him towards Friends, and opening one by one their testimonies to his understanding. His old master seemed rejoiced to see him, and clung to him with affection; and his schoolfellows received him with open arms."

Though but about sixteen years of age, he saw plainly the danger of living an easy, unconcerned life in conformity with the fashions and customs of the world, and that the surrender of the will unto Him who endured the cross, despising the shame for us, was called for in respect to the use of the plain language and garb. That ancient precept seemed to be revived in his experience. " Put away

2*

the strange gods that are among you, and be clean, and
change your garments." This he was strengthened, not
without trials to his incipient faith, to yield to; and soon
found a path widely different from that of the world, and
the only right one for him to walk in. But the Lord, who
had called for the sacrifice sustained therein, and in His
own good time changed the wilderness of trial and conflict
into a fruitful field; and he was enabled to realize with
the eye of faith, that the Christian's home and treasure
are elsewhere than here; and in consideration thereof he
faithfully practised that denial of self, and the maintenance
of the daily cross, which the Truth ever leads into, and
by which alone the peace of mind he so greatly coveted,
could be secured.

His Journal continued:

But to proceed with my own experience, I had many
solitary walks by night and by day, wherein I saw my
situation, and was clearly convinced by that Divine Light
within my heart, a portion of which is given to all to
profit with, that I was a daily transgressor, and that if I
continued therein, my portion would be with the miserable
at the close of life, which I was well assured also I had no
lease for. Being earnestly concerned for my salvation, I
renewed my former promises of amendment of life; but
not being deep enough, and not having come to the true
watch-tower, I was easily led astray by the enemy of my
soul, who indeed is as a roaring lion seeking whom he may
devour. But I could not give up to live an unconcerned
life; and after renewing my covenant with my merciful
Lord, I had, during these seasons, great peace of mind.

When I had entered the sixteenth year of my age, my
father having become a member of the Society of the

people called Quakers, and my mother withdrawing from the Baptist meeting, we removed within the compass of South Kingston Monthly Meeting of Friends, in the State of Rhode Island. After our removal my father hired me out to work by the month; where I had an opportunity of going to Friends' meetings, which were many times held in silence. About the end of this summer, I was very much awakened: being sensible that I was living too much at ease, and seeing many who I thought were running in the broad way that leads to destruction, and fearing my part would be with them, I again besought the Lord to look down upon me and help me; and in this distress of mind I promised to obey him in whatsoever he required of me, however in the cross to mine own will; and I soon saw it was my duty to use the plain language, and also to have my clothes made plain, and one day having been at work alone, and coming to the house where I then resided, and feeling it laid upon me to begin to use this new language, and expecting to be derided on that account, it greatly humbled me. But He who had made me sensible of my duty, strengthened me to perform the same, blessed be His holy name forever. And, as I expected, so it proved, for the young man who lived at the same house, on hearing the alteration in my speech, derided me in such a manner as to make it very trying. But when I came to be alone, I found great inward peace for thus giving up to use the plain Scripture language.

Moreover, having worn my hair long, as was then the fashion, I also found it my duty to cut it off. The next First-day morning, feeling my mind drawn towards Friends, and to their meeting, I went home to my father's house, in order to attend it. My father and mother were glad to see me with the change in my appearance. But

my sisters, who were older than myself, said they were
sorry I had spoiled my head of hair. But they knew not
the peace I felt for so doing. I went to Friends' meeting
this day, and found it my duty likewise to go to meetings
in the middle of the week, as well as on First-days. I
have since mourned to see such a neglect in the attendance of religious meetings, which plainly shows that they
who do so, are not enough concerned for their salvation.
Having now conformed in respect to having my clothes
made plain, and being diligent to attend meetings, I believed it required of me to request to be taken under
Friends' care as a member of their Society; and they
took an opportunity with me on the occasion, and encouraged me to persevere in well doing; but waited, as I
suppose, to see what proof I made of an orderly life and
conversation. By not keeping on my guard, the enemy
of my soul got some advantage over me; but not so as to
hinder me from going to meeting: nevertheless, the sweet
precious life which I before experienced, I felt greatly to
decrease. Oh! how needful it is to keep on the watch-
tower, *the only place* to grow in grace, and to bear fruit
that will be acceptable to the great Husbandman.

I continued in this situation about three years, without
much growth in religious experience. Yet I believe the
Lord had me in his remembrance, and knowing my intentions were good, preserved me from gross evils, and
mostly from running into hurtful company. During these
three years I had considerable acquaintance amongst
Friends, and being somewhat sensible of the high and
holy profession they made—that of obedience to the light
of Christ within man, God's gift for their salvation—and
seeing many of them, as I was sensible, take but little
heed thereunto, it was a great stumbling-block to me in

such a weak state as I was in, and sometimes almost discouraged me. Oh that we that make so high a profession, may not offend the little ones, or the pure principle in others; to whom we should be as a city set on a hill that cannot be hid; that they, beholding our good works, and strict obedience to the light of Christ, may glorify our Father who is in heaven. I likewise saw many worthy Friends whose good example was as lights to me; and some whose doctrines were very precious and edifying to my mind; which opened my eyes to see I must not feed on the failings of others, but rather that a sense of their misconduct should be a warning for me to be more faithful. And I discovered that the Lord was with this people, favoring them that were obedient, and cautioning and reproving them that were unfaithful. Oh! may these lukewarm ones be awakened to a sense of their situation before it be too late.

When I was about nineteen years of age, I was again visited with the Day-spring from on high, wherein my love to my God and my friends was renewed; and I saw clearly it was my duty to offer myself to the care of Friends again, acquainting my father therewith. Friends appointed a committee to visit me on my request; and, after the regular proceedings in such cases, I was received a member.

The death of my dear mother about this time was a great trial to me. It occurred on the 12th day of the Eighth Month, 1792. I was present when she departed this life; she having been a weakly and afflicted woman more than twenty years.

CHAPTER II.

MARRIAGE WITH ALICE SHEFFIELD, AND HUMBLE SETTING
OUT IN LIFE. BELIEF THAT HE WOULD BE CALLED TO
THE MINISTRY, AND EXERCISES PREPARATORY THERETO.
REMOVAL TO THE NEIGHBORHOOD OF RENSSELAERVILLE,
N. Y. REMOVAL TO MIDDLEBURG, N. Y. OBSERVATIONS
ON HIS EMPLOYMENT AS A TEACHER. DEATH OF HIS
FATHER. APPEARS IN THE MINISTRY. REMARKS ON
THE COMFORT EXPERIENCED IN THE ATTENDANCE OF
MEETINGS FOR WORSHIP.

BEING now received into the Society, I attended meetings diligently; and found it my duty to observe the good order thereof, and to take the good counsel and advice of Friends, which I prized as a great blessing; and felt myself favored that my lot was cast among a people whom the Lord had raised up to show forth his praise. And I am confirmed in the belief, that if they continue to make the Lord their refuge, no weapon formed against them shall ever prosper, and the tongue that rises against them in judgment shall be put to silence: for the Lord will arise for the help of his people, and his enemies shall be scattered.

When I had entered the twenty-first year of my age, I was married to Alice Sheffield, daughter of Samuel and Elizabeth Sheffield—a member of our Monthly Meeting of South Kingston; it being on the 12th day of Twelfth Month, 1793.

These dear young Friends, in their early housekeeping, began in a very circumscribed manner. A Friend who

visited them, thus described their home : " It consisted of
but one room, without any closet and a few shelves in one
corner to hold dishes, etc. Very few of our Friends have
known the poverty that he knew ; and very few, even
among the stronger-minded ones, attained to what he did,
not as respects preaching, but in the interest in his conversation and his ready answer to all that presumed to call in
question any of our fundamental doctrines and testimonies."

Feeling myself more confirmed in the faith of the Society, I believed it was my place to attend Quarterly and
Yearly Meetings ; which were seasons of good instruction
to me. I often sought the Lord when alone for His counsel, and he was graciously pleased to manifest His will to
me, which made me willing to part with all, yes—to sell
the glories of the world to purchase the field wherein the
pearl of great price lay. And many times when alone, I
did believe if I was faithful to Divine manifestations in
my own mind, that I should be called to declare to others
what the Lord had done for me.

Much of my outward employment from the time of my
being married was teaching school : and having many
children, Friends and others, placed under my care, I
found it always best to ask counsel of Him who is the
great Lord and Law-giver, that I might know how to instruct these dear children thus committed to my care, not
only in the instruction necessary to fit them for business
in this life, but also to train them in the fear of God, and
in His nurture and admonition. And when I was careful
and waited on the Lord for direction, I had great comfort
in conducting my school.

When I had entered the 28th year of my age, my dear

father was removed by death. And for the loss of him my heart truly mourned; remembering his godly concern in the latter part of his days to instruct us in the way we should go. Oh! that children would hearken to the good counsel given them by truly concerned parents. I have often felt everything alive within me moved, by seeing inconsiderate, disobedient children slight and disregard their parents' good advice, whose hearts have been filled with anxious care, and no doubt many times they have strewn their tears in consequence of their children's disobedience; it may be after they have gotten out of their power to restrain them. May these things be treasured up in the hearts of children; and may they remember the great and ancient command, " Honor thy father and thy mother, that thy days may be long in the land which the Lord thy God giveth thee." And also to remember, that to slight and disobey parents, is a sin of no small magnitude; and that those who do so, are making a bed of sorrow to lay their head upon one day or another.—But, dear youth, the desire of my heart is, that you may shun this source of sorrow, by obeying your parents in the Lord; so shall you be as a staff to their age, and as balm to their declining nature.

Soon after my father's decease, which was on the 2nd day of Second Month, 1801, I saw clearly that if I was faithful, I would soon be called to the work of the ministry. And on the twenty-second of the same month, upon a First-day of the week, at our meeting at the lower meeting-house in South Kingston, I uttered a few words in the dread and fear of Him, the great Shepherd of Israel, who had thus made known to me my duty at that time; and I felt great peace as a reward for obedience. This strengthened me; and I was thereby encouraged to draw near oftener than the morning to wait upon the God of my salvation, who alone had become my guard and guide. Thus I endeavored to be faithful and obedient, and found that language to be verified which was spoken from the Lord by Samuel to Saul, the first anointed king over Israel : " To obey is better than sacrifice, and to hearken than the fat of rams." But O that none may presume to speak in the name of the Lord, without His holy influence, and the word of command laid upon them! Then only will such experience the answer of peace in their own bosom. On the contrary, if they offer an offering of their own preparing, they may expect to receive this language : " Who hath required this at your hand to tread my courts ?"

I many times had to go down as into Jordan, yea to the very bottom thereof. Oh! none can know the tribulated path the Christian has to tread, but those that walk therein. But it is the highway to holiness; the very way the blessed Saviour trod; and all His followers must become acquainted with it. For it is through many tribulations that any one enters the kingdom. I well remember one day being deeply tried, as to an hair's breadth, so that I was just ready to conclude I was forsaken, when I put up my cries to the Lord, and appealed to Him who knew the sincerity of my heart, for help and strength. Upon which the language of David was presented to my mind : " Why art thou cast down, O my soul? and why art thou disquieted within me? Hope thou in God; for I shall yet praise him for the help of his countenance. O my God, my soul is cast down within me : therefore will I remember thee from the land of Jordan. Deep calleth unto deep at the noise of thy water-spouts; all thy waves and thy billows are gone over me. Yet the

3

Lord will command his loving kindness in the day time, and in the night his song shall be with me, and my prayer unto the God of my life." And this encouragement was given me from the Fountain of all good, as I believe; and so I felt the seas to be stilled, and the raging, foaming waves to cease; blessed be his holy name forever. I did not for several years find it my duty very often to appear in public testimony in our meeting, but often felt it my place to wait upon the Lord out of meeting, as well as in meetings; and found as David said, that "He inclined unto me, and heard my cry:" and graciously appeared for my comfort and consolation, yea with the healing balm of life under his wings.

When I was about thirty-two years of age, I believed it best for me to remove with my family into New York State, within the compass of Coeyman's Monthly Meeting. But I had many serious considerations about this removal, it being a matter of great importance to me; and in the Ninth Month, 1805, I went into that country in company with my brother-in-law Joseph Collins, to see it; which visit was satisfactory; and in about five weeks after my return, I removed with my family, having the unity of my friends herein. Being favored with a prosperous journey, we got well here, and I was truly thankful to my great Lord and Master; and finding many sympathizing friends, I was comforted in their company. Although I had many times to descend into Jordan, even to the depths thereof, yet these truly baptizing seasons were times of my greatest improvement and growth in the best things. For the law is a light, the commandment a lamp, and the reproofs of instruction the way of life. And it is in the valley of humiliation that the Lord doth instruct his people.

I endeavored to abide in this Jordan spiritually with patience, and to endure various dippings therein, until He was pleased, by the lifting up of his holy countenance, to bring me out of these trials, and to enable me to bring up stones of memorial to the honor of His name. And as David praised God for his mercy, so doth my soul praise him, saying, "Bless the Lord, O my soul, and all that is within me bless his holy name. Bless the Lord, O my soul, and forget not all his benefits : who redeemeth thy life from destruction ; who crowneth thee with loving kindness and tender mercies." "Oh Lord my God, thou art very great ; thou art clothed with honor and majesty : who coverest thyself with light as with a garment ; who stretchest out the heavens like a curtain ; who layeth the beams of his chambers in the waters ; who maketh the clouds his chariot ; who walketh upon the wings of the wind ; who maketh his angels spirits ; his ministers a flaming fire."

As I was concerned to perform my duty in whatever the Lord required of me, I found it right to visit some neighboring meetings within the compass of our own Monthly Meeting. Wherein, notwithstanding I had many favored seasons, yet He who knew what was best for me, led me again and again into the valley and shadow of death. Oh! this is the cup our Saviour spoke of, and this is Christ's baptism, which all his true disciples must partake of. Oh, dear brother and sister, whoever you are, do not think to reign with Christ in glory, unless you are willing to partake of His bitter cups, death and sufferings. And in order to bear these trials, so as not to forsake your dear Lord and Master, you must pray for patience to endure the turning of His holy hand upon you. And may you remember for your encouragement, that if you keep the word of his patience, He will keep you in the hour of temptation. Oh give not out, my dear exercised brother or sister, but hold on thy way. Help is laid on One that is mighty; and He is willing to save all those who forsake all to follow Him; and when the time of refreshing shall come from the presence of the Lord, all those that have patiently endured their trials, shall witness the winter to be past, the rain to be over and gone, the flowers to appear on the earth, the time of the singing of birds to be come, and the voice of the turtle to be heard in their land.

When I had lived about two years within the compass of Rensselaerville Particular Meeting, where I first removed when I came from the State of Rhode Island, I believed it right again to remove to a little meeting at Middleburg, about ten miles distant, it being held under the care of the Monthly Meeting, and but two meetings a month. I had a desire to attend all our religious meetings, and not knowing there would be a meeting established there, it caused me to examine the ground of my removal. But making them a visit, and attending one of their meetings, they felt very near to me, and I was favored in this meeting, in a good degree, with the Heavenly Father's love, and my mouth was opened in testimony to His blessed truth: and having to believe, if the few Friends of the place remained steadfast in the Truth, there would be a meeting established there, after weighing the matter in a serious manner, and advising with some of my friends of Rensselaerville, I thought it would be safe for me to remove thither; though I was loath to part with friends of that meeting, as many of them expressed they were with me. And some of their spirits I had felt very nearly united to mine in the heavenly journey. May the Lord preserve them in His holy fear.

Christopher Healy often experienced a being introduced again and again into the furnace of humiliation and trial, that so not only the dross and the tin, but the reprobate silver might be consumed, whereby a vessel meet for the inscription of "Holiness unto the Lord" should be wrought. He was often brought into a state of mourning and lamentation. But could as oft acknowledge with the Psalmist: "Thou hast put off my sackcloth, and girded me with gladness." The following from his memoranda, clearly prove this:

In the latter part of 1807 I removed to Middleburg, and when there was no meeting there, I found it my duty to go to Rensselaerville Meeting of Friends, they still feeling very near to me; and I was often favored with the Lord's holy presence in them to my satisfaction and comfort. But our meeting was soon allowed, that is once a week, which I believe was in a good degree overshadowed by the wing of Ancient goodness, who is the life and support of all our religious meetings; and who is the bread that cometh down from heaven. Oh then, saith my soul, may we be concerned oftener than the morning light, to wait upon Him, and pray for our daily bread; and He, who is rich in mercy, will not fail to hear our prayers, and to fill our souls, in His own time, with the soul-sustaining bread of heavenly life, and cause us to draw water out of the well of salvation. Then shall we experience the mountain of the Lord's house to be established in the top of the mountains; and have the pleasant prospect of all nations flowing unto it. And feelingly can my mind unite with the Psalmist who said, "Great is the Lord, and greatly to be praised in the city of our God, in the mountain of his holiness. Beautiful for situation, the joy of the whole earth, is Mount Zion, on the sides of the north, the city of the great King. God is known in her palaces for a refuge. For lo, the kings were assembled, they passed by together. They saw it, and so they marvelled; they were troubled, and hasted away. Fear took hold upon them there, and pain. Thou breakest the ships of Tarshish with an east wind. As we have heard, so have we seen in the city of the Lord of hosts, in the city of our God; God will establish it forever. We have thought of thy loving kindness, O God, in the midst of thy temple. According to thy name, O God, so is thy praise unto the ends of the earth: thy right hand is full of righteousness. Let Mount Zion rejoice, let the daughters of Judah be glad, because of thy judgments. Walk about Zion, and go round about her; tell the towers thereof. Mark ye well her bulwarks, consider her palaces; that ye may tell it to the generation following. For this God is our God for ever and ever; he will be our guide even unto death."

On the fourth day of Second Month, 1808, I attended our own meeting in the middle of the week, and soon after I sat down in the meeting, I felt the Heavenly Father's love to spread, and it was as a shower of celestial rain, which refreshed many of our minds; and though our number was small, I did believe that ancient promise was verified, that where two or three are gathered together in Christ's name, there will He be in the midst of them.

The next First-day following, at the same place, the Lord's mighty power was present, and did enable me to open Truth's doctrine to my own comfort, and to the encouragement of the sincere hearted, and to the strength of the feeble-minded. Blessed be the name of the Lord who is our strength, and without whose presence all are poor. O may my soul be truly humbled before the Lord, that I may learn contentment, and also to suffer hunger, as my God sees meet. For blessed are they that experience a true hunger and thirst after the heavenly bread and water of life, for they shall be filled in the Lord's own time.

At our next Monthly Meeting we were allowed a meeting as before hinted, twice a week; which was an encouragement to our little number; and we esteemed it a favor from the Good Hand, who cares for those that cast their care on Him. And feeling my heart to abound with thankfulness, under a sense of the powerful word of life, my soul was poured out in gratitude and praise to the great Author of all our blessings.

25th of Fifth Month, attended our Monthly Meeting, where an exercise came upon me to request men and women Friends to sit together, in order that I might clear myself of what lay upon my mind. And having the unity of both meetings herein, I was favored to lay before my brethren and sisters the great difference between faithfulness to the Lord and unfaithfulness: remembering the words of the Lord, by the mouth of his Prophet to revolting Israel, saying: "She did not know that I gave her corn, and wine, and oil, and multiplied her silver and gold, which they prepared for Baal. Therefore will I return, and take away my corn in the time thereof, and my wine in the season thereof, and will recover my wool and my flax given to cover her nakedness." This will be the punishment of all the disobedient. The Lord will take away the blessing and talents from them, if they will not improve them, and withdraw His manifold favors from them, and leave them in darkness. But unto faithful Israel—the true church of Christ—who live in obedience to God their Heavenly Father, the encouraging language of Isaiah the prophet, which also arose in my mind to communicate, may be applied : " For Zion's sake will I not hold my peace, and for Jerusalem's sake I will not rest, until the righteousness thereof go forth as brightness, and the salvation thereof as a lamp that burneth.— And the Gentiles shall see thy righteousness, and all kings thy glory ; and thou shalt be called by a new name, which the mouth of the Lord shall name. Thou shalt also be a crown of glory in the hand of the Lord, and a royal diadem in the hand of thy God. Thou shalt no more be named forsaken ; neither shall thy land any more be termed Desolate ; but thou shalt be called Hephzibah, and thy land Beulah : for the Lord delighteth in thee, and thy land shall be married. For as a young man marrieth a virgin, so shall thy sons marry thee ; and as the bridegroom rejoiceth over the bride, so shall thy God rejoice over thee." Under these encouraging prospects my soul doth lift up its head in hope. And the language presented : " O Zion arise, and shake thyself from the dust of the earth, and put on thy beautiful garment, even the white robe of righteousness, purity, and holiness, in which thou shalt be presented to the Lord a royal priesthood, a holy nation, a peculiar people, zealous of good works."— After this time I went through many heighths and depths, sometimes feeling almost forsaken of any good ; and many times was made very sensible that the true watch-tower was too much neglected by me ; which was the occasion of my feeling myself forsaken, and sometimes to prove my faith and hope in God. But blessed be his holy Name forever, it was not long before he returned, and I felt myself comforted in His holy presence. For He loves His poor, humble, dependent children, and will arise for their help.

Seventh Month, 1808.—Attended meeting on the First-day of the week at Stanton Hill. The forepart of which I sat under great weakness. But light and life arising towards the conclusion, I was favored to clear myself of an exercise that I had been under for some time, to the comfort of many faithful burden-bearers. Many of the dear youth being present, my mind was largely opened to them, in the love of our Heavenly Father; and also to the parents, showing them the great obligations, we as parents are under, to train up our tender offspring in the nurture and admonition of the Lord; and that if we neglect this, and our children make themselves vile, and wound religion through their impiety which is oftentimes chargeable on the neglect of parents and masters while the children are under our care, we shall stand accountable for them. Oh dear parents, and such that have the care of children, my mind is enlarged towards you, on account of the little lambs committed to your trust. I fear if the children should become aliens and strangers to God, and the commonwealth of his chosen Israel, the blood of many of their precious souls will be chargeable to you. While the debt contracted on your part will, I fear, be such as you shall find it difficult to fully discharge.

This favored meeting was of the Lord, the fountain of all good. And may no praise be given to the creature, but all the praise, glory, honor, and renown be ascribed to our Father in heaven, who enables, through the influence of his son Jesus Christ, to open Truth's doctrine to our own admiration; and well may we say, it is the Lord's doings, and marvellous in our eyes. Oh thou ever blessed

Shepherd of Israel, keep me in the low valley of humiliation; and suffer me not to take my flight on the Sabbath-
day—a day of joy and favor from the Lord to my poor
soul—but lead me in thy wisdom, and by thy right hand,
so shall I be enabled, at thy command, to teach transgressors thy ways, and to speak a word in due season to
them that are weary: so shall the praise be given unto
Thee for ever.   Amen.

Christopher Healy, with every other child born of the
Spirit, had felt his need of the "liberty of heart derived
from heaven." And no doubt experienced, through submission to the effectual working of the Lord's power, the
growth into dominion of that incorruptible seed and word
of God, which liveth and abideth forever.   And also the
encouraging promise, "In Christ Jesus neither circum-
cision availeth anything, nor uncircumcision, but *a new
creature.*" And "As many as walk according to *this rule,*
peace be on them, and mercy, and upon the Israel of
God." His diary proceeds:

14th of Eighth Month.—This morning I felt my mind
measurably brought under the government of the Prince
of Peace, which gives the victory over our wills and inclinations: and a fervent desire attended that others may
witness the same. Which as we dwell under the precious
dominion thereof, causes our love to flow to God, and
through him to all mankind. This Prince of Peace is
thus spoken of by the Prophet: "There shall come forth
a rod out of the stem of Jesse, and a Branch shall grow
out of his roots: and the spirit of the Lord shall rest
upon him, the spirit of wisdom and understanding, the
spirit of counsel and might, the spirit of knowledge, and

of the fear of the Lord." This is Christ Jesus; and if
we will hearken to His counsel, and obey His holy requirings in our own hearts, we shall witness the wolf and lion-
like nature within us to be slain and reduced to love.
Then shall we experience as the fruits of the Government
of the Prince of Peace, what the prophet declared: "The
wolf shall dwell with the lamb, and the leopard shall lie
down with the kid; and the calf, and the young lion, and
the fatling together; and a little child shall lead them.
And the cow and the bear shall feed; their young ones
shall lie down together: and the lion shall eat straw like
the ox. And the suckling child shall play on the hole of
the asp, and the weaned child shall put his hand on the
cockatrice's den. They shall not hurt nor destroy in all
my holy mountain: for the earth shall be full of the
knowledge of the Lord, as the waters cover the sea." O
blessed day indeed: and is only experienced by such as
witness the new birth to be brought forth in them; yea,
of being born again of that incorruptible seed and word
of God, that liveth and abideth forever.

CHAPTER III.

ENGAGES IN A RELIGIOUS VISIT IN COEYMAN'S PREPARA-
TIVE MEETING, N. Y.   REMARKS ON THE EVILS OF THE
USE OF AND TRAFFIC IN SPIRITUOUS LIQUORS.   WARNS
A NEIGHBOR ON ACCOUNT OF HAVING A MAN WHO PRE-
TENDED TO BE A SOOTHSAYER IN HIS HOUSE.   STRENGTH-
ENED IN A TIME OF DEEP TRIAL BY THE UNITY OF HIS
FRIENDS.   VISITS A MAN AND WARNS HIM AGAINST
PREACHING FOR HIRE.   REMOVES WITHIN THE COMPASS
OF COEYMAN'S PREPARATIVE MEETING.

I INFORMED my friends at our Monthly Meeting, that
it was on my mind to visit a few Friends' families in the
compass of Coeyman's Preparative Meeting. And the
meeting uniting with me therein, it left me at liberty to
perform the same, in company with an elder and sympathizing brother belonging to that meeting. I went to the
said Friend's house on Seventh-day, the third of Ninth
Month, 1808, preparatory to the visit. The next morning
before meeting, we went to see one of the families; and a
favored time it proved; wherein my heart was truly humbled under a sense of the importance of so great an undertaking; it being the first visit that I had ever made in
this way of going from house to house. After this we
went to meeting at Stanton Hill; wherein I was favored,
I believed, with the word of life to mine own humbling
admiration. O may I give Him all the glory to whom it
is due. Who alone can appoint, anoint, and qualify for
His great work and service. Many of my dear brothers
and sisters were brought very near to me in this meeting;
and the word of comfort and consolation flowed freely.

The nursing fathers and mothers were encouraged to persevere. The lukewarm were warmed; and the dear youth invited. After meeting we performed the rest of our visit to a good degree of satisfaction. Returning next morning, we went to see one of my companion's neighbors, a woman that appeared to be near her end. I found a concern to lay before her the necessity of a preparation for death; also that some were received at the eleventh hour. She expressed great satisfaction with the visit. The same day attended a meeting appointed at Henry Post's, which proved a trying one, though it ended to some satisfaction. After this meeting, returned home to my family.

O Lord! when I remember thy loving kindness to me, a poor worm of the dust, my spirit is humbled under a sense of thy condescending love. O may I ever dwell in the low valley, where thou art pleased to visit, and feed thy flock. Yea, by the side of still waters, and in the midst of green pastures, where such shall rest under the banner of thy love.

21st of Ninth Month.—Attended our Monthly Meeting at Coeyman's; where we were favored with the company of several Friends, who were appointed by the Yearly Meeting to attend the subordinate meetings with a minute of advice, containing a living concern and travail of the Yearly Meeting, for a reformation herein. The company and gospel labors of these, were truly strengthening and edifying to many of our exercised minds; and, I believe, had a powerful tendency to reach the witness in many of the lukewarm among us. There was also a word of invitation, in the love of the gospel, to the dear youth. One part of the Yearly Meeting's advice, together with that of its committee, proved relieving to my mind, viz., that of

4*

the evil connected with using spirituous liquors any otherwise than as a medicine. For I had believed for some time, that no person while under the influence of good, could, when in health, partake of an article so destructive as this to the human race. I also believe, if professed Christians of all denominations were to live under the circumscribing power of the Spirit of Jesus Christ, that a lesser quantity would serve them as a medicine. O may all professing the Christian name consider these things! And may such as are in the unnecessary use of this destructive article—destructive to both soul and body—and which is affecting the peace of so many families, and *especially those who are buying and selling, and making themselves rich by the profit thereof,* consider whether they are not of that number our Lord said offended his little ones that believe in Him! In love to your souls, I leave these lines to be read when I am in another state of existence.

On the First-day of First Month, 1809, I felt my mind relieved from a close trial that had been resting on it for some months, and at times so heavily that had not the Lord in His loving kindness reached forth His helping hand, I must have been utterly discouraged. But now, under a renewed sense of His goodness to me this day, I am brought to renew my covenant with Him whom I feel to be my only Lord and Lawgiver. The prayer of my soul is, that I may be preserved so watchful and careful as with His holy help, never to depart from my covenant with Him. Oh what a comfort those feel who are engaged to live near to the great Fountain of all good, from whence doth flow the sweet refreshing stream that waters the soul. These are they that can praise Him in truth in the land of the living. Oh blessed Redeemer, remember those in every quarter of the world, whom thou hast given largely to partake of afflictions. Reach forth Thy mighty Hand of power, and place it underneath, that they may not sink. Endow with patience to bear all trials that thou permits to come upon us; for thou alone can enable to persevere into obedience unto holiness. Unto Thee, O Lord, belongs all the praise for evermore. Amen.

On the 9th of Fourth month I felt my mind drawn to go and see one of my neighbors who had a man residing with him who pretended to have a familiar spirit, whereby he could tell what had or what would come to pass, taking pay therefor. Feeling the indignation of the Lord against such conduct, I found it laid upon me to go the next day, which I did; and told my neighbor if he allowed this man thus to proceed in his house, he would be partaker with him in the plagues with which he would be visited as a reward for his iniquity: for it is an abomination in the sight of the Lord. This neighbor said he was obliged to me for my visit; and appeared to be affected with what I had to say to him; and said he had felt uneasy about it himself; and further expressed that he believed my message was of the Truth. In a few days after I was informed that he had put a stop to such conduct at his house. For this act of obedience I felt great inward peace. Oh may I continue in humiliation before the Most High. After this time I had several highly favored meetings, wherein we were truly comforted together in the name and with the presence of the Lord.

Perhaps there are but few who have been called to the work of the ministry, that have not at times known the accuser of the brethren, who is ever watching to hinder the work of the Lord, and if possible utterly to discourage and to destroy, to introduce his subtle reasonings, which if listened to, and heeded, tend only to bewilder and to blind.

Christopher Healy did not escape this "slough of despond;" but through the help of the ever-present, ever-effectual Helper, and that of his friends, he got safely out of it.

His allusion to worthy elders, among whom his lot was now cast, who sympathized with him in his great poverty of spirit, and who were alike willing and able to go down with him into baptism and death, must have proved particulary helpful to him in comforting his drooping spirit. Being able also to speak a word in season to his weary and ofttimes heavy-laden soul: which "fitly spoken" word, Solomon in his Proverbs beautifully compares to "apples of gold in pictures of silver." May the Lord in his never failing mercy continue such Aarons and Hurs to His church, who as faithful burden and standard bearers, keeping the word of His patience, and watching unto prayer with all perseverance, may thus be instrumental in upholding the hands that hang down through weakness, and in effectually turning the battle to the gate.

At our Monthly Meeting in the Third Month, I found it laid upon me to put Friends in mind of the awfulness and solemnity of worshipping the great God; and that no offering, except of His own preparing, will be accepted by Him. For the Lord knows in whose hearts it is to serve Him. I had likewise a word of comfort to the mourners in Zion. After the meeting of business came on, the enemy of my poor soul, who is always ready to destroy, made me believe that I had disturbed the silence of the

meeting for worship, and thereby offended the Lord, and
burthened my friends. The which brought my soul into
mourning, and I sat as with sackcloth on my loins, and
my head in the dust. And almost despairing I put up my
prayers, cries, and tears to my God, to whom I could appeal in sincerity of heart. But O, my spirit was bowed
to an extent I never remember to have witnessed, but
blessed be the Holy Helper, when I was just ready to
sink, He put forth His Holy Hand for my help. After
meeting, such were my feelings, I thought it best to desire
the ministers and elders to stop, that I might have an
opportunity with them: that so they might correct or
advise me. And when we met, the Lord met with us,
and gave me strength to inform them how it had fared
with me through the meeting for business. When, instead
of correction from my brethren, I had their unity and
near sympathy with me in my deep baptism; which fully
healed up all the wounds that my poor soul had experienced this day.

O may all that are concerned to appear in the ministry,
be careful to know the word of command from the Holy
One, and not let a good desire for the people be sufficient
to raise them up in the ministry. But remember, O exercised brother or sister, who art called to the work of the
ministry, that in order that thy offerings be acceptable to
God, or beneficial to the people, thou must feel with the
apostle the necessity of the woe. Yea, woe be unto thee
if thou preach not the gospel. Then if the enemy of thy
soul seeks to discourage thee, and to destroy thy faith, and
thou be thereby brought to fasting, thou shalt witness the
Holy Hand to be underneath thy head to keep thee from
sinking; and when the time of fasting is over, thou shalt
witness the company of holy angels to administer to thy

hungry soul, and thine heart shall rejoice with songs of praise to thy Heavenly Father through Jesus Christ. Which, blessed be the Lord, was my happy experience on my way home after this Monthly Meeting.

The neighbor before alluded to, whom I was constrained to go and see on account of having the soothsayer, as he professed to be, in his house, in a short time being convinced of our principles, requested and became a member of our Monthly Meeting.

In this year, 1809, it came livingly in my mind to go and see an hireling priest. But weighing the concern, not being willing to go too fast, and desiring the Lord to direct me aright in what I believed was from Him, after a time of waiting and proving the fleece both wet and dry, I felt renewed and strengthened from the great Minister of ministers. And one morning believing the time had come to make the priest this visit, I went, beseeching the Lord to go with me, well knowing that without His help, I was unable to perform it according to His will. And blessed be His Holy Name, He was pleased to be my companion and helper. For when I came to his house, the Lord renewed my strength, and opened my way to have an opportunity with him. Feeling my mind clothed with the love of our Heavenly Father, I, in a solemn manner, said to him, I have come in the spirit of restoring love to tell thee that the Lord God of heaven and earth is not well pleased with thy preaching for hire. And if thou continues so to do, the things that belong to thy peace will be hid from thine eyes. But if thou wilt refrain, and live under the power of the cross of Jesus Christ, thou shalt become acquainted inwardly and experimentally with Him whom to know is life eternal. He was tender and loving, and invited me to stay. But feeling myself clear, I acknowledged his kindness, gave him my hand and bid him farewell. He said he wished me well. I told him I wished him well. And so in love we parted; and I went on my way with an humble heart; rendering the praise to my Heavenly Father, who is a present help in the needful time.

The latter part of Eleventh month, 1809, I removed with my family within the compass of Coeymans' Preparative meeting, where I opened a school. Soon after my removal I was brought into great poverty of spirit, but I found many sympathizing friends there. Among them, dear brethren and sisters who were willing to go down into Jordan with ministers. Such elders are indeed worthy of double honor; and some of those worthy Friends were made instrumental in comforting my drooping spirit, by speaking a word in due season to my weary mind; which about this time was plunged into deep baptisms. This language of encouragement from my friends proved as words fitly spoken, which were to my soul as apples of gold in pictures of silver: being sanctified by the Lord.

CHAPTER IV.

HAS A MEETING IN THE DUTCH SETTLEMENT OF SCHO-
HARIE. EXPERIENCE OF THE ENJOYMENT OF DIVINE
FAVOR. REMARKS ON THE SUFFERINGS AND RESURREC-
TION OF CHRIST.

Soon after our Monthly Meeting in the First Month,
1810, I attended a meeting at Coxsackie's, appointed for
Samuel Carey; and a highly favored one it proved. The
doctrine of the Gospel dropped as oil, and distilled as
dew on the tender grass, to the refreshing and comforting
of many minds. Some expressed their sense of this before they left the house. O may all the glory be given to
Him, who alone is worthy forevermore. After this we
had many large and favored meetings at Stanton Hill,
which is called Coeymans' meeting, to the comforting of
many minds, they being owned and accompanied by the
great Head of the church, which alone makes good meetings.

Having for months felt living desires to make a visit to
the people of Schoharie, a settlement of Dutch people
who were very little acquainted with Friends, I was very
much discouraged about it at times, thinking it would
not be well accepted by them; there having never
been any Friends' meeting at that place. This made it
the harder to give up to. But many times, when my
mind was comforted in the Lord, this visit, or a meeting
there, looked pleasant. And after weighty deliberation
thereon, together with the advice of my friends, I set out,
in company with a worthy Friend from our meeting, on

the 14th of Third Month, and rode to John Drake's.—
The next day attended Friends' Preparative Meeting at
Oakhill, which was small. After the meeting, John Drake
joining us, we set out for Schoharie; the distance being
about fifteen miles. It being very cold, and we riding on
horseback facing the wind, it proved very tedious; and I
feeling somewhat cast down in mind, fearing I had been
too forward in making this visit, which was also the means
of drawing my friends from their homes, the thoughts of
it brought me very low. But appealing to Him who I
believed turned my mind to this place, beseeching Him to
go along with us, blessed be His holy name, He was
pleased to condescend to strengthen and comfort our
minds. We reached our friend Joseph Efners, who was
the only Friend in that place, before dark.

A school-house being obtained to hold a meeting, it
was held the next day accordingly. A considerable number of the Dutch people came, though the weather was
trying; and were very civil. And blessed be the Helper
of Israel, he appeared to our comfort in this meeting.
The universality of the grace of God was fully declared
to the people; showing that a portion thereof is given to
all to profit with; and that it is His holy law that he has
placed in our hearts, even at an early period of our lives;
condemning us for evil; and that it is obedience to the
same that justifies us, and gives us the answer of peace in
our own minds. It was also showed them that the gospel
was free; and that Christ's ministers could not be hired
to preach, but as they received freely, so they must deliver
the same to the people. It seemed to me that the minds
of the people, toward the latter part of the meeting, were
tendered with a degree of the Heavenly Father's love.
So that I believed, while standing on my feet amongst

them, that He who called me to go and see this people, was, in His great love and mercy, pleased to overshadow the meeting this day, and to tender their minds toward us and our testimonies; and caused the meeting to end to our comfort and satisfaction. The people spoke lovingly of us, and invited us to their houses; and some of them felt near to me, while their countenances bespoke their satisfaction.

We rode from thence to Middleburg meeting, distant about eight miles, and lodged at David Gurney's. I was glad to meet with Friends of this place. And a meeting being appointed the next day, our friend John Drake appeared in supplication, much to the comfort of my mind. But it was my lot to be silent, except towards the close of the meeting, when I informed them that solemn silence was acceptable to God, and that I had been as clearly convinced as ever I was, that good will for the people was not a sufficient qualification to preach the gospel. For had that been the case, my mouth would have been largely opened amongst them. This day we had another meeting about five miles from Middleburg, at Jonathan Mosher's, in Rensselaer, several Friends accompanying us from the former place. In which, after we took our seats, I gave up to be silent. But unexpectedly I was drawn to declare the word of life to the comfort of the humble-minded, and to the stirring up of the careless. Here we parted from Friends, and rode to Amos Mosher's, whose wife was a Methodist. They inviting us to tarry all night with them, we did so. They were young and recently married. The young man being under a concern of mind for his best welfare, we had a comfortable visit with them. His wife said their house was always open to Friends. She said she had seen it her duty to be plain in her dress and address; and her countenance declared the sincerity of her mind.

We attended Friends' meeting next day at Rensselaerville; these two young people coming to the meeting. And the Lord was pleased to comfort us together, and I was led to declare how attentive a faithful soldier of Christ would be to the Captain of his soul's salvation; even to obey His command in all things. As I stood on my feet in this meeting, I felt the word of life to increase; and the true mark and badge of discipleship was clearly brought before the view of my mind in the words of our Lord: "By this shall all men know that ye are my disciples, if ye have love one to another." A portion of this love spread over the meeting, and caused it to end to our humbling admiration. After this meeting, we had a sitting in a family wherein the humbling power of Truth broke forth and distilled as the dew on the tender grass, the hearts of those present being tendered and much broken. I believe this opportunity will not soon be forgotten by them. After this we went to Caleb Spencer's, and staid that night, and next morning returned home. I was truly thankful to the Lord for so sympathizing a companion as my friend proved to be in this short visit.

On the first day of Fourth Month, 1810, I attended a meeting appointed at a sick woman's request, about seven miles distant. Soon after I sat down in the meeting, I felt the presence of the Good Master near, and I was soon raised upon my feet with these words. "When a man's ways please the Lord, he maketh even his enemies to be at peace with him." Oh, the advantage and favor those receive from the Lord, that live in His holy fear, and obey his commands. How safe is their dwelling-place. What encouragement there is to persevere. How these will be protected. For "He that dwelleth in the secret place of the Most High, shall abide under the shadow of the Almighty. I will say of the Lord, he is my refuge and my fortress: my God; in him will I trust. Surely he shall deliver thee from the snare of the fowler, and from the noisome pestilence. He shall cover thee with his feathers, and under his wings shalt thou trust: his truth shall be thy shield and buckler. Thou shalt not be afraid for the terror by night, nor for the arrow that flieth by day; nor for the pestilence that walketh in darkness, nor for the destruction that wasteth at noonday. A thousand shall fall at thy side, and ten thousand at thy right hand; but it shall not come nigh thee. Only with thine eyes shalt thou behold and see the reward of the wicked. Because thou hast made the Lord which is my refuge, even the Most High thy habitation, there shall no evil befall thee, neither shall any plague come nigh thy dwelling." I was helped from this Scripture testimony to encourage all present to attend to the gift of God, or seed of the kingdom in the heart. So should we know a safe dwelling-place in the Lord. I was much enlarged thereon to my own humbling admiration, and to the consolation of many present.

Fourth Month, 2nd.—Returning from my school at evening, my mind as I walked was fixed on heavenly things, and I felt a stream of Divine love to flow into my soul, whereby my inner man was greatly refreshed. And my spirit breathed forth songs of praise to the Lord, beseeching Him to preserve my soul alive, and keep me obedient to His commands. This heavenly flow of Divine love continued with me until late in the night, and my cup did overflow with joy at the goodness of the Lord to me. Eye has indeed not seen, nor ear heard, neither hath it entered into the heart of man, while in his degenerate state, to conceive the good things the Lord hath in store for them that love, obey, and follow Him with all their hearts. Oh blessed Redeemer! Thy presence is sweet; and by me is preferred before corn, wine, or oil: yea, to the riches of the Indies. Thou art infinitely to be preferred to gold. For Thou canst give eternal life; and at thy right hand are rivers of pleasures for evermore, saith my soul.

Our meetings at Stanton Hill being very large on First-days, owing to a great number of people besides our members attending, my soul was often prostrated before the Lord, both in and out of meeting, craving in secret prayer His Almighty aid, and that he would keep me in a true, humble, waiting state of mind in these gatherings, that so I might experience my strength renewed in Him; and know Him, the great Shepherd of Israel, to put me forth and go before. O God! the work is thine, and thou canst carry it on either immediately or instrumentally as pleaseth Thee. Therefore, may I ever wait in solemn silence before the ever blessed Saviour to lift me upon my feet. So shall I, through Thy mighty power, and gospel light and life, teach transgressors Thy ways; and sinners, through Thy redeeming love and power, shall be converted unto Thee. O may I never stir up nor awake the Beloved of my soul until He please. Then I believe He will often cause His doctrine to distil as the dew, and as the gentle rain on the tender grass. For when He, the God of Israel, is pleased to arise, then shall His enemies be scattered. I well remember what our Saviour said to the Scribes and Pharisees: "My time," said He, "is not yet come; but your time is alway ready." And I am well confirmed in the opinion, that all true ministers must wait His time, before they can preach His gospel; and must not attempt to feed on the manna of yesterday, but know their strength renewed day by day, by the alone sustaining bread.

Fourth Month, 13th.—My mind was led to consider the beauty of holiness, and in a particular manner what benefit the dear youth would receive, if they would be so wise as to embrace religion in the morning of their days! What snares and temptations of the enemy of their soul's happiness they might avoid, by covenanting with, and adhering to the great Shepherd and Bishop of their souls, before their minds become biassed by the god of this world. O how pleasant is the morning of life when no clouds obstruct the light of the Sun of Righteousness; when the mind feels clear; when obedience keeps pace with knowledge; and no condemnation covers the soul. Such mornings may truly be said to be mornings without clouds. Our Heavenly Father, under the law, required a lamb of the first year without blemish; but now, under the gospel dispensation, He calls for a broken heart and contrite spirit. Moreover, dear youth, unto these he looks that are poor in spirit: and will, as they continue faithful, show them His heavenly kingdom. But all your offerings must be without blemish, even the whole heart, without any mixture of the creaturely will. For the feast, the heavenly feast that Christ will come unto, must be kept with the unleavened bread of sincerity and truth. Although some high-minded youth may look upon the path of self-denial and the daily cross, as too mean a road for them to walk in, especially at so early a period of their days, falsely imagining that thereby they shall lose all their comfort in this life! But, dear youth, let me inform you from my own experience, that these are the suggestions of the enemy of our peace. For never can there be found such joys and comfort in earthly things, as those witness who can say in truth, Thy will be done in my heart as it is done in heaven.

And may I, while writing these lines, adopt the language of one formerly who had proved that one day in the Lord's courts is worth a thousand elsewhere, saying, "I had rather be a door-keeper in the house of my God, than to dwell in the tents of wickedness." O how sweet is the presence of our Lord and Saviour to those who choose Him for their portion, and obey His sweet voice. It is as marrow to their bones, and health to all their flesh. Safe indeed to feel preserved within the hollow of His Holy Hand.—Remember, dear youth, that our great Lord and Master when on earth declared: "Whosoever shall seek to save his life shall lose it;" that is, to save his life of pleasure and vanity, shall lose his eternal life: but he that is willing to lose his life of pleasure and vanity in this world, and cleave to Christ and *become His disciple through self-denial and the daily cross to his own will*, shall not fail of preserving it, or of having a place in Christ's kingdom.

Fifth-day, 19th.—Being this day plunged into a great sea of trouble, wherein my soul was deeply tried, my supplication to the Lord was after this manner: O Lord, stretch forth Thy holy hand of help and deliverance; for without Thee, as Thou knowest, I am not able to bear up nor keep my head above the mighty waves of this tempestuous sea. Therefore, O blessed Lord, if it be thy will, manifest thy power, and work deliverance for thy poor servant. Thou knowest I love thee, and thy glorious cause above my natural life; which I refuse not to lay down if it should please thee to call for it. I love thee above all things here below; and long to feel a refreshing stream from thy holy fountain. O blessed Lord of life and glory, be pleased to cause the morning dew, and celestial rain to descend and water my poor soul as thou hast aforetime often done to thine own honor. O Lord, give me patience to bear my trials until it shall please thee to bring me safely through them. Amen.

After an allusion to our blessed Lord's query to Peter, three times repeated, " Lovest thou me?" with the great duty of feeling and knowing the prevalence of this love in ourselves, first and before all to Christ, ere we can be strengthened and enabled to feed His sheep, or speak a word in season to them that are weary; with some allusion also to the birth, life, miracles, sufferings, death and resurrection, and despised appearance, in the world's view, of Jesus Christ of Nazareth, our Saviour, Christopher Healy proceeds thus to comment upon that most satisfactory sacrifice of the dear Son and Sent of God for man's salvation :

What could be more affecting than the manner of His (the Saviour's) death? with the resigned situation of his soul, conveyed in the following language: " Oh, Father, if it be possible let this cup pass from me: yet not my will, but thine be done." This cup, this bitter cup of death and suffering he drank for us! Oh may we so live under the power of his cross to our own wills, as to have true fellowship with him in his sufferings : so shall we be benefited by his death. And when our blessed Lord arose, having conquered all the powers of darkness, how comfortable it was to his disciples to hear the glad tidings: Behold I go before you into Galilee, there shall ye see me. So shall the faithful servants of Jesus, that continue with him through suffering and death, arise with him in newness of life, and witness the Saviour's promise verified, that where he is, there shall also his servants be.

8th of Tenth Month, 1810.—This day I am thirty-seven years old. O Lord! as I grow in years may I grow in grace; and in the knowledge of our Lord and Saviour Jesus Christ, whom to know is life eternal. Therefore, Lord, suffer me not to transgress thy holy law. Wean my affections more and more from every thing here below; and set my heart wholly on thee. Thou knowest the many weaknesses that surround me; but thou art my strength in weakness, riches in poverty, and the only hope of eternal life. O make me willing to be wholly thine, in body, soul and spirit; and to become as passive clay in the hand of the potter. Thou art the great Potter. Mould and fashion me into a vessel of use in thy holy house. O Lord, I once more resign my life and my all unto thee. Even this evening do I resign myself to be disposed of as thou shalt see meet. Therefore, O Lord! visit my iniquities and my transgressions, if any there be in me, with thy rod and thy stripes; and continue thy loving kindness, even thy Spirit of Truth, that leads and guides into all truth; which doth at this time enable my poor soul to give thee the praise, the honor, the glory, to whom it is due. Amen.

CHAPTER V.

REMARKS ON THE PRECIOUSNESS OF TRUE UNITY. RELI-
GIOUS CONCERN FOR THE CHILDREN IN HIS SCHOOL.
VISITS A SICK WOMAN, A MEMBER AMONG THE METH-
ODISTS, AND ATTENDS HER FUNERAL.

EARLY in the Eleventh Month of this year, I attended
our Quarterly Meeting, which was a low time with me.
The evening following, visited a sick woman, who departed this life next day; which brought me to look closely
into my own case. The same night when I went to bed,
it pleased my Heavenly Father to visit my poor soul with
the Day-spring from on high, wherein my heart was so
overcome with his loving-kindness, that I spake of it to
my friend who lodged with me; for sleep, in this joyful
state of mind, departed from my eyes. I saw clearly that
holiness became God's house forever; and felt a secret
prayer for further purification. The next day, in company with my before mentioned friend, I visited a dis-
consolate widow, and had a religious opportunity in the
family; wherein the Lord gave me a word of comfort to
the bereaved one, which I believe sweetened the bitter cup
of her afflictions, that she had lately drunk so large a
portion of.

The next being First-day, accompanied by the same
Friend, I went to Crum Elbow Meeting. Soon after I
sat down in the meeting, I felt the unity of the one Spirit,
in the bond of sweet peace to spread over us; and in the
comfort thereof I was raised upon my feet, and the Lord
was unto me, I believe I may say, mouth and wisdom.

The language of David was presented to my mind: " Behold, how good and how pleasant it is for brethren to dwell together in unity! It is like the precious ointment upon the head, that ran down upon the beard, even Aaron's beard; that went down to the skirts of his garments; as the dew of Hermon, and as the dew that descended upon the mountains of Zion; for there the Lord commanded the blessing, even life forever more." Upon this subject I was lengthened and strengthened this day, blessed be the name of the Lord; who alone can qualify to preach the gospel. May the praise be given to him, to whom it is only due. After this meeting, I returned home with a degree of sweet peace.

The winter following, I attended but few meetings except our own; being in my usual employment of teaching a school. O, saith my soul, may I so walk before the dear children committed to my care, that I may, as way opens in the truth, administer counsel to their tender minds! Having a large number of small children in my school, I was often brought to consider the importance of my trust, not only in respect to their outward education, but also to endeavor, through Divine assistance, to turn their tender minds in the way of Truth; teaching them that " the fear of the Lord is the beginning of wisdom," and to depart from evil is understanding. One day having a larger number than usual, and many of their minds appearing tender, I was led to beseech the Lord to be near them; and in secret did put up my petition on this wise: O Lord! visit the dear lambs under my care with the Day-spring from on high. Cause them, dearest Lord, to remember Thee, their Creator, in the days of their youth; while their minds are tender. And strengthen me, thy poor servant, to instruct them in thy fear; that

we may feel thy presence to be with us, which will enable
us to give thee the praise henceforth and forever more.
Amen.

Fifth Month, 1811.—Attended our Quarterly Meeting;
and the latter part of the same month our Yearly Meeting
in New York, to good satisfaction. Many Friends from
distant parts attended this annual gathering, whose gospel
labors were strengthening to my mind.

On my return home, I was informed of the death of
one of my near neighbors—a Friend—whose departure
was sudden and unexpected. Oh how needful it is to be
prepared for death; seeing it will sooner or later arrest
us all!

Eighth Month, 18th, I visited a sick woman who was
near leaving the world. She appeared in a comfortable
state of mind; had her senses well; and manifested her
satisfaction with my visit, by requesting a religious opportunity in her family. Feeling my mind drawn thereto,
I asked the people present to sit down in a quiet manner,
there being several of the Methodist persuasion present;
the sick woman being also a member of that meeting.
After a time of silence, my mouth was opened in gospel
love, and concluded in supplication to the Lord, to the
tendering of most present; and to the comfort of the sick
woman, who, at our parting, signified the same. For we
parted in an affectionate manner, I not at all doubting, if
enabled to make a happy end, that I should meet her in
everlasting peace. She lived but a few hours after this
interview.

The next Third-day I was at her burial. A Methodist
minister also attended, and a number more of their church.
There were likewise some Friends, and many of other
denominations there. When I took my seat in this meet-

ing, a living desire arose in my mind, that the Lord would
be pleased to keep down forward spirits, and instruct by
his own power. Soon after the meeting gathered, a man
brought a stand with a Bible on it. This minister and I
sat side by side in a quiet manner for some time; which
no doubt appeared strange to some of them. But I believe he felt something that forebade his proceeding in his
usual formal manner. After a while he got up; but did
not take his Bible for a text, but spoke something in allusion to the solemnity of the occasion. He then kneeled
in prayer. After which he spoke a little, but soon expressed that he found it right for him to leave the service
of the meeting, saying, he believed the Spirit of the Lord
was at work with some present; and so sat down. Where-
upon the meeting remained silent for some time. My
mind was truly brought to wait on the Lord, and my
strength was renewed in him. After a period of sweet
silence, a man of a forward spirit, who had been in the
way of speaking in their meetings, got up and spoke; but
the power of the Lord was against him, and he pretty soon
sat down. Directly after this, I felt the power of Truth,
as a live coal from the holy altar, to touch my heart,
whereby I was raised on my feet, and my mouth opened
with the declaration: Christ is the fountain of living waters,
unto which all may come and drink to the satisfying of
their thirsty souls. Enlarging thereon, the Lord was
pleased to favor with his gospel power and life-giving
presence, which only can enable any to preach the gospel;
for which divine favor my soul doth bless his holy name.
After I sat down, the Methodist minister arose and said
he was now confirmed in what he had before felt. He
expressed his satisfaction with what was said, and desired
the people to remember the counsel of our friend, as he

called me, adding, they had been faithfully warned. He
kneeled again, and then sat down. After which we remained a time in silence. I then offered him my hand,
which he received in a loving manner, and so the meeting
concluded to the satisfaction of most present. The minister expressed his love, and we had some agreeable conversation, parting in a loving manner. Oh how good it
is to trust in the Lord; for I believe he gave the victory
this day.

Some time after this, I was invited to attend the burial
of an aged woman—not a member with us—living about
five miles distant. It being on First-day afternoon, and,
as I was afterwards informed, notice being given of it at
their different meetings, a large concourse of people attended. I went to the meeting in great poverty of spirit,
and took my seat with my whole dependence on the Lord;
who is strength in weakness, riches in poverty, and a
present Helper in every needful time. But let none dare
to arise to speak in his name, until he gives the word of
command. I was led to show the people the preciousness
of time. That it waited not for man, nor tarried for the
sons of men. That it was more precious, because in time
only can we prepare for a never-ending eternity. I was
led clearly to open the Apostle's testimony where he
saith: "If ye live after the flesh ye shall die; but if ye
through the spirit do mortify the deeds of the body, ye
shall live." And also, "To be carnally minded is death,
but to be spiritually minded is life and peace." I was
much enlarged thereon to my humbling admiration.—
The presence of the Lord was near, and many were sensible thereof. The meeting concluded with tender advice
and counsel to the youth.

After this meeting, a Baptist preacher came to me, and

said he was glad to see me for the first time. And said he felt such unity with the counsel to the youth, that he was sorry he had not publicly declared it. I told him I wanted no praise; but enjoined if there was any good done to give the praise to whom it was due. He parted with me in a loving manner; and said, "Go on in the strength of the Lord." Oh may all praise be ascribed to the Shepherd of Israel, without whose blessed help we can do nothing. Oh join me, reader, to give him all the praise, and let the creature be abased as in the dust.

CHAPTER VI.

VISITS MEETINGS AND FAMILIES NEAR RENSSALAERVILLE, N. Y. VISITS RHODE ISLAND QUARTERLY MEETING, AND SOME MEETINGS IN CONNECTICUT. LETTER OF DORCAS BROWN. LETTER OF LYDIA WEEKS. LEAVES HOME TO VISIT FRIENDS AND OTHERS IN EASTON AND FERRIS-BURG QUARTERLY MEETINGS. DEATH OF HIS WIFE. LETTERS OF MARY VARNEY. LETTER OF JOHN WILBUR.

In the Second Month of 1812, Christopher Healy informed his Monthly Meeting of a prospect of religious service in some neighboring meetings with their families. It granting him the requisite liberty, he set out the 27th of the same month, accompanied by a Friend of his own meeting. In some of these opportunities he writes of his way being much closed up; but at others, enlargement through Holy Help, was experienced.

His diary thus continues:

Berne meeting was crowded, and the Lord was pleased to favor with His holy presence. Truth's doctrine dropped as the dew, and as the gentle rain, to the comfort of many minds. This afternoon was at an appointed meeting about four miles from Berne, held at the widow Coles'. I was led to open to the people the mystery of Ezekiel's vision concerning the dry bones; showing them that there are many at the present day, who are as dry and lifeless as those the Prophet beheld in the valley. Oh may the Lord by His mighty powerful voice, shake the dry and barren minds of the children of men, and cause them to behold their situation; that so they may cry for help, and that the Lord may be pleased to breathe the breath of life into them, that they may stand up and become an army for the Lord, to fight in his glorious cause: the weapons thereof being not carnal, but mighty through God to the pulling down of the strongholds of sin.

After attending a few more meetings, he returned home, with, as he states, a thankful heart to the Lord; and found his family well.

On the 13th of Ninth Month of the same year, his friends of the Monthly and Quarterly Meetings respectively of which he was a member, having granted the needful certificates, he started on a religious visit to Rhode Island Quarterly Meeting, and some meetings in the State of Connecticut. He speaks of the parting from his dear wife and family as trying, this being the farthest from home he had yet been; but of her giving him up as cheerfully as he could expect. With his friends Nathan and Ruth Spencer he proceeded pretty directly to Canaan, in Connecticut, where he writes—

We found a few Friends. Had a meeting to good satisfaction; and afterwards an opportunity with the members by themselves; which proved strengthening to our minds as well as theirs. There appeared to be a few among them that were engaged in the blessed cause, and who were good examples to others. From thence we went to Hartford, and had a meeting with Friends. It was somewhat trying in the early part, but towards the conclusion more favored. I was led to declare the necessity of a living engagement in the Truth, that we might become as lights to the world; and my friend Ruth Spencer, in sounding an alarm. We found some well engaged Friends at this place, though the number was small. From others we parted with almost aching hearts, beholding their want of spiritual life; which ever causes the true mourners in Zion to weep.

After going to and from several meetings, with but little remark in reference to them, he came on the next First-day week to Hopkinton, where he writes—

Many attended, not of our Society. It was a highly favored meeting. Many of the dear youth having been received by convincement in this meeting within a few years, their company and countenances refreshed my spirit: feeling the living engagement of their minds and fellowship in the truth. Had a meeting this afternoon about four miles from Friends' regular meeting-place at the house I removed from when I went into New York State. Many of my former neighbors attended and were glad to see me. Though this meeting was trying in the forepart, it ended to good satisfaction. Next day had a meeting at Rickmonton, at Friends' meeting-house, where it appeared that there was want of attention to the direction of the great Physician of value, by which means some of them remained sick and wounded, causing us to leave the meeting with heavy hearts.

The next Fifth-day attended the meeting at the lower meeting-house in South Kingston. Information that we intended to be at this meeting having spread, many not of our Society attended. The Great Master was pleased to crown it with His heavenly light, and the doctrine of the gospel dropped as the dew and as the gentle rain to the watering many minds. This is the place that I first publicly espoused that cause which is dignified with immortality, and crowned with eternal life. This afternoon had a meeting at the court-house on Little Rest Hill, and many people attended. Here I was led to declare Christ Jesus to be the only way of life and salvation. That he was the stone that was set at naught by the builders of old, but was then, and is still, the head of the corner. I was favored to set before them the blessed effects of obedience to the spirit of Truth in the heart, to the consolation of many minds present. This meeting concluded in fervent supplication to the only preserver of men.

Sixth-day had a meeting at Wickford, wherein I was silent; but our friend Ruth Spencer had a few words by way of testimony. In the afternoon, attended a meeting appointed for us at a Baptist meeting-house about three miles from Wickford, which was owned and crowned by the good Master. Several that were there, after the meeting concluded, expressed their satisfaction, and that their minds had been sweetly comforted. First-day attended Friends' meeting at Greenwich. In the afternoon, one appointed for us at a Baptist meeting-house, about seven miles from Greenwich, near to the cotton factories of that place. A blessed meeting it was. Many of the people attended. The principles of truth were clearly opened, and seemed to have place in many minds.

Second-day had a meeting at Foster, which was small but to our comfort. After meeting, dined at B. Collins'. In a religious opportunity in his family, the children were very tender; and parted with us in a sweet frame of mind. From thence we rode to Rowland Green's; who was gone on a religious visit in the Southern States. His wife and children received us very affectionately. Next day had a meeting at Scituate; very few Friends belong to this meeting, but general notice being spread, many others came; and the great Shepherd was pleased to make himself livingly known amongst us, who is the crown and diadem of all our meetings. Some expressed their satisfaction in this meeting in a very moving manner.— Fourth-day had a meeting at Cranston, to good satisfaction. Dined at Sylvester Weeks'. He and his wife, Lydia—she being a worthy minister—are as a father and mother in Israel. In the afternoon rode to Providence, accompanied by our kind and loving friend Dorcas Brown; and by William Jenkins, a young man that came out to meet us at this meeting. Lodged this night at Daniel Anthony's, who is the parent of our friend Ruth Spencer, and father-in-law to Job Scott. They received us gladly.

Fifth-day, 8th of Tenth Month, which was my birthday, had a meeting at Providence. Sat the meeting through in suffering silence. Sixth-day visited families at Pautucket. Found great want of a living engagement among them. Seventh-day, had a meeting at Cumberland; where light and life gave the victory. Several Friends came where we dined, and we had a comfortable oppor-

tunity together, which proved consolatory. First-day
attended Friends' meeting at Smithfield lower meeting-
house. Here, through our blessed Helper, judgment was
laid to the line, and justice to the plumb-line; and we
were mutually comforted together. Daniel Anthony and
daughter accompanied us to several of these meetings.
First-day afternoon, attended a meeting appointed for us
at Friends' meeting-house in the town of Providence;
which was large; some few colored people being among
them. I was largely opened to speak on Daniel of old.
Oh, saith my soul, may we of the present day have that
holy zeal and faith that Daniel had! I also had a word
of encouragement to the colored people, to the tendering
of some of their minds. One of them followed us to the
house where we stopped, and in a very tender manner
expressed the satisfaction and love he felt.

Second-day, rode to Swansea; and at one o'clock attended a burial, where the friends of the deceased had
requested a Friends' meeting, and many attended. It
was a favored time. At three o'clock this afternoon, attended a meeting appointed for us in Friends' meeting-
house at Swansea, which was large and greatly favored.
Third-day, in the forenoon, we were at Freetown. It
was an exercising time in the fore part, but ended to a
good degree of satisfaction. It the afternoon had a meeting at a small village about two miles from Freetown.
This was small, occasioned by the young men of that
place being called upon that day to perform military
duty. My mind not feeling clear, I desired another
meeting in the evening, which was much united with;
particularly by their minister, who not only gave his attendance in the afternoon, but expressed his satisfaction.
The evening meeting was large, amounting it was thought

to as many as four hundred people. The captain of the training company, when he dismissed them, requested their attendance at the meeting. It proved a precious season. The peaceable kingdom of Christ was clearly held up to their view. After meeting, the minister invited us home with him, and treated us very kindly. Oh may we never forget the tender mercies of our God! who is the great Minister of ministers; and only can give ability to preach the gospel; and also to send it home to the hearts of the people, and seal it on their minds.

Fifth-day, attended their meeting at Providence. And after it, the meeting of Ministers and Elders, to good satisfaction. At six o'clock in the evening had a meeting appointed for the colored people of the town. It was thought there were more than four hundred of these attended, with two hundred white people or more. It was a solemn meeting. The doctrine of the gospel flowed freely. It was clearly opened to the people, that God had no respect of persons, but in every nation, he that feareth Him and worketh righteousness, shall be accepted of him. And as the rivers of old that went out of the garden of the Lord, parted and became into four heads, and one part watered the land of Ethiopia, so doth the grace of God and stream of gospel love, flow to the people of color. It was a season not to be forgotten by many. Some of these poor people were heard to say, Oh what a good meeting we have had! How I wish, said one, that some of my acquaintance had been here! One of them towards the close of the meeting, in a solemn manner, testified to the goodness of the Lord, saying, "Had I the riches of the Indies, I would willingly part with it all, for the love I now feel." May the praise be given to the Lord who was evidently near this evening, and whose presence alone makes good meetings. Blessed be his holy name forever.

After this he had or attended meetings at Newport, Portsmouth, Tivertown, Conanicut Island, Boston Neck, Tower Hill, Hopkinton, Providence, Bristol, Greenwich, Wickford, North Kingston, Cranston, Swansea, and at Warwick. The last meeting, he writes, " was a precious one, wherein the people were shown that the travels of the children of Israel of old, were a type of the Christian travel towards the heavenly Jerusalem, the holy Mount Zion, the city of the living God, whose walls are salvation, and whose gates are praise." He appointed a few more meetings at factories, and some among other religious societies, where he was treated with much kindness and respect; and then, parting with his friends, set out for home, which he was enabled to reach safely, and was joyfully received by his dear wife and family: being truly thankful to the Lord for his preserving hand, that, as he writes, " kept me, and brought me safely home to my family and friends with the reward of peace." He was absent on this journey about ten weeks, attended more than sixty meetings, and rode upwards of one thousand miles.

While on this religious errand, the following letters were written. They show the esteem, in some wise, which Friends there had for him, with their appreciation of his gospel labors. They are thus indorsed by Christopher Healy:—" Some letters received by my wife while I was in Rhode Island."

Providence, 31st of Tenth Month, 1812.

Dear Friend:—Though personally unknown to me, I take the liberty of thus addressing thee. Having been

some days in company with thy beloved husband in
attending meetings, it has tended to create a near sympathy with him, and also for thee in his absence from
thee. Thy care is great in superintending so large a
family of little ones. But, my dear friend, I would have
thee to remember, that formerly there was a reward for
those that tarried at home. Yea, we read that they divided the spoil. And I have no doubt but this will be
thy enriching experience; and that thou also wilt share
largely of the Father's love, by thus resigning the precious
partner of thy life, to the disposal and service of his
blessed Master. The Lord has indeed anointed and appointed him to perform the service in which he has been
engaged since he has been in our parts, strengthening him
to fervently and affectionately labor for the good of souls;
and to the exalting of that grace by which the Apostle
said, "I am what I am." And, O! saith my soul, may
he continue on the right foundation, keeping a single eye
to his Holy Head and Leader, Christ Jesus, the Rock of
ages; that he may more extensively labor, if required, to
the awakening of thousands to the knowledge of the
truth; which I have no doubt will be the case, as he keeps
humble and reverently dependent upon the alone putting
forth of the Shepherd of Israel, the only safe Leader and
Guide, who has already led him about and instructed
him, and opened to his understanding the treasures of
wisdom and knowledge, and revealed the mysteries of the
kingdom to him. May he therefore continue faithfully
ministering in the ability which God giveth.

I have been with him at fifteen meetings; in most of
which he was greatly favored; some of them being particularly heart-tendering seasons, I hope long to be remembered by many to their lasting improvement. I said in

mine heart, it is the Lord's doings and marvellous in
mine eyes.   And oh! what might this power effect for
many more if submitted to? There is nothing that digni-
fies and exalts like the truth; and none are so happy as
the followers of it.   Although it leads in a straight and
narrow path, it leads to peace; even that peace that the
world can neither give nor take away; while how desirous are those that enjoy the possession of it, that all
mankind may live in the same. For this they labor, and
are willing to spend and to be spent if it may be to the
gathering of but one precious soul.

Thy husband is nearly through the meetings that he
expected to take, and will probably, after attending our
Quarterly Meeting, look toward home.

Thine affectionately,

DORCAS BROWN.

Swansea, 5th of Eleventh Month, 1812.

Beloved Friend:—I thought I felt a precious liberty to
salute thee in endeared affection, having not only to feel
with thy dear husband since his lot has been cast in this
land, but with thee in thy present tried situation. It is
often consoling to my mind to believe, that the law that
was made for the benefit of those that stay by the stuff is
in full force, having never been repealed. And I am
comforted in a fresh belief, that as thou abides in the
faith and in the patience, thou wilt be favored to partake,
not only with thy precious Christopher in his sufferings,
but also in his cup of heavenly consolation: which, if I
have any sense and feeling, he has had at times to overflow. I have been at several meetings with him, in which
he has been wonderfully favored to divide the word aright,
to the strengthening and encouraging many who were

almost ready to say, Who shall show us any good? That
I have said in my heart. It is the Lord's doings, and marvellous in mine eyes! Oh! saith my soul, may He have
the praise of his own works; that so whatever we do, may
be to the honor of his great and excellent name.

Thy dear husband has had many meetings among those
not of our Society; for which I think him eminently
qualified. I have travailed with him, in my feeble capa-
city, fervently breathing for his preservation on the right
ground; and that he may be favored to see the right time
of returning to thee, and to reap the rich reward of entire
dedication. As his visit seems drawing to a close, I hope
and have no doubt in my mind, that as he keeps an eye
single to his great and good Master, that He will graciously condescend to be with him in returning to his
outward habitation, giving the enjoyment of that sweet
peace that is only purchased by obedience, and is more to
be preferred than corn, wine, or oil; which peace I have
had to believe, thou would be a sharer in. As thou keeps
near to the Fountain of all good, He will not only be a
father to thy children, and a tender husband unto thee,
but will keep thee in the hour of temptation, and when
thou art separated from thy richest earthly comfort.—
And as dear Christopher keeps his place, he will find, if I
am not very much mistaken, that though he has tender
ties, he must turn his back upon them, and do whatever
his Divine Master biddeth him to do.

My dear husband wishes to be affectionately remembered to thee; and saith he feels a near unity with Christopher. We are at Swansea, where we have come to
attend our Quarterly Meeting. It is near the hour of
gathering, so I bid thee farewell.

LYDIA WEEKS.

At the next Monthly Meeting succeeding his return from this journey, he again laid before it an exercise which had for some time attended his mind, to make a religious visit to Friends and others within the compass of Easton and Ferrisburg Quarterly Meetings. His friends uniting with him herein, he was set at liberty to pursue his prospect. This journey, requiring him to leave home so soon again, is alluded to as a close trial to both him and his dear wife, who, as will be seen, departed this life, in the mysterious providence of our Father in heaven, leaving ten children, the oldest not seventeen years of age, before his return again to the afflicted remnant of his family. He left home on the 1st of First Month, 1813, and rode to Jacob Gurney's, a worthy Friend who had given up to be his companion; saying, he believed it to be his duty to accompany him in this journey.

They attended meetings pretty steadily within the limits mentioned. But as little is said in reference thereto, except the fact of doing so, it might seem more tedious than otherwise to the reader to insert them all here. The diary states that on " First-day we attended Friends' meeting at Queensbury, which was large. Notice being given of our intention of being there, and a funeral also occurring at the same time, caused most of the people within some distance to be collected together. The uncertainty of time, and that all flesh is as grass, was clearly held up to their view; and, that the dispensation which we of the present day live under, is the gospel dispensation, whereof Jesus Christ is the great Minister: who declared his kingdom was not of this world. I may say, under a humbling sense of Holy Help, that He was unto me this day mouth and wisdom; and many were reached with the incomes of the Father's love. May all praise be given to the great

King, who holds the treasures of wisdom and knowledge. The meeting concluded in solemn supplication. Thus we parted in that love, which enables to drink into one cup, and closely binds together."

After an appointed meeting at Lake George, he alludes to being introduced to a young man about twenty-one years of age, who had received a gift in the ministry. He says, " May he be preserved ! What good examples such are to those that are young, as well as to some that are more advanced. My dear young friends, how doth my heart, while writing these lines, flow with tender solicitude for you, that you may closely attend to the law of the Spirit of life, the light of Christ in the heart, which ever has and ever will prove to be a fountain of life to preserve from the snares of death."

It was while he himself was an invalid at Troy, on this labor of love, that he first heard of his dear wife's illness; and very soon after of her death; with that also of his mother-in-law. How true is the language of the poet :— " Woes cluster: rare are solitary woes." This seemed to be an unexpected and very heavy stroke to him. He says :

I was weighed down with trouble. Think, dear reader, of the bitterness of my spirit on my own, and my dear children's account! But I hope I did not exceed right bounds. Though my heart did ache with sorrow, so that I seemed like sinking under it, I craved of the Lord to be resigned to His will, and He, the tender Shepherd of Israel, regarded my cry, and consoled me by His precious presence. I carefully searched the ground of my leaving my family, and could appeal to my God that my intention was to obey him, and follow his requirings; and

I dare not think that I had done wrong in leaving them. Thus I tried to resign all to His blessed will, and to renew my covenant with Him, promising the great Lord of all, the remainder of my days.

He returned to his lonely home on Fifth-day, the 11th of Third Month, 1813, having been absent about two months, attended seventy-three meetings, and travelled more than a thousand miles.

His wife died, as already referred to, the 6th of Third Month, 1813, as if going into a sweet sleep. She much lamented the bereaved condition her children would be left in, and greatly desired her husband's and their welfare. The last words she was heard to utter were: "Come, and let us go to the house of the Lord."

His journal further states, that—

Through the blessing of the great Caretaker, who opened the hearts of sympathizing friends, I was favored to place my children to my satisfaction; and then removed myself to my much beloved friends Benjamin and Martha Gurney's, where I met with a very cordial reception. Oh, may the blessing of heaven rest upon them, and upon those that have the care of my dear children, who I desire may be trained in the fear of the Lord. I am well satisfied with my home. Greater care could not be taken, than is taken by those kind friends with whom I live; and if they that give only a cup of cold water in the name of a disciple were not to lose their reward, how much more shall the blessing descend on those, who, out of a sense of duty, do so much for one left as I am. We live together in that love and true Christian fellowship that enables to drink into one cup. Behold how good and how pleasant

it is! May the Great Shepherd guard and keep us thus
united together in the ever blessed truth.

During Christopher Healy's absence from home on this
visit, divers letters of encouragement and sympathy were
written either to his wife, or to himself, near the time of,
and after her decease. From these we select the following. To the former, dated Charlotte, 2d Mo. 10th, 1813,
there is this indorsement by C. H. "A letter from Mary
Varney to my wife."

"My Dear Friend:—Though personally a stranger to
thee, yet having been favored to attend several meetings
appointed by thy endeared companion, I felt something to
arise in my mind after this manner: What a blessing it
is to be favored with such an husband, who prefers the
welfare of his fellow-creatures to every outward tie! Oh,
my endeared friend, mourn not too much for the loss of
his company; for how has he been strengthened, through
Holy Help, not only to sound an alarm to the ungodly,
and to invite the wanderers home, but also to speak a
word in due season to comfort them that mourn in Zion!
Oh, how has he indeed been made an instrument in the
hand of our God, to encourage these, and take them by
the hand, as it were, in their solitary and depressed situa-
tions. I have great cause to number this among the
favors with which the great Preserver has blessed me, at
a time when I was ready to say in my heart, 'who shall
show me any good,' or can I much longer endure under
the weight of discouragements which I feel? Oh, that I
might walk worthy of all the favors conferred on me by
His Almighty Hand, who has wrought wonders indeed.
May'st thou, dear sister, be strengthened to give thy dear
husband up, though he may be called to lands unknown,

and to places far distant from hence. If this should be, He that has called him to leave all that is near and dear in life, will be a husband to thee in his absence, and a father and caretaker to thy beloved children. I have felt a sympathy with thee not to be described fully by words, nor conveyed by ink and pen. Thus with a salutation of love unfeigned, I affectionately bid thee farewell,   MARY VARNEY."

The next letter, addressed to Christopher Healy, seems almost prophetical of that forthcoming chastening, which suddenly and forever severed his dear companion from him.—

"Charlotte, Third Month 4th, 1813.

"My endeared Friend,—That regard which I believe Truth itself raised in my mind for thee, is by no means impaired; but often, very often, since we parted has it been revived, with fervent desires, I trust, for thy prosperity as well as my own. In seasons of greatest retirement, my spirit has craved His holy aid for thee, my endeared friend, believing many trials are allotted thee, on account of the testimony He has given thee to bear for His name and truth before the people. It has frequently occurred to my mind, while viewing the favors conferred on thee while with us, whether the enemy will not be suffered to buffet and to try thee still more! But may thy faith fail not, my endeared brother. He that has been with thee in six troubles, will not leave thee in the seventh, as thou abidest steadfast. I remember, my endeared friend, to whom I am writing; and it is not with a view to teach thee, but as things simply arise in my mind, so I drop them in that freedom which I trust true friendship confers.

"I have felt myself much alone since I saw thee; and it frequently revives on my mind, 'I am like a pelican in the wilderness;' and there seems but One to whom I dare to make my moan; and I have found him all sufficient. Indeed he has not only enlarged my heart towards my fellow creatures, but given me that confidence in his Almighty power that enables to testify that He will give ability to answer His requirings, even to be mouth and wisdom, yea all in all, to those who trust in Him alone. May my soul bow in humble reverence before him at all times, in remembrance of his mercies and great condescension to me, a poor unworthy child. I have felt like one relieved from a great weight of distress since thou wast at Lincoln; for which relief, may gratitude fill my mind to His adorable name. But thou knowest, my dear friend, the unwearied enemy is never wanting on every hand, and when he cannot prevail to sink the poor tried one below all hope, he will endeavor to creep in, in some other way—perhaps to exalt the mind, and to make it appear somewhat in its own view. May thy prayers be for me, that my faith fail not in the trying hour; but that I may be sustained and supported to the praise of His ever worthy name.   MARY VARNEY."

The following, from the same, holds out the cordial of tender sympathy to his bereaved and afflicted mind.—

"Granville, Fifth Month 4th, 1813.

"My endeared Friend Christopher Healy,—I have had frequently to remember thee in thy lonesome situation. But I trust the great Caretaker will care for thee, and sustain and bear up thy mind under the many trials which in his wisdom he may permit. We read that many are the afflictions of the righteous, yet the Lord delivereth out of them all. I should esteem it a great favor to see thee once more; but whether this will ever be is very uncertain. Oh that we may dwell where we may be as living epistles written in each other's hearts! I believe that whilst I remain in time, and am favored to live in the truth, I shall not forget thee, my beloved friend, who was made an instrument for my help. I have thought many times since, that I seemed to myself in a new world where a free air circulated. Truly I have cause to praise His great Name that works wonders. May I dwell in humility all the days of my life; and give the honor and praise to whom it is due. If thou feels a freedom to write a few lines to me at any time, they will be very acceptable. After hearing of thy great loss, and as I was musing on thy case, it seemed to arise in my mind to write. I am thy friend. I trust, though I feel at times as the least in the flock, desiring thy sympathy.

"MARY VARNEY."

John Wilbur also thus writes to him on this sorrow-stirring occasion:—

"Hopkinton, Fifth Month 23d, 1813.

"Dear Friend Christopher Healy.—We received thy kind salutation of Twelfth Month last,—which was very acceptable. I had written a few lines previous thereto, in order to send thee, but finding that thou wast from home, I omitted forwarding them. But as they were penned under some sensibility and anticipation of an afflictive dispensation to be meted thee, I think it may not be altogether improper to enclose and forward them at this time. I can tell thee, Christopher, that I ever desire, while here, to be in such a situation of mind, as to be able to sympathize with the afflicted, and to be willing to take my share in whatever sufferings are permitted to assail any of my near and dear friends; knowing, from a little experience, that the commiseration of a friend, when I have been afflicted, has been as a precious cordial to my mind. And now my desire is that thou mightest be enabled to bear up in thy present bereaved situation, leaning on that Beloved which I hope thou art not bereaved of. Notwithstanding the desire of thine eye and of thine heart is taken away as with a stroke, yet I trust there is One, who, although invisible to thine outward eye, thou art favored to behold, and thy heart to be fixed upon; who is altogether lovely; yea, far surpassing all earthly ties or outward possessions, on which the mind may rest and have hope. All earthly enjoyments are subject to change; but this, the Beloved of souls and Father of all, is the same yesterday, to-day, and forever. He will never wholly forsake those that love Him, and rely on his supporting power, but he will bear them up as on eagle's wings, and often bring them into quiet places, and speak comfortably unto them; giving them, as it were, vineyards of precious fruit, and the valley of Achor for a door of hope; making them sometimes to sing his praise as in the vigor of youth.

"When I take a view of thy late service, I am ready to say, that I think thou hast cause to be thankful that thou gave up thereto. For had there been a holding back therein, peradventure it might have added greatly to thy affliction when otherways deeply tried. But now I think thou may'st be comforted in reflecting that thou hast endeavored to fulfil the several services pointed out as time and ability were afforded. May'st thou therefore be enabled to say that this dispensation is from the Lord; and to adopt the language of Job, that tried servant formerly, 'The Lord gave, and the Lord hath taken away; blessed be the name of the Lord.'

"My wife has been afflicted with sickness for about a month; but is rather on the mend. She desires to be remembered to thee, and expresses much feeling and sympathy for thee under thy late loss and afflictions. Similar feelings are also mentioned by many of thy friends hereaway. I remain affectionately thy friend,

JOHN WILBUR."

CHAPTER VII.

ATTENDS THE YEARLY MEETING IN NEW YORK. VISITS MEETINGS IN EASTON QUARTERLY MEETING. RELIGIOUS ENGAGEMENTS AT HOME. VISITS FRIENDS AND OTHERS IN THE EASTERN AND SOUTHERN PARTS OF NEW YORK, AND IN PHILADELPHIA YEARLY MEETING. INCIDENT RELATED OF HIS ENTERING A BALL-ROOM.

THE diary is resumed :—

The latter part of the Fifth Month of this year (1813), I attended our Yearly Meeting at New York. The several sittings thereof were favored with the presence of our Holy Head, who is the life and crown of all our religious meetings. There I met with some of my dear brethren and sisters from the northward, where I had made my late visit; and in remembrance of the sweet unity and fellowship we had one with another, we were glad and rejoiced to meet again, believing that the love of Jesus had bound us together. After my return, I attended some burials, and had a number of meetings within the

compass of our own Monthly Meeting; most of which
were favored. When at home, particularly, I was exceedingly lonely, and my feelings not to be described;
visiting my children brought sad and sorrowful recollec-
tions, especially to hear some of them express the loss of
their dear mother. But many times, in the midst of
these seasons, the great Caretaker was not wanting with
the comfort of His Holy presence. Oh may He continue
to be my companion! And I have no doubt He will, if I
can but be preserved His devoted servant.

On the 2nd of Ninth Month, I left home in order to
visit my sister, Sarah Main; and to have some meetings
within the compass of Easton Quarterly Meeting; having
the concurrence of my friends herein. Was at Easton
on First-day, and was glad to see and sit with Friends of
this meeting, as well as many that were not members;
being favored to participate in that love, that hath no
bounds. Afternoon at Cambridge, where the precious
water from under the threshold of the door of the sanctuary, did flow and become a river to swim in; and we
rejoiced in the Lord's presence. Many Friends and
others that attended when I was here before, were at this
meeting.

The Fifth-day following, I attended Friends' week-day
meeting at Queensbury. This meeting being composed
mostly of Friends, I desired no notice to be given except
to such. Here I had to set before my brethren and sisters
the purity of our profession, and the Rock from whence
we were hewn. Also how our ancient Friends not only
suffered for the cause of Truth, but obtained the victory
through Christ Jesus their Leader. He was made perfect
through suffering; and how highly it behooves us—as
professors of the same holy faith—to be willing to suffer;

and through and over all to stand for the cause and the testimony; that it may not, through our unwatchfulness, or any other means, fall in the streets. I did believe, while standing in this meeting, that if Friends keep to their peaceable testimonies and practice, as well as profession, that no weapon formed against them shall ever prosper. For, as it is written, " When a man's ways please the Lord, he maketh even his enemies to be at peace with him."

I visited some Friends' families in this place; and on Sixth-day came to my sister's, in the town of Greenwich; and we were rejoiced to meet again. Seventh-day had a meeting in the neighborhood, which the Master was pleased to own. In the afternoon held one at Whipple City, which was small; and I not feeling clear, requested another in the evening, which was readily granted; and a large meeting it was. Here the glorious gospel dispensation was clearly set forth, with the benefit those receive who live under the peaceable government of Christ; and how inconsistent all outward wars and fightings were with such a dispensation which was ushered in with the anthem: "Glory to God in the highest, and on earth peace, good will toward men," which all such as profess Christianity claim to live under. This meeting continued near three hours, and was a heart-melting season. The people appeared loath to leave their seats when the meeting was over. Here I parted with my dear sister; and a heavy parting it was to us both. May she be favored to live in the truth, and to have the company of Him, who comforts those that mourn in Zion.

Shortly after this he returned home. In another short visit he writes of being at a meeting at Othniel Phelps';

who, with his wife, had been convinced of Friends' principles. "May they continue," writes Christopher Healy,
"in what is made known to them to be their duty; so
shall their endeavors be crowned with success in the holy
warfare, the weapons whereof are no more carnal, but
mighty through God to the pulling down of strongholds."

On First-day, the 20th of Ninth Month, Christopher
Healy attended his own meeting at Stanton Hill, "wherein," he writes, "the doctrine of the gospel was clearly
opened. Many people, not of our Society, attended, and
a refreshing time it was. May the praise be given to our
gracious Helper. At the close of this meeting the epistle
from the Yearly Meeting in London was read. The hearing of which brought a sweet covering over the meeting;
and it broke up in a solid manner. On the Fourth-day
following, attended our week-day meeting. Almost as
soon as I had taken my seat, these words came into my
mind: 'Without faith it is impossible to please God.'
On which I enlarged, showing to my beloved friends, that
the faith which pleases Him works by love and purifies
the heart. I was greatly engaged thereon, to the reaching the blessed witness in the hearts of many. This
meeting concluded in solemn supplication to the King of
heaven; and I believe will not soon be forgotten."

Obtaining certificates from his respective meetings, he,
on the 6th of Twelfth Month, 1813, left his home, to perform a religious visit to Friends, and those not of the
Society in the eastern and southern parts of his own
Yearly Meeting; and to the same class within the limits
of the Yearly Meeting of Philadelphia. His journal
states, that after taking a solemn leave of the family

where he made his home, it being a precious season, he
pursued his journey cheerfully; having commended his
dear children to the protection of the guardian Shepherd
of Israel. After attending a few meetings, he writes of
tarrying one night at Zopher Green's; whom he repre-
sents as a worthy father in Israel, his counsel and advice
being precious to him. He alludes to their dear children
also as those that were walking in the Truth; and then
adds, "Oh how helpful young Friends may be to one
another, by being good examples; and this not only to
each other, but to the world at large. What a comfort,
too, such are to their religiously concerned parents!"

This worthy Friend accompanied him to the next meeting. Notice being given, it was large and much favored;
proving to many a watering season. After meeting, he
visited a Friend's family in the neighborhood; "wherein," he says, "the Great Master favored with that counsel
which is bread to the soul. A heart-tendering season it
was to the dear youth present. May it remain with them
as a nail fastened in a sure place, and the praise be given
to Him who alone is worthy."

After visiting several meetings and families, with but
little comment thereon, he, with his companion, Samuel
Seaman, passed into Pennsylvania, and attended Strouds-
burg, Easton, Plumstead, and Abington meetings, and
thence on Third-day, to Thomas Scattergood's, in Philadelphia, who kindly accompanied them to the three
Monthly Meetings in the city. The memoranda continue:—

These were mostly favored meetings; and Friends of
Philadelphia showed us much kindness. Sixth-day, accompanied by Thomas Scattergood and Thomas Norton,

we attended a meeting appointed for us at Germantown.
In this meeting I was led to speak of the glorious gospel
dispensation, contrasting it with that of the Law. That
the outward wars, under the dispensation of the Law, are
to be spiritualized; and it is thus that they convey divine
instruction to us of the present day. For the day pro-
phesied of by Jacob of old, has come to pass that "The
sceptre shall not depart from Judah, nor a lawgiver from
between his feet, until Shiloh come; and unto Him shall
the gathering of the people be." This Shiloh, which is
Christ Jesus, is come to teach his people Himself; and
happy are those who are taught of the Lord: for great
will be their peace. I was very much enlarged on this
subject, to my own comfort and satisfaction, and to the
tendering of many minds. Near the close of the meeting,
Thomas Scattergood stood up and said, that the gospel
dispensation had been clearly pointed out, and spoken to
in a lively manner; and his heart was made glad that
these things were so cleared up.

First-day, was at Horsham meeting. Many Friends
and others attended. It was a time of favor. The manner in which our Saviour was born; the way in which
he was preserved from the wrath of Herod; his life and
doctrine; and the benefit and blessed effects of his spirit
on the mind, were clearly spoken to; and I believe it was
a profitable season to many present. One aged Friend,
after meeting, greeted me kindly; and told me I had
labored faithfully amongst them; and said, "thou wilt
have thy reward." Second-day was at Buckingham
Monthly Meeting, where I had to remind them of our
great and holy profession. They were exhorted to live
consistently therewith, that they might be lights in the
world. Third-day attended Monthly Meeting at Sole-

bury; and that evening had an appointed meeting at Buckingham, which was large. Fourth-day at Wrightstown Monthly Meeting; and in the evening attended a meeting appointed for our Friend T. H., from New York: a favored time. This meeting was at a village called Newtown. Fifth-day was at Middletown Monthly Meeting; and had a public meeting in the evening. Sixth-day at Falls; and a public meeting in the evening.

All of these meetings were owned by the Shepherd of Israel. Friends were mutually comforted, and my soul had to rejoice in deep humiliation before the Lord, from whom all our strength doth flow. Seventh-day had a meeting at Makefield, where many hearts were tendered; and it was evident that the good Shepherd watered and fed his flock; and opened their minds to see his glorious rest, that he had prepared for those that follow him. That evening had a sitting in a family, to satisfaction.

First-day morning, my dear companion, Samuel Seaman, parted with me, and returned home. We parted in that love that had enabled us, while together, to drink into one cup. I came that day to Bristol meeting. Here the Lord caused his baptizing power to descend, which made my cup to overflow; and many hearts felt living praises to ascend to our Heavenly Father. Oh Lord! Thou who art strength in weakness, and whose living stream doth water thy poor depending children, I have great cause to be humbled before thee, for thou hast never failed to help in the needful time, as my faith has been unshaken, and mine eye and expectation has been unto thee. Oh! may I be preserved in an holy dedication of soul unto thee, for truly I have found there is none like unto thee, who hast the words of eternal life. Under a realizing sense of thy great power and merciful hand ex-

tended to me in this remoteness from my own abode, do I
bless thy great Name.   It is thy love that has opened the
hearts of Friends in this land, as well as the hearts of the
different denominations of professing Christians, to hear
the blessed words of truth.   How often has thy word, O
Lord, been as a fire and as a hammer, to the melting and
breaking everything that opposes thy glorious reign.   Be
pleased, Oh blessed Father, in and through thy beloved
Son, who alone can preserve under the operation of thy
truth, to keep those whom thou hast reached unto in thy
loving-kindness; that they, with my poor soul, may be
strengthened to ascribe all honor and glory, might and
power, unto thee, and to thy dear Son, for evermore.   Amen.

Second-day attended a meeting appointed for me at
Byberry.   I felt great weakness to attend my mind in
the morning, which continued until I sat down in the
meeting; but as I endeavored to keep mine eye to Him
who is strength, He did prove to be strength in my weakness; and truth reigned over all.   Many not of our Society attended, and among them were some colored people.
The great Master descended and did break and hand the
bread of life to the multitude, to the rejoicing of the dear
children of the heavenly family.   Third-day, at a village
called Smithfield, had a very crowded meeting.   Fourth-
day, attended Friends' meeting at Byberry; a very large
meeting.   Afternoon we were at Bustleton.   Fifth-day
at Holmesburg; they were large, and favored by the
overshadowing of Divine love, that caused many hearts
to rejoice.   Sixth-day had a meeting at a place called
Goosetown.   Seventh-day, at a village called Milford; a
more crowded meeting I have not been at in this land.
The Great Master made known his loving-kindness, and
many rejoiced in his presence.

First-day, crossed the Delaware to Trenton, and was at
Friends' meeting there, which was small. Staid that night
at Joshua Newbold's—a precious family. There met me
here a kind Friend by the name of Simon Gillam, a minister. Had a meeting appointed next day at Trenton.
Third-day, at Stonybrook. Fourth-day, at Bordentown.
Fifth-day at Crosswicks. Sixth-day, at Lower Mansfield;
and in the evening at Bordentown. Seventh-day at Upper
Mansfield; mostly favored meetings. At the last meeting came two kind Friends, Robert Pitfield and Elizabeth
Allinson, from Burlington, to meet us.

First-day attended meetings at Burlington, both fore
and afternoon; where we had the company of our beloved
friend Henry Hull. General notice being given, the
meetings were large, and owned by the Master of our
assemblies. Here belong our aged friends, John Hoskins,
George Dillwyn, and John Cox. In the evening, made
three religious visits in the town, viz., at John Hoskins',
William Allinson's, and Nathaniel Coleman's. These
were precious seasons; the families being alive in the
Truth. This when accompanied by the Shepherd of
Israel, which was our happy experience, makes such seasons refreshing. This evening returned to Robert Pitfield's; whose wife is a living member, which causes her
conversation to be refreshing to a weary mind. She is
but twenty-five years of age. Here we parted with our
kind friend Joseph Satterthwaite, who had been with us
for several days. Next day Robert Pitfield took us in his
carriage to a meeting at Westfield. Third-day to one at
Rancocas. After meeting we went home with our friend
Samuel Wills, where we were sweetly refreshed both in
body and mind, feeling the Great Master was there.
Fourth-day attended a meeting at Mount Holly. Fifth-

day, one at Moorestown. Sixth-day at Newtown. That
evening we crossed the Delaware to Philadelphia: and
Seventh-day rested. First-day morning was at meeting at
the Northern district.

He then attended in succession the Monthly Meetings
of Chester, Darby, Goshen, Concord, and Wilmington,
together with the Almshouse of Chester County, during
one of the evenings; and on the next, which was Seventh-
day, he attended the select Quarterly Meeting in Philadelphia. Resuming the journal—

First-day morning, I attended the meeting at Arch
Street; wherein I was silent. Afternoon, at Pine Street;
where I was again silent. Second-day, attended the general Quarterly Meeting at Arch Street. Our friend Henry
Hull was favored in testimony. Towards the close of the
meeting for worship, I had a few words to offer. Third-
day, had a meeting at Frankford; which was to satisfaction. Fourth-day, at the select Quarterly Meeting of
Abington, wherein I was favored. Fifth-day, the Quarterly Meeting. The business of Society was transacted
with brotherly love and condescension, and concluded to
the encouragement of each other. Sixth-day attended a
meeting appointed for us at Merion. Rode that night to
Edward Garrigues'. Seventh-day, rode to Darby; and
rested at Thomas Garrett's, who are loving and kind
friends.

First-day, at Darby meeting, which was large, being
composed of Friends and those not of our Society. It
ended to mutual satisfaction. That evening rode to Concord. Second-day, attended the meeting of Ministers and
Elders. Third-day, that for discipline; wherein, through

Divine help, I was favored to relieve my mind, to my
comfort, and the satisfaction of many. After meeting,
rode to Philip Price's, who, with his wife, went with us
to Caln Quarterly Meeting. I had many stripping and
baptizing seasons, about this time, but was favored to
abide in the patience. At this Quarterly Meeting I was
helped, towards its conclusion, to relieve my mind. Staid
that night at J. K.'s. Next day attended a meeting by
appointment at Westchester; wherein I was silent, being
resigned to the will of my Divine Master. That afternoon
rode to Thomas Garrett's, at Upper Darby, where our
dear friends were glad to see us. Seventh-day, reached
the neighborhood of Byberry. Next day attended meeting there, where were a great number of people of different professions. It was a precious meeting by and through
the help of Israel's King, who doth anoint afresh for his
work and service, as he is waited for in humble patience.
Oh! blessed and adored be the name of the great Minister of the sanctuary, who still remains to be mouth and
wisdom to those that stir not up nor awake him until He
please.

This afternoon rode to Isaac Parry's, attended by a
young Friend by the name of James Thornton, grandson
of that eminent minister James Thornton, of Byberry.
Second-day had a meeting at the almshouse of Bucks
County, with the sick and afflicted. This is the second of
this description that I have found it my duty to visit
since I have been within the limits of this Yearly Meeting.
Oh, what lessons of deep instruction these have been to
my mind. My pen is not able to represent to the full,
my sympathy with these poor creatures. Some have lost
their reason, so as to be quite distracted. Some are crip-
ples. Some groaning with severe pains, who expressed

that they did not expect to live many days; exclaiming,
"O! if I could but be happy, it is all I ask." How thankful they were, that we thought so much of them as to
have a meeting with them. It seems to me that pure
religion, under the immediate, quickening power of the
great Opener, leads to visit these. Oh, may I never forget
these seasons; and may you, that read these lines, be
favored to feel as I now feel. If so, it will humble the
mind as in the dust, and raise living intercessions, that the
Lord would bless these poor creatures; and although they
receive, as it were, their evil things in this life, that they
may be prepared for endless rest at last. Second-day
afternoon, had a meeting at Doylestown, which ended to
a good degree of satisfaction. Third-day, made a visit to
a settlement of Germans called Mennonists. They are a
plain people; both young and old being exemplary in
this respect. They have also a testimony against war.
The meeting was a satisfactory one; and they expressed
their thankfulness for our visit to them. That afternoon
rode to John Watson's. Next day attended Bucks Quarterly Meeting of ministers and elders, held at Wrightstown. In the afternoon had an appointed meeting about
six miles distant, at a public house. Fifth-day was at the
Quarterly Meeting, to good satisfaction. Sixth-day had
a public meeting at Wrightstown, appointed at nine o'clock
in the morning. It was a large and favored meeting.
Another at Yardleyville in the afternoon. That evening
came to our friend John Miller's, who with his family are
choice Friends. Here I was joined by William Taylor, a
dear and truly sympathizing friend and help-meet. He
has also a precious gift in the ministry, though not so
large as some.

After visiting a few more meetings, with some families in and about Bristol, and crossing the river into the neighborhood of Burlington, he went to Vincentown, where he had a meeting on First-day, the 6th of the month. He thus again writes:—

It was attended mostly by those not of our Society. Here we were sweetly refreshed together. In the evening had a meeting with the few Friends by themselves; wherein the Truth was held up; and our principles, with our high and holy profession, opened in primitive purity; and they were exhorted to cleave thereto. This was a precious little meeting; and notwithstanding there appeared a great slackness in some, yet I believe they felt renewedly concerned to double their diligence. We parted in great love; our minds being drawn near to each other. Oh, how precious is the love of Truth! How it unites together.

Second-day, had a meeting at Lumberton, in a Methodist meeting-house, to good satisfaction. From here I went home with my dear friend Josiah Reeve. Next day had an appointed meeting at Upper Evesham. Fourth-day at Easton. Fifth-day attended the Monthly Meeting at Moorestown. Here the honest-hearted were comforted; the lukewarm were warned; and the dear youth invited. Sixth-day at Evesham Monthly Meeting. Seventh-day, Monthly Meeting at Upper Evesham. Here the Divine Master enabled to lay justice to the line, and judgment to the plumb-line. The meeting concluded to the comfort of many. First-day was at Cropwell, a branch of Upper Evesham Monthly Meeting; a large and satisfactory meeting. Second-day at Haddonfield Monthly Meeting. Silent, except a few words in the meeting for discipline.

This meeting was hurt by the youth going out at the close of the meeting for worship; some of them tarrying a considerable time. Oh that all Friends, old and young, might be careful how they disturb the quiet of meetings by coming late, or going in or out unnecessarily. Remembering that both meetings for worship and discipline, *ought to be held in the authority of truth.* Then they will prove edifying and strengthening.

The next Fourth-day attended the select Quarterly Meeting at Haddonfield; wherein our friend Richard Jordan was greatly favored. That evening rode to Benjamin Swett's, distant about four miles. He and his wife are worthy ministers. Fifth-day was at the Quarterly Meeting of Haddonfield. It was an open time, the glorious truth being in dominion; of which many present were sensible. Richard Jordan, a father in our Israel, concluded the first meeting in solemn supplication; and under the precious covering granted, Friends' minds were prepared to transact the weighty concerns of the church. That evening rode to Benjamin Cooper's. He and his family are good examples, and prefer Jerusalem's welfare to their chiefest joy. Although they have considerable of this world's goods, yet they have the blessed cause at heart. This tends to keep the worldly disposition in subjection to the power of Truth; whereby if they continue to live in the same, they will be enabled to be good stewards. May this consideration have place in the minds of those who have large possessions.

Christopher Healy attended some more meetings, principally within the limits of the Southern and Western Quarterly Meetings; also the almshouse of the State of Delaware, a service for which his sympathizing mind with the afflicted, seemed particularly to draw him. He then went to Westtown School, to which he thus alludes: "Had a meeting with the scholars, which was a precious season. Oh, the innocent sweetness that was felt among them!" Not long after this he rode to Philadelphia, preparatory to the Yearly Meeting. The diary resumed:—

Seventh-day attended the select Yearly Meeting, which was divinely favored. First-day, five meeting-houses were opened for worship. Second-day, the 18th of the Fourth Month, 1814, the business of the Yearly Meeting commenced; which through the several sittings thereof, was owned by the Great Shepherd, and conducted in brotherly love and condescension. It concluded on Sixth-day, the 22nd of the month. Our beloved friend, Thomas Scattergood, left this yearly meeting on Fourth-day, being unwell: which illness increased, and proved to be the prevailing fever. On First-day evening he resigned his soul to Him that gave it. Though his family and the church have met with a great loss, yet for him they have no cause to mourn. He has left a sweet savor behind him, and his memory will be pronounced blessed. He has been as a father to me. May we that are left behind, follow him as he followed Christ.

Our friend had some religious service on his way, but except this, he proceeded pretty directly from Philadelphia Yearly Meeting to that of New York. The memoranda continue:—

Seventh-day, the 21st of Fifth Month, attended the Yearly Meeting of Ministers and Elders. And on Second-day that for business came on. Through the several sittings of this Yearly Meeting, the Divine Master was pleased to favor us. We had the company of William Flanner, from Ohio, Micajah Collins from New England, and many other strangers. The meeting concluded on Fifth-day, the 26th.

After the conclusion of the Yearly Meeting, he turned his face homeward; taking some meetings on his way. One with the Methodists, which, he writes, he had had a prospect of for nearly three years, proved to the relief of his mind. He reached home on the 10th of Sixth Month, 1814. To which, in his journal, allusion is thus made:—

Rode home to my dear friend Benjamin Gurney's, where I was kindly received; and can say I feel a thankful heart to the Lord, who, by His divine voice called me forth, and by his divine power preserved and strengthened me to perform what he required, to the praise of his own eternal Name. I was out on this journey six months and ten days; attended two hundred and seven meetings, and travelled by computation two thousand miles.

The following circumstance, which it is believed took place while he was a resident in the State of New York, is not in Christopher Healy's journal; but its authenticity being substantiated by a Friend who heard it from his own lips, we have thought good to present it here. It tends to show not only the respect which was paid him by citizens of his neighborhood, but also the power of the Spirit, which wrought in and through him to the conviction of many minds.

"We had been speaking," says the writer of this, "of the trials and faithfulness of Sarah (Lynes) Grubb, and

Christopher remarked, that other Friends were sometimes brought into close trials of faith. In confirmation of this, he said he was once travelling on the 4th of the Seventh Month, and the time had fully come for feeding his horse. It was a few miles from Albany; and he stopped at a tavern kept by two brothers whom he knew very well, and put his horse under the shed. The hostler came and gave the horse his oats. Presently the sound of a fiddle was heard in the house, and Christopher knew there must be a dance going forward. He became a good deal disturbed, under the thought of what people would say if he should be found on such a day, at a tavern where a dance was going on. It would bring discredit, he thought, on his profession. He quickly decided to proceed; and was about mounting his horse, when he heard the language, ' Thou must go into the dance room!' This he thought was out of the question, and a delusion, and he'd do no such thing. So he rode off slowly, but with a heavy mind. Feeling so uncomfortable riding, he dismounted and tried walking; but it was no better; the exercise continued. Again he heard the voice, and again strove to put it away as a delusion. The third time the admonition was ' Perhaps thou wilt never have another opportunity to warn these people.' ' If it comes to that,' said Christopher, ' I must go back.'

"Mounting his horse, he returned to the tavern, put it under the shed to finish the oats, and proceeded into the house. The senior of the young men who kept the house, he found in the bar-room, and inquired of him if he might go into the dancers' room? Though doubtless astonished, the landlord said, ' You may, Mr. Healy, if you desire it.' On being requested to do so, he also went with Christopher up-stairs and opened the ball-room door.

The floor was occupied by the dancers, and the fiddler was engaged in his vocation, when the unexpected appearance of the plain Quaker burst upon their astonished vision. Instantly the tones of the fiddle ceased, and the dancers retired to the seats placed around the room. The junior landlord came forward instantly, seeing his gain was likely to be disturbed, and said, 'Oh, Mr. Healy, you can't preach here?' 'But,' said Christopher, 'only let me ask the young people a question. Would you be willing to get into the quiet a little time?' The company very generally gave assent; but the young landlord interposed, and said, 'Any other time, Mr. Healy, we shall be glad to hear you, but positively not now.' 'Well,' continued our friend, 'If thou wilt not suffer it, I shall be clear, and must leave it on thee.' He then departed, and went with a light and cheerful heart on his road.

"Some time after, Christopher met with the young landlord, who told him that he had felt very much troubled whenever he had thought of having stopped him from speaking to the dancers; and desired him to have a meeting appointed in that dance-room, and he would take care to have all the company that were then present invited. The proposal took hold of Christopher's mind, and after consulting with the select members of his Monthly Meeting, he felt easy to appoint a meeting in this large room of the tavern. Very especial care was taken by the young landlord to have all the company of 'the Fourth' present, and Christopher added, 'That he never remembered to have had a more satisfactory meeting; the floor being a good deal wet with the tears of his auditors.' After the meeting was over, the young landlord told Christopher, that his object in going into the room at the first was so far accomplished, that there was not another sound of the fiddle, or a single dance after he went into the room that day; but that they all departed to their respective homes as though they had been at a Quaker meeting."

CHAPTER VIII.

MARRIAGE TO SARAH MILLER, OF BUCKS CO., PA. PAYS A RELIGIOUS VISIT TO SOME PARTS OF THE NEW ENGLAND STATES. PAYS A SOCIAL VISIT, WITH HIS WIFE, IN PENN- SYLVANIA. HOLDS MEETINGS IN CONNECTICUT, MASSA- CHUSETTS AND RHODE ISLAND. VISITS THE WESTERN PART OF NEW YORK STATE; AND SOME OF THE INDIAN TRIBES THERE. VISITS THE SOUTHERN AND WESTERN STATES. AGAIN VISITS SOME PARTS OF THE SOUTHERN AND WESTERN STATES. INTERVIEW WITH FOUR MEN UNDER SENTENCE OF DEATH AT GOSHEN, NEW YORK. REMOVES TO BUCKS CO., PA., AND OPENS A SCHOOL. VISITS FRIENDS AND OTHERS IN THE NORTHERN AND EASTERN STATES. VISITS FRIENDS AND OTHERS IN NEW YORK AND UPPER CANADA. LETTER TO HIS WIFE. RE- MARKS AFTER HOLDING MEETINGS WITH INDIANS.

On the 12th of Tenth Month, 1814, Christopher Healy was married to Sarah Miller, daughter of John and Sarah Miller, of Bucks County, Pennsylvania. She being one that he believed would make him a helpmate in the Truth.

After his marriage, he did not go much abroad, until on the 24th of Tenth Month, 1815, with the unity of his Friends, he left home to pay a religious visit to some parts of the New England States. While on this visit, after a favorable allusion to the parents and children of a family in which he was much interested, he thus concludes: "May all parents consider the importance of their trust, which is nothing less than being *guardians over them for the Lord.*" He also alludes to a satisfactory meeting he had at Bath, upon which he makes the following remarks: "I often say in my heart, good is thy word, O Lord! Worthy art thou to be waited upon and obeyed. May I never move without thy anointing being renewed upon my spirit. So shall I be enabled, through Thy power, to teach transgressors thy ways, that sinners may be converted unto Thee."

After this, again resuming the diary, he says :—

I was at Durham meeting, which was very large; many not of our Society being at it. My mind was deeply humbled before the living God; and herein my soul was brought truly to wait upon Him, and in Him was my strength renewed. I was afterwards enlarged in the doctrines of Truth. May my soul be kept humble, and may such seasons be sanctified to the people for their improvement in the way of life and salvation. From here I wrote the third letter to my dear wife. When I contemplate our separation for the Truth's sake, my soul is thankful to the Lord; who is able to strengthen to bear this and every other cross, and will, if we continue faithful in all to Him, enable us through mercy, finally to wear the crown. The following intercession also arose in my heart at this time on her behalf: Mayest Thou, dearest Father, be to her precious mind as an husband; and so strengthen her that she may not repine. Fill her soul, if it be thy good pleasure, with thy good things; that so she may joy in the Lord, and rejoice in the God of her salvation.

May we, though far separated from each other, yet be sweetly united in thy Holy Spirit; and at all times give Thee the honor and the glory, who can and will make hard things easy, and bitter things sweet.

This journey throughout appears to have been to the satisfaction of Friends where he travelled, and to his own peace. One little extract from the record he has left of it, shows who was his sufficiency; and where and how his strength was sought and found, viz: "Oh, dearest Lord, keep me sufficiently humbled under a sense of my own inability to do any thing that will advance Thy glorious cause!" Upon reaching home,—we quote again from the journal:—

My dear wife and family received me with joyful hearts. We felt thankful to the great Preserver of men, that he had not only led forth, but brought again in peace. Blessed be the name of the Lord. I was absent on this journey eleven weeks; travelled one thousand one hundred miles; and attended over sixty meetings.

About three weeks after my return home my wife and I went to Pennsylvania to visit our relations; and had a number of satisfactory meetings thereaway. In attending Bucks Quarterly Meeting, my heart was brought into mourning to see in so many of the young people a departure from our testimony in relation to plainness.— Counsel was given suitable to their states. May it be sanctified to the dear youth. The meeting ended well. We found our relations well, and returned home in about seven weeks.

Christopher Healy did not at any time long rest from religious service abroad. In the Sixth Month of the year

now reached (1816), not feeling his mind clear of the
New England States, he again went forth, and held some
meetings in Connecticut, Massachusetts, and Rhode Island,
and attended the Yearly Meeting there. He returned
home in about five weeks, with the reward of peace.—
"Blessed," he hereupon writes, "be the great Shepherd,
who, when he puts forth, goeth before."

His next concern was a visit to the western part of the
State of New York; and to have some meetings with the
Indian tribes there. Obtaining the unity of his Friends,
he left home on the 5th of First Month, 1817. He had
a number of meetings, both among Friends and others,
including the Indians; of which he states, particularly in
allusion to the latter, that they were to great satisfaction.
He was from home about six weeks.

On the 12th of Eighth Month, 1817, Christopher Healy
writes: "I took an affectionate leave of my dear wife
and tender children, and being joined by my kind friend
Robert Nelson, proceeded on a visit to the Southern and
Western States." Of this journey our dear friend has left
but little, except an account of the meetings he attended,
and the places at which he tarried. After getting home, he
thus records his gratitude: "May the Lord be praised for
ever—the great Minister of ministers—who hath brought
me again to my precious family in peace. My soul is
humbled under a consideration of these favors." And
shortly after, his pen thus dwells upon the Lord's mercies,
and sets forth his praise :—

What shall I render, O Lord, unto Thee for all thy
benefits? Thou that redeems from destruction! Thou
that crownest with loving kindness and tender mercies!—
May'st thou continue to preserve from temptation, and

deliver from evil; and strengthen me, O Lord, to perform thy requirings. It is Thou, Blessed One, that can bend my mind, and enable me to say, Thy kingdom come: Thy will be done in my heart, as it is done in Heaven. So shall my poor soul praise Thee, who alone art worthy. Amen.

Feeling his mind again drawn in gospel love to visit some parts of the Southern and Western States, he left home therefor, with the unity and sympathy of his Friends, on the 19th of Eleventh Month, 1818, accompanied by his friend and former companion, Robert Nelson. On his way southward, he attended Bucks Quarterly Meeting; and had an appointed meeting at Trenton, which he writes was large and much favored. At Germantown he records being exercised strongly against the love of the world. Arriving at Baltimore, he says, "I received a truly sympathizing letter from my wife, which cheered up my mind." In this city he attended the Monthly Meeting for the Eastern District, which, he writes, was "to some satisfaction." The Western District "somewhat trying." A public meeting being appointed in the evening, it was large. He says,—

I went to it under great poverty of spirit. After a time of reverential silence, feeling the power of supplication poured forth, my poor soul addressed the Throne of Grace. Then was the way open to minister from these words, "If any man have not the Spirit of Christ, he is none of his." Showing from thence the necessity of *being in Christ*, that so our salvation may be sure. This meeting ended to our great comfort.

Next morning visited two sick Friends; one of them

being near her end with a cancer in her breast. Oh the sweetness of her spirit! Her cup was made to overflow with Divine love. She was patiently waiting and quietly hoping; and it was evident she was borne up of Him who is everlasting strength. May the Lord continue to be her support to the end.

Passing into Ohio, under date of the 5th of First Month, 1819, he thus writes:—

Was at Flushing; a crowded meeting. The doctrine of the peaceable kingdom of the Messiah was held up to view, which lays waste the kingdom of Antichrist. Oh! may this be the happy experience of all mankind. At Zanesville, on First-day, attended a small meeting of Friends. Had hard labor, but was favored to relieve my mind. Oh the love of money! which, while men covet after, they err from the faith, and pierce themselves, and those that are concerned for their welfare, with many sorrows.

At Waynesville, Springborough, Lebanon Court House, he held meetings; and in the evening one at the same place, for the Methodists. These, he writes, were large and favored. "The minds of the people were opened to receive the truth, and many hearts were comforted. My own soul could say, great is the Lord, and greatly to be praised in the city of our God, in the mountain of His holiness."

Next day he attended Friends' meeting at Cincinnati; and in the evening appointed one, which was held in a Methodist meeting-house. "A very large number attended; and a favored time it proved. Blessed be the name of Him who is the Helper of his people. Next day visited some that were sick, including one at the poor-house—a young man who went from New York to this western country in search of his father; but did not find him. Meanwhile he was taken sick, and being out of money was conveyed to the almshouse." When Christopher Healy went in to see him, he perceived he was dying, and he lived but about seven hours afterwards. The case of this poor stranger excited much tender feeling in the mind of Christopher Healy. The same evening he had a meeting for the people of color, to their mutual comfort. "How true it is," exclaims C. H., "that the Ethiopians shall stretch out their hands to God."

He got to John Miller's, his father-in-law, where he left his family on the 27th of Second Month; and states that he found his dear wife and family all well; and were greatly rejoiced to meet again in the Truth. That the reward of sweet peace was granted them, in resigning each other for the sake of that cause which is dignified with immortality, and crowned with eternal life. From here, on their way home, he attended some meetings; and being at the house of one of his friends, he was informed that there were four men in Goshen jail, about twenty miles from where he was, under sentence of death; having committed murder. His memoranda thus gives the affecting relation :—

Feeling my mind drawn to make them a visit, in company with two of my friends, I went. The jailor seemed kind, and was willing we should make the poor criminals a visit. He also, in a respectful manner, waited upon us to the different apartments of the prison. Oh what a shocking sight were these poor creatures! In a religious opportunity, some of them were much affected, and wrung their hands with grief. My soul was deeply stirred while I sat with them. All but one were sensible of their wicked deed. That one appeared hard-hearted. One, a colored man, honestly confessed the deed, and said he was hired for money. He said keeping bad company had brought him there. I asked him if he had found forgiveness? He said not; but he meant to beg to Jesus as long as he lived. I felt to say to the poor man, that if he continued in that humble, begging state, I believed he would find pardon. I felt very desirous that these poor objects of pity would be enabled to obtain forgiveness. I thought this sad scene was as great a sermon as ever I heard. Oh may these lines prove a warning to those that read them.

On Fifth-day, the 18th of Third Month, 1819, they reached home with thankful hearts to the Preserver of mankind. He adds, "Blessed be his holy Name forever."

The following summer and autumn he attended Nine Partners, and Stanford Quarterly Meetings; and had a number of meetings with those not of our Society; which yielded peace.

In the Ninth Month of 1820, he visited the meetings in the western part of the State of New York. Was absent from home about three weeks, and returned with the incomes of his Master's approbation. This year (1820), he removed with his family to Bucks county, Pennsylvania. He thus alludes to it in his journal, which is, for a time, resumed:—

Having for some time believed it would be right to remove with my family to Bucks county, and having settled my outward concerns, and my children being willing to part with us, we took a solemn leave of children and friends in the Eleventh Month of 1820, and came hither. My family consisting of myself and wife, with four small children. We settled within two miles of the Falls Meeting, and were comforted in being among our friends. We had also many precious meetings together, which were owned by the good Master's presence. Soon after settling here, I opened a school near our home, many children attending. This is an employment which always suited me, when I felt released from travelling on Truth's account. I continued my school, only attending meetings at home, with some neighboring ones, until in the spring of 1822 I opened a concern that had rested with weight on my mind, to pay a visit in gospel love to Friends and others not in membership with us, in some parts of the Northern and Eastern States. Obtaining the unity of the Monthly and Quarterly Meetings, I left home in the Fifth Month, accompanied by my dear Friend Moses Comfort, an elder of the same Monthly Meeting. We appointed some meetings on the way, which we attended to satisfaction. Getting to New England Yearly Meeting, held in the Sixth Month, we met with our dear friend George Withy, from old England.

After this, upon coming to Nantucket, he says :—

We had some very large meetings on this island; the inhabitants seeming ready at the notice given. We were here one week. Were at both their Monthly Meetings; and parted in much tenderness and love. From here we went into the State of Maine, and travelled as far eastward as the Kennebec river. Then returned through New Hampshire and Vermont to New York; and had many precious meetings. From thence to Long Island. Here we found some Friends very uneasy concerning sentiments held by Elias Hicks; who lived at Jerico, on this Island. Some of us had been doubtful for several years of his soundness in the true faith of our Lord Jesus Christ.— After our visit on Long Island, we returned to New York. Hence by Shrewsbury and Rahway, on home; and found my dear wife and family well.

His journal continues: "Staid at and about home, visiting meetings, and attending to such concerns as Truth required of me, until in the Twelfth Month, 1823, having previously opened a concern to perform a visit, in gospel love, to Friends and those not in membership with us, to some parts of New York State, and Upper Canada, I set out with my brother-in-law, John Miller, Jr., as companion. We went by New York, up the North river, and had many favored meetings with Friends and others."

While out on this visit, he thus wrote to his wife:—

Queensbury, 12th of First Month, 1824.

My dear and loving Wife:—I embrace the opportunity this morning to inform thee of my health. I received thy letter, which made me to rejoice. I am comforted in finding thou art so thoughtful concerning the great work that thy dear husband believes himself called to. May the Holy Hand bear thee up in thy lonely seasons, and mayest thou, my dear bosom friend, pray for me, that my faith fail not. So shall I be resigned to our Divine Master's will, and also cheered by the hope that we will meet again in that love in which we parted. I may tell thee, that the Good Hand that called me to go forth has been near, and we have had many favored meetings with Friends and those not of our Society. Yesterday we were at Queensbury, where the Good Master's presence was our crown. May He have the praise, who alone is worthy. Our present prospect is next to go towards Black river. I have found Friends, so far, in this northern country, generally sound in the faith. O, may the Lord preserve this people, whom he has raised up to show forth his praise, in the true faith of our Lord and Saviour, Jesus Christ.

And now, dearly beloved, we sympathize together.— Though far separated from each other in body, we are present in spirit, serving the Lord. May we be enabled to have our faith strengthened by the blessed promise to those that love the Lord more than wife or children, houses or lands—They "shall receive an hundred-fold, and shall inherit everlasting life." In this belief we were joined together; being well assured we should have to resign each other to our Divine Master's disposal. Farewell in the everlasting Truth.

Thy loving husband,

CHRISTOPHER HEALY.

Wishing to get to the Half-Year's Meeting in Upper Canada, they crossed the river St. Lawrence. This was attended with much difficulty; owing to the ice on the river being too thin to bear their horses, and yet so thick as to prevent the use of boats. After much risk and toil they finally got safely over; when they all for a time sat down, and felt their hearts bowed in thankfulness to the Great Preserver of men for His merciful help and protection. Before parting with the ferryman and his helpers (a large number having assisted in getting them over the river), they asked for the fare across. The ferryman said: "I consider we have risked our lives for the sake of help-

ing you on in the line of your duty, and I cannot take
money for it." And the rest all agreed therewith; saying, we were perfectly welcome to all they had done; and
that they were thankful in being able to help us on our
way. We were favored to get to the Half-Year's Meeting
at West Lake in good season; and had a comfortable
time with Friends there. Also visited most of the meetings belonging to the Half-Year's Meeting, and had some
meetings among different tribes of Indians: I trust to
their, as it was to our comfort.

Oh these poor children of the wilderness, how my heart
feels for them! When I contrast *our* favored situation
with *their* sufferings, I am humbled as in the dust. I have
believed when sitting in meetings with them, that every
thoughtful mind, if made acquainted with their situation,
must feel sympathy and tenderness for these, our poor
afflicted brethren and sisters in the creation of an Almighty Father; they being also equal objects of redeeming grace. My desire is while writing these lines, that it
may sink deep in the minds of all the white people,
especially our rulers, to consider their case; and remember our Blessed Saviour's saying, "As ye would that men
should do to you, do ye also to them likewise." I fear that
many who profess to be the followers of Christ, fall short
of living up to this rule that our dear Lord has laid down.
Oh may it not only be remembered in the case of the poor
Indian, but in that of the afflicted sons and daughters of
Africa, yea, likewise, in all our dealings one with another.
For true Christian principles will surely lead to the faithful observance of this blessed rule.

After feeling my mind clear of Upper Canada, we
crossed the Niagara river a little below Buffalo, and came
into the United States. After which, we had a meeting

with the Buffalo Indians. This tribe is a part of the Six
Nations. Red Jacket and Cornplanter, with another Indian chief, and a large collection of other Indians, both
male and female, came to this meeting. They sat remarkably solid; much becoming such an occasion. I spoke by
an interpreter that Red Jacket brought with him. It was
a favored time. From thence we travelled homeward
through the States of New York and New Jersey, taking
meetings on our way. Upon reaching home I found my
family well. O, may my soul give the glory to Him,
who is glorious in holiness, and ever worthy of all praise.

CHAPTER IX.

REMARKS ON THE DOCTRINES OF ELIAS HICKS, AND EF-
FORTS USED TO STOP THE PROGRESS OF ANTI-CHRISTIAN
SENTIMENTS IN THE SOCIETY OF FRIENDS. VISITS FRIENDS
AND OTHERS IN THE SOUTHERN STATES. SOLEMN MEET-
INGS WITH SLAVEHOLDERS AND SLAVES. LETTER OF
NATHAN HUNT. THE SEPARATION IN THE SOCIETY OF
FRIENDS CAUSED BY DOCTRINES PROMULGATED BY ELIAS
HICKS, AND OTHERS. ATTENDS NEW YORK YEARLY
MEETING IN 1828.

THE journal of Christopher Healy next proceeds to
portray that disaffection and lapse in religious belief,
which in the eventful year of 1827, culminated in the
separation of so large a number from our religious Society. Christopher Healy, in his journal, says:—

About these days (1824) there was much appearance of
unsoundness among our members. Elias Hicks had made

some visits amongst us, to the grief of many, both in city
and country. Our members began to have different sentiments respecting the divinity of our dear Redeemer; and
this divided feeling increased very much amongst us, so
that the harmony and unity began to be lost. And it
must be so; for in proportion as the true faith in our
Lord Jesus Christ is forsaken, the unity of the Spirit in
the bond of peace, and true fellowship of the saints, comes
to be broken. A great concern was felt by many of us,
to stop the progress of this dividing and disorganizing
spirit; for it seemed as though it would destroy all harmony and fellowship, and comfort of love in our religious
Society. But adored be the name of Israel's Shepherd,
who cares for his own sheep, and calls them, and leads
them as lambs in the midst of wolves; even wolves in
sheep's clothing. For some of these that had departed
from the faith once delivered to the saints, so as to deny
that Jesus who suffered without the gates of Jerusalem as
the Saviour of the world, and yet profess a great love for
us and our young people, we could do no other than bear
our testimony against.

In 1828, while attending Bridgewater Monthly Meeting, New York, Christopher Healy felt drawn to open
and support the doctrine of the divinity of our Lord Jesus
Christ, by authority of the Holy Scriptures, and declared
it to be the doctrine always held by the Society of Friends.
These errors, which the principal leaders of the Separatists
of that day propagated, were brought into view by quota-
tions from their printed discourses. It was distinctly
stated that, notwithstanding they professed to believe in
Christ, if they would confess their real sentiments, it
would be found they denied that He who was born of the

10*

Virgin Mary, and respecting whom it is declared, that, "when He bringeth the First Begotten into the world He saith, let all the angels of God worship Him," is the Saviour of men. Instead of acknowledging the Son, to whom it is said, "thy throne, O God, is for ever and ever: a sceptre of righteousness is the sceptre of thy kingdom," the Separatists declared that the Almighty could never set Jesus Christ above us, for, if He did, He would be partial,—thereby endeavoring to destroy the divine and glorious character of the Son of God,—while they pretended to believe in his light shining in the heart.

This development of the unbelief of Elias Hicks had a very convincing effect on a number in the meeting, who did not appear to have understood his opinions fully, and the various shifts and glosses used to inculcate them. This conviction was rendered still more complete, by some remarks of Hugh Judge, who had, unhappily, in his old age, fallen in with these errors. He observed, that he had not heard a word that had been spoken, but felt a great weight of darkness upon his spirit. He then endeavored to give, what he considered to be the sentiments of Friends; making them appear very outward in their views; and in order to exhibit the spirituality which he had attained to, he declared that he did not believe Jesus Christ, who was born of the Virgin Mary, to be the Saviour; and near the close of his speech said: "My Saviour never was crucified:" thus denying Him to be the Saviour of whom the apostles declare, "We preach Christ crucified: to the Jews a stumbling-block, and unto the Greeks foolishness; but unto them which are called, both Jews and Greeks, Christ, the power of God, and the wisdom of God." This effectually confirmed the observation before made by Christopher Healy, that if they would confess their real sentiments, it would appear they did not believe the Lord Jesus was the Saviour; and appeared to have had a settling effect on those present.

In the Twelfth Month of 1824, he paid a religious visit to Friends of the Southern States; also to slaveholders with their slaves. He had many large and satisfactory meetings. After one of which, he could adopt the following language: "In the Lord's presence *there is life,* and at his *right hand rivers of pleasure forevermore.* May my poor soul continue to be humbled in the dust before Him." His own account follows:—

In Virginia I was joined by a kind friend and elder, James Stanton. We had a large public meeting at Muffleborough, in a Methodist meeting-house. Four Methodist and two Presbyterian ministers attended; also a great number of slaves and slaveholders; so that the house could not hold them, but many stood in the yard where they could hear. A solemn stillness prevailed over the whole assembly. It was evident the heart-melting presence of the Divine Master covered the meeting; and ability and strength were given to declare the doctrines of the gospel, and the righteous testimonies thereof.— Many minds, both of slaveholders and slaves, were tendered; and my own soul did secretly praise the Lord our God.

After having many meetings in the lower part of Virginia, we came to Piney Woods meeting of Friends in North Carolina, where notice of our desire to have a meeting was given to slaveholders and their slaves. A large number attended, and the meeting was favored with the life-giving presence of our Holy Head and heavenly Shepherd. We passed from thence down to Elizabeth

City, having a number of large meetings on the way.—
The masters and slaves expressed their great comfort in
our visit to them.   Here we saw many poor colored people, very aged, whose heads were white, walking with
staffs, and some with two, to enable them to get about.
Oh how my heart did feel for these!   When they came
to shake hands with us, tears were trickling down their
faces, expressing at the same time their great thankfulness to the Lord for our visit to them, such poor creatures.

Next morning I received a visit from a Methodist minister, who expressed a desire that I might have another
meeting with them and their slaves; and said there would
more come together than did before, for they were all
glad of the meeting.   I told him I must see my way
clear, before I could make another appointment.   He said
he was early convinced that slavery was wrong, and that
he had missed it exceedingly in purchasing any.   That if
any way opened to free them, he would give them their
liberty.   The slaveholders that I spoke with, generally
acknowledged the evil of slavery.

After weighing the request of the minister, I was most
easy to leave the place.   On our way up the State from
Elizabeth City, we came to Rich Square, in Northampton
county, at the time of the Quarterly Meeting; where I
met with our friend William Forster, from Great Britain.
The Quarterly Meeting of business was favored.   Next
day we had a public meeting.   Many of both whites and
blacks could not get into the house.   The meeting was
owned by the Divine Master, who was this day mouth
and wisdom: and I could adopt the language, "In thy
presence there is life, and at thy right hand rivers of
pleasure forevermore."   May my poor soul continue to
be humbled in the dust before Him.   From thence we

rode about two hundred miles up the State to New Garden, where we had a meeting. And one also at Deep River, which was a favored time. Next day we had a meeting on our way to our aged friend Nathan Hunt's, who was a living minister, bringing forth fruit in old age. He kindly accompanied us, and his company and gospel labors were strengthening to my mind. We had a number of favored meetings together, and then came to New Garden to attend the Quarterly Meeting to be held there. It was a favored time; blessed be the good Shepherd of the sheep, who putteth forth his own, and goeth before them. May they always be willing to follow Him, either in suffering or rejoicing; so shall He be glorified in them. After this Quarterly Meeting, except a few meetings on our way, we came almost directly home, and found my dear wife and family all well. Oh may my soul always remember how good it is to trust in the Lord and never doubt his precious promises, that He will never leave nor forsake those that trust in Him!

From letters written to Sarah Healy during her husband's absence on this visit, tending to encourage her in her loneliness, and conveying their sense of his ministerial services among them, we select the following from the pen of Nathan Hunt:—

"Springfield, Guilford Co., N. C.,
Third Month 11th, 1825.

"Dear Friend:—Thy husband came to our house last Third-day morning, and attended our Monthly Meeting on Fourth-day; in which his divine Master furnished him with understanding to bring forth out of his treasures things new and old, to the comfort, edification and encouragement of the mourners in Zion; and to caution and counsel the lukewarm and careless professors. I attended public meetings with him Fifth and Sixth-days, and also on Seventh-day with a large company of people. There were masters and some slaves in all of them. He has shown himself to be a workman that need not be ashamed, dividing the word aright; wielding the sword with dexterity and skill; and applying Gilead's healing balm to wounded souls. He feels particularly near to many of us, because he comes in *the good old way*, and we understand him, being like face answering to face in a glass. He is as bone of our bone, and flesh of our flesh; a brother indeed; and we will have no other doctrine than that which he preaches.

"If thou, dear heart, feels sometimes lonely and sorrowful, let this thought cheer thy mind,—my dear husband is making many glad; and they that go forth weeping and sorrowing, doubtless shall come again rejoicing, bringing their sheaves with them. This I believe will be the blessed experience of thy bosom friend, and your coming together will be like the rejoicing of the righteous. Oh how comforting the promise is, 'The Lord will keep him in perfect peace whose mind is staid on Him, because he trusteth in Him.' These become like Mount Zion, that never can be removed. Many such gracious promises we find in the Scriptures of truth to animate and strengthen us in the weary pilgrimage through time, that we may keep the eye single to the Lord, in what situation soever He may be pleased to place us in his house. For it appears some have to go forth to battle, and some to stay by the stuff; but all share alike in the spoil. The beauty is, for every one to be in their allotted station. My dear wife and myself are prepared to feel with thee and thy dear husband, in your separation, as it has been often our

lot to be separated for the work's sake. But it mattereth
not what may be the pathway through the changeable
scenes of this uncertain world, be it rough or smooth, if at
the end we may but be favored to enter through the gates
into the city, where the enemy will cease to trouble, and
the weary be at rest.

"My dear wife unites in near and dear love to thee.

I am thy affectionate friend,

NATHAN HUNT."

Here our friend again alludes to the unsound views
then being disseminated by Elias Hicks, and some of his
adherents :—

The unsound principles promulgated by E. H., had now
increased very much within the compass of our Yearly
Meeting and several others, viz., New York, Baltimore,
and Ohio ; which broke the harmony and peace wherever
those principles prevailed ; causing doubts and denials of
the divinity of our Lord Jesus Christ, and of his propiti-
atory sacrifice for the sins of the whole world. Elias
Hicks having travelled in several Yearly Meetings, and
books being circulated holding forth the same unchristian
views, all had the effect to make a very gloomy appearance over our Society ; and caused many of us to mourn
and lament in the language of the prophet: "Oh that my
head were waters, and mine eyes a fountain of tears, that
I might weep day and night for the slain of the daughter
of my people." This awfully disorganizing and dividing
spirit went on, till in the Fourth Month of 1827, at the
time of the Philadelphia Yearly Meeting, this disaffected
and unsound part of the Society drew off ; and in the
Tenth Month of the same year, established what they
called a Yearly Meeting of their own. This seemed to

relieve Friends of much trouble; and opened a way for us to testify against them in the order of Truth and discipline. Oh! how my soul remembers the afflictions and sorrows—the wormwood and the gall—that I, as well as many others, had to feel and taste of during this great conflict. "Oh my soul, come not thou into their secret; unto their assemblies, mine honor, be not thou united."

Again, after a reference to the very trying occurrences in New York Yearly Meeting in the Fifth Month, 1828, which he attended, he writes:—

Upon the conclusion of the Yearly Meeting, I went in company with the Yearly Meeting's committee as far as Bridgewater; and a trying and proving season it was. Oh the sorrowful state of those that deny the Lord that bought them! The meetings mostly divided. The unbelieving part manifesting that they went out from us, because they were not of us. After the Monthly Meeting at Bridgewater, I returned home, taking meetings on the way. Friends of our Yearly Meeting felt near to each other after such a load of darkness had been removed from us. But I could not help mourning the loss of many that were evidently carried away by the leaders of the separation, in a dark and cloudy day. May the Lord of the vineyard be pleased to open their understandings, and restore them to the fold again. And it is my heart's desire and prayer to the Lord our God, that those also who have been the means of thus dividing in Jacob and scattering in Israel, may, if it be not too late for them to see their error, be brought to confess that Holy Redeemer whom, as their only Saviour, they have slighted and despised.

CHAPTER X.

EMBARKS ON A VISIT TO FRIENDS AND OTHERS IN GREAT
BRITAIN AND IRELAND. LETTER TO HIS WIFE. LETTER
OF ANN JONES. LETTER OF WILLIAM EVANS.

CHRISTOPHER HEALY, as his journal states, having for
several years felt his mind drawn to visit in gospel love,
Friends, with some others not of our Society, in Great
Britain and Ireland, obtained a certificate of the unity of
his Monthly, Quarterly, and Yearly Meetings for this
service. The full time, as he believed, having arrived,
on the 2nd of the Sixth Month, 1831, he went on board
the ship Algonquin, William West, master, and after
taking an affectionate leave of his dear wife and numerous
friends who accompanied him to the ship, he, the same
day, sailed from Philadelphia; having for companions,
bound on a similar errand, Jonathan Taylor of Ohio, and
Stephen Grellet, from Burlington, New Jersey. They had
several meetings, both morning and evening, with opportunities also for reading portions of the Holy Scriptures;
the captain, who was very kind and courteous to them,
sitting with them; and many of the passengers and sailors
likewise giving them their company. They had an unusually smooth and pleasant passage, and on the 29th of
the same month cast anchor before the city of Liverpool.
Next morning they went on shore, and it being Friends'
usual meeting day, they attended it. Christopher Healy
writes: " It was a comfortable meeting, and I can say my
soul felt humbled as in the dust for the blessing and favor
of Heaven in bringing us safely over the mighty deep."
" He that made the heavens and the earth," he continues,

" the sea, and the fountains of waters, can control them
at His pleasure." They visited a number of Friends'
families in and about Liverpool, with some of the sick
and the aged. On First-day morning they also together
attended the same meeting, and on the following Fourth-
day morning Stephen Grellet left for London, and Jonathan Taylor for Manchester; Christopher again attending
Liverpool Meeting on Fifth-day. He says it was a precious meeting, and very confirming to him that he was in
his right place. He adds, "May my soul wait for right
direction. And may the Shepherd of Israel keep and
preserve my dear wife and children, to whose care I have
resigned them."

He held some more meetings in and about Liverpool,
of one of which he records, that " the blessed Redeemer
was pleased to overshadow the assembly, and to crown
with his living presence. May He alone have the praise."

Taking coach from here, he and his companion came,
amongst other places, to Nantwich, where a Monthly
Meeting was held. Here he says, " We met with our
dear friends George and Ann Jones, who had not long
since been in America on a religious visit. We were
truly glad to see each other; and could thank our divine
Master and take fresh courage." At Colebrookdale, on a
First-day, he had a public meeting, which was large.—
Christopher was opened both in doctrine and counsel.—
He adds: "May it be remembered; and may I never
forget the loving kindness of the great Minister of ministers, who alone can rightly teach what to declare among
the people, and when to be silent."

At Sidcot, he thus writes: "A considerable number of
Friends belong to this meeting, who have a school under
their care; of which a large proportion attended the

meeting. It was a very good time. Counsel flowed freely to parents and teachers, that they should instruct the children in the fear of the Lord. Advice was given likewise to the dear children; many of whom were much tendered. May it be long remembered. Had a meeting at the same place in the evening, to the joy and rejoicing of many; which was acknowledged by those not of our Society in a feeling manner. May the Lord have all the praise, to whom it is due."

At Chatham he writes: "A large public meeting in the evening. A precious quiet spread over us; and it proved a solemn, favored time. May such seasons not be forgotten. It is the Lord's doings, and marvellous in mine eyes."

At London, he attended the Quarterly Meeting of Ministers and Elders for London and Middlesex. Here he met with his friend and fellow passenger and countryman, Stephen Grellet, and his aged friend Thomas Shillitoe, of that land; who had been in America on a religious visit. This meeting was to their comfort, being truly glad to see each other. Next day, Christopher Healy attended the general Quarterly Meeting, which was large. He was silent; but Sarah (Lynes) Grubb was largely engaged in the ministry; as was Thomas Shillitoe.

About this time he wrote to his wife; from which the following is extracted :—

Stoke Newington, Tenth Month, 10th, 1831.

My Dear Sarah :— * * * I have just finished visiting all the meetings in London and Middlesex Quarterly Meeting, and am this morning going to attend the Morning Meeting of Ministers and Elders in London. Then I expect to take meetings through the different counties towards Scotland. Yesterday was at Tottenham meeting, which is about six miles from London. Here our dear friend Thomas Shillitoe lives. I drank tea with him and his dear wife, who is eighty-six years old; seven years older than her husband. They both attended meeting with me—a large meeting of Friends. I had a public meeting at four o'clock for others, which was large, and solemnly quiet. Soon after I took my seat in meeting, the testimony of the apostle was presented to my mind: "There is therefore now no condemnation to them which are in Christ Jesus, who walk not after the flesh but after the Spirit. For the law of the spirit of life in Christ Jesus hath made me free from the law of sin and death;" on which important subject my mind was clearly opened to explain to the people the necessity of attending to this law of the Spirit of life.

* * * Dear Thomas Shillitoe says he remembers thee perfectly well, and also his being at our house. He desires to be affectionately remembered to thee. Thomas preaches the gospel in his old age, in life and power. Oh how encouraging it is to see such dear Friends, and to believe they are planted in the house of the Lord, and to see them flourish in the courts of our God; bringing forth fruit in old age.

My mind is abundantly engaged in public meetings, and the minds of the people are very much opened to hear the truth of the gospel as it is in Jesus, through the teaching of his grace and Holy Spirit in their hearts.— Oh! saith my soul, may they be willing to *obey*. Then will they have a sure foundation to build upon, even Christ Jesus, who was the foundation of old, and remains to be the everlasting Rock against which no storm nor tempest can prevail. My heart is full of gospel love while I am writing to thee, my dear companion, believing thou canst read and understand the feelings of my heart.

After the expression of tender regard and counsel for his dear children, whom he respectively named, he thus concludes :—

Give my dear love to father and mother, and all our dear friends. May they be favored to know the sweet presence of the Lord Jesus in their religious meetings.— And now, in dear and tender love, never to be quenched by many waters, nor distance, nor time, I take my leave, and bid thee farewell in the Lord.

CHRISTOPHER HEALY.

At Uxbridge he attended a meeting of Friends; which he writes was "a trying time;" and then adds, "as it has often been with me since being in this land. I often go mourning on my way. Oh the unfaithfulness that prevails!" "At Luton," he says : "I was led to speak in a very plain manner, and felt that the service was owned by the great Head of the Church, and that it was to the edification of the people." At the house of his kind friend John Smith, of Thirsk, he was taken dangerously ill of bilious colic. By this he was confined three weeks. He thus alludes to the kind care of this family towards him :—

It could not be possible for more care and sympathy to have been bestowed than was by these kind friends, together with my dear companion, Joseph Hopkins, whose attentions seemed to be to every want of mine. May the Lord bless each and all of these for such sympathy and kindness to a stranger in a strange land. Just as I was recovering, news came of the death of my dear and much

11*

beloved friend Jonathan Taylor; who departed this life at the house of Mary Lecky, at Kilnock, in Ireland. He came to England in the same ship that I did; and for the loss of him I did truly mourn. Yet from the account I had of his departure, I have no doubt but that he made a happy close.

The following letter from his friend Ann Jones, alludes to this illness, and also to the death of Jonathan Taylor; and on other accounts is well worthy an attentive perusal:—

"Stockport, Eleventh Month 23d, 1831.

" My dear friend C. Healy :—I can very truly tell thee that it has not been for want of fellow feeling, in near sisterly sympathy with thee, that I have not sooner given thee a written proof of my remembrance, but for want of health and ability for the employ. My mind has followed thee and our other transatlantic brethren, with feelings of more than common interest: and that not only as one who knows 'the heart of a stranger' in a land of strangers, but also as one who knows a little of the bonds and afflictions which *abide* those who go forth as advocates of the doctrine of the cross, and of the gospel of Christ Jesus our Lord, in a day, when, because iniquity abounds, the love of many waxes cold. I think the apostle says, 'we count them happy *which endure*,' and blessed indeed are they who endure to the *end:* who *strive* through the faith of the gospel to persevere in patience in the path of duty till He who hath called to the service, and apportions to each his share or measure of suffering and of labor, shall see meet to say, 'It is enough.'

" I heard some days ago of thy serious indisposition at

Thirsk : but having no direct or very recent account, am
at a loss to know where to address a letter to thee. Nevertheless I am disposed to try, not only to give thee an assurance of our near sympathy with thee, but also to say, that
if thy state of health and religious feelings and engagements will allow of thy coming to rest awhile with us, we
do most freely and gladly offer thee a home with us, till
thou art so far recruited as to allow of thy travelling safely
in our damp climate. By no means questioning the kindness or want of hospitality of Friends where thy lot is
cast—I trust and believe thou wilt not lack either—but
as one who knows the great difference between this climate and that of America, and how little English people
in general are aware of the need which Americans have
of more warmth, from fire, clothing, &c., than is necessary
for the English constitution ; neither would I by any proposal of mine, like the old prophet formerly, be the means of
turning or drawing a fellow-servant out of the right way,
and yet if thou couldst see thy way to *rest* awhile with
us, and not go to Scotland or Ireland, till the winter has
at least partly passed away, I should be glad. I know not
where our friend J. Wilbur is, but on hearing of your
prospect of going together into Scotland at this season of
the year, I could but desire that if you did go, it might
be with the assurance that it was the *best* you could do.

I do not forget that He whom we desire to serve, is all-
sufficient to carry His servants through all the perils and
difficulties they meet with, in the discharge of their duty
to Him : but 'wisdom dwells with prudence,' and it is
requisite for us to try whether we may not safely keep on
the side of (shall I say) human prudence, where two ways
are before us. Thou wilt perceive I only propose ; with
an assurance of a hearty welcome to thee if thou canst

find thy way hither where, and in the neighborhood, there is no lack of people who have souls to save or to lose.

"I shall hope to hear from thee on the receipt of this. If thou canst not suitably write thyself, request some friend where thou art to write in reply.

"As there is no doubt thou wilt hear of the removal from works, (undoubtedly) to blessed and glorious rewards, of our dear friend Jonathan Taylor, at Kilnock, in Ireland, I think I must give thee a few particulars relating to dear Jonathan Taylor's latter days, his illness and close. He was at meeting at Dublin, and had good service. His concern was principally to the young people. He and his companion Jacob Green, had visited all the meetings in Ireland except three; and attended the three Quarterly Meetings. Jonathan Taylor appeared to be low, and not quite well, and on H. S., Jr., asking him when he expected to go to England, he replied he did not know, he could not tell when he should leave Ireland; but wished to go to Mary Leeky's at Kilnock, to rest awhile. He was at Dublin Meeting on First-day morning, and Kingstown in the afternoon: had an appointed meeting at Wicklow on Second-day: returned to Dublin where he was at meeting on Third-day—silent. After meeting complained of being unwell; and spent the time in Dublin and the neighborhood until Sixth-day. He said he had taken cold. Friends observed a remarkable sweetness in his countenance. Sixth-day, the 28th, went to Kilnock very unwell; worse when he arrived; went to bed immediately; and was not up afterwards. Inflammation of the lungs came on: his mind much abstracted from outward things: he expressed that he felt resigned. Dr. Harvey went from Dublin on the first instant to see him: bled him which afforded some relief, but the doctor found him too weak to bear the depletion necessary to remove the inflammation : continued gradually sinking, and was frequently heard supplicating to be released. On First-day the 6th of Eleventh Month, this dear disciple fell asleep in Jesus, on whom he firmly believed ; and for whose Name's sake he had patiently suffered. This will be a heavy stroke to his wife and daughter. And whilst we mourn their and the church's loss, are bound to unite in the language, ' Blessed are the dead which die in the Lord,' &c.

" I have written more than I expected when I began ; and am reminded it is time to close. My husband is well. He unites with me in the above invitation, and in the salutation of love and sympathy.

Thy friend,

ANN JONES."

The following are extracts from a letter of our late beloved friend William Evans, to Christopher Healy while in England :

" Philadelphia, Twelfth Month, 22d, 1831.

" My Dear Friend :—Thy very acceptable communication, written at Hartford, 7th of Tenth Month last, was duly received, and tended to quicken our feelings in that fellowship we have long enjoyed with each other, and which has not been diminished by the temporary separation we are subjected to for the work's sake. Thou art often the subject of our thoughts and conversation, and it has been pleasant to hear by letters from some of our English Friends of thy movements, which, though we have had no very particular accounts, are satisfactory. If we are the servants of Christ, it is not probable we shall please all men ; for there are those who with all their profession of his religion, are nevertheless in heart enemies of the cross; they cannot bear the foolishness of his gospel, and it is not proper that such should be fed with food that gratifies their vain and superficial minds. But the unity of the true Seed, those who are acquainted with the afflictions of Joseph, is truly desirable and this, I doubt not, thou wilt be favored with.

"It is very difficult to form a correct judgment of the state of the church in England without being there; but from what we hear, and from what we know of the visitors to this country, it is evident there is a difference in the tribes. A class who profess much head knowledge with some experience, and another who are less concerned about that which is gathered by the wisdom and talents of man, and more deeply engaged to descend into Jordan, where they may, from season to season, witness the washings of regeneration and the renewings of the Holy Spirit, by which they are made quick of understanding in the Lord's fear, and prepared to receive and communicate the language of the Spirit unto the churches. To meet with such as these, and to mingle with them in the fellowship of the Gospel of Christ, which is often the fellowship of suffering, is truly strengthening, and indeed, though seemingly paradoxical, it is cheering. Those who know much and whose time seems always ready for doing, have a strong aversion to the doctrine of suffering—they do not like to look on what is called the gloomy side, but are in danger of compassing themselves with sparks of their own kindling, the end of which will be sorrow. To the traveller in the Lord's cause, it is however a consoling reflection, that help is laid on one that is mighty; who can preserve in heights, and sustain in depths, and mercifully furnishes, as he is waited upon, with wisdom and strength from his sanctuary, to enable him to steer through the various difficulties which surround him, and to set up stones of memorial that hitherto the Lord hath helped him.

"Fellow-pilgrims, particularly those employed in the same work, cannot but desire for each other, that they may in all their goings forth be thus favored, that the Great Name may be honored and exalted, and the answer of sweet peace be poured into their bosoms, when the allotted labor is accomplished. That this may be thy experience is our affectionate trust and desire, as we doubt not it would be thy prayer for us under similar circumstances.

"According to thy request, I wrote to thy wife informing her of thy letter to us, thy health and comfortable getting along; and held up to her view the standing ordinance in Israel, that those that remain with the stuff, faithful in their allotment, were to participate in the spoils, equally with them who went to the battle. After visiting the meetings of Burlington and Shrewsbury and Rahway Quarters, I went into Bucks in the Ninth Month last, and was at the Falls Meeting, where I saw her. She appeared to be in good health, and told me she had then recently had letters from thee.

* * * "I was at all the meetings in your Quarter, which being attended by few others than the members, were small, except the Falls. In all of them are to be found some exercised Friends, who are the salt, which, through divine mercy, preserves the body; otherwise, the external appearance furnishes but little to cheer with the hope of a succession in the church in some parts. Upon these the weight of exercise on account of others and the cause at large must fall, and there seems no safe alternative but to give themselves up cheerfully to spend and be spent for the sake of our poor shattered Society. * * *

"Our meetings are held in quiet, for which we have cause to be thankful; but the great want of religious fervor makes them at times very trying. Ease and prosperity seem to be the bane of religion. One to his farm, another to his merchandise, and others to their worldly comforts and delights, lessens the number of laborers for the springing up of the water of life, and throws an undue weight upon others, who often feel greatly discouraged with the little evidence of fruits proportionate to the labor bestowed upon such, and the trials we have just emerged from. We endeavor to keep hold of the hope that brighter days are ahead, but how far, seems often wrapt in much uncertainty. Times and seasons are in the Lord's hand, and he can cause light to break forth from obscurity, and darkness to become as the noon-day. For the cause sake, and for the children, and those who may be looking towards Zion, one cannot but desire that the brightness of the everlasting light might shine forth more conspicuously and availingly amongst us. * * *

My wife desires me to present her love and say thou hast her wishes for thy preservation and safe return.— We shall be glad to hear from thee again.

From thy affectionate friend,

WILLIAM EVANS."

CHAPTER XI.

VISITS IRELAND. RETURNS TO ENGLAND. LETTER OF MARY
J. LECKY. LETTER OF SAMUEL REYNOLDS. LETTER OF
JOSEPH THORP. EXTRACTS FROM LETTERS OF C. HEALY
TO HIS WIFE. LETTER RESPECTING THE CHARACTER OF
C. HEALY'S RELIGIOUS EXERCISES IN ENGLAND. REMARK
OF JOHN BARCLAY ON HIS CHRISTIAN FEARLESSNESS.
EXTRACTS FROM LETTERS OF THOMAS CHRISTY WAKE-
FIELD AND JACOB GREEN. RETURNS TO AMERICA. NO-
TICE OF AN INTERVIEW WITH A YOUNG MAN IN ENG-
LAND ON THE DANGER TO FRIENDS OF JOINING WITH
PERSONS OF OTHER RELIGIOUS DENOMINATIONS IN BE-
NEVOLENT ASSOCIATIONS.

GOING to Ireland, Christopher Healy visited Belfast,
Lisburn, Lurgan, Moyallen, Grange, Richhill, Dublin,
Ballitore, Carlow, Waterford, Youghall, and Cork. "The
meeting at Cork," he says, "was a laborious time at the beginning; but, through hard labor, way opened and strength
increased, until Truth reigned over all. Blessed be the
name of the Great Head of the Church, who alone can
give strength for his work and service." From thence he
went to Clonmel, Limerick, Roscrea, Mountrath, Mount-
mellick; and returning to Dublin, took steamer for Liverpool.

Extract from a letter written by Mary J. Lecky, dated
Second Month, 12th, 1832,—and addressed to Sarah
Healy:—

"In the City of Cork he had a meeting with Friends;
a remarkable season. He wrote me that it was a very
open-time, but J. Hopkins told us more fully that he

thought it would be almost worth coming from America
for such a meeting. From Munster he took a few meetings of Leinster Province in his way to Dublin, where he
arrived the 6th of last month. He left for Liverpool on
the 10th, leaving a sweet savor on the minds of his
friends, I believe, where he visited them in this land. In
Dublin, which is a very large particular meeting, he had
much service with Friends on First-day forenoon, and
with those of other professions in the afternoon; favored
seasons. It was sweet to sit under his ministry."

After returning from Ireland to England, he held many
public meetings, the most of which he records were to
good satisfaction. He thus alludes to one of them :—

The doctrines of Truth being opened, an hireling ministry, with the subject of war, as being inconsistent with
the gospel, and contrary to the command of Jesus, was
closely spoken to. The necessity of taking up the cross
of our holy Redeemer before we can become his followers,
was also dwelt upon. It being only as we do this, through
obedience to the teaching of his grace, that we can have
our fruit unto holiness, and in the end everlasting life.

The following letter from Samuel Reynolds, of Dover,
was written to Christopher Healy some time in the year
1831:—

" Beloved Friend :—An opportunity offering of sending
thee a few lines, I felt unwilling to let it pass by without
expressing my deep regret in not being favored with thy
company at Dover; the more when I reflect that I might
have availed myself of the more full expression of our
mutual feelings on those things to which there appears too
much reason to apply the words: ' That which now letteth

will let, until it be taken out of the way.' Thou hast done what thou couldst, I believe may truly be said; and in that thy feet were turned another way, the burden must rest upon those unto whom they were first directed; but unto such, who although in a far inferior degree have become companions in travail for the suffering seed, there is brought an increase of exercise and sympathy with those who wish well unto our favored Society. The language of my spirit at times is, when viewing the ravages that have been made within our borders by a conformity to the spirit of the world: Surely we shall one day fall by the hand of the enemy.

"With the salutation of dear love, in which my wife unites, I desire very sincerely that thy portion may be a rich reward of heavenly peace and comfort as thou passest along in the Master's service, and when thou hast completed this, thy work of labor and love, thou mayest be favored largely to partake of the joy of thy Lord.

"I remain thy truly affectionate friend,
            SAMUEL REYNOLDS."

The following letter, received by Christopher Healy about this time, from Joseph Thorp, who had for a time been his companion, alludes to his instructive and entertaining conversation,—a talent for which our dear friend was remarkable; and which is so well remembered by those who had the pleasure of listening to its animating flow. Perhaps, too, there were no subjects dearer to his heart, or upon which he was more wont to enlarge, than the doctrines and testimonies of Friends, of which mention is made in the letter. We well remember hearing him say, with much emphasis of manner, "These (Quaker) principles are the dearest principles on the face of the earth." May none of us, professors of the same precious truths, be either lukewarm in their support or be ashamed of their faithful maintenance among men; remembering the dear Saviour's own words: "*Whosoever* shall be ashamed of me and of my words, *of him* shall the Son of man be ashamed when he shall come in his own glory, and in his Father's, and of the holy angels."

"Halifax, Second Month 27th, 1832.

"My dear Friend Christopher Healy:—As I fear I shall hardly be able to meet thee during thy stay at Stockport, as I rather had hoped to do, I thought I would at any rate drop thee a line if it were only to assure thee that we do bear thee in affectionate remembrance.

"I was truly reluctant to surrender my privileged office when I did, but the ties of the dearest attachment, the fear that I should be wanted in the business at home, and the little indisposition of which I spoke to thee, and which rather increased for a few days afterwards, seemed to make it prudent to return. And though I parted from thee, yet in mind I have gone with thee. I have thus had thee *my* companion often every day. I have marked thy progress; have felt interested in it; and whilst my heart hath breathed fervently for thy preservation, and that thou mayest be favored to return in peace to the bosom of thy family, I have felt answered in the belief that He will keep, who hath called thee; and that He will preserve thee 'in the work whereunto he hath called' thee.

"I have much pleasure in calling to remembrance the subjects upon which thou touched in thy conversation; and I hope the valuable instruction contained in it, will not be quite lost to me. Thy remarks on our principles and 'peculiarities,' too, have raised and confirmed them in my esteem; and though thy plain and powerful speaking may almost startle us who have perhaps been too much used to smoother things, yet we cannot but acknowledge that these are indeed *the Society's first principles, from which we have too much glided away,* and that to ourselves almost imperceptibly. * * *

"I remain thy assured friend,

JOSEPH THORP."

Christopher Healy went to London on Seventh-day, the 12th of Fifth Month, 1832, in time to attend the Yearly Meeting. His journal states that up to that time, he had travelled thirty-seven hundred and fourteen miles, and attended two hundred and eighty-five meetings. In London he stopped at the house of his friend John Sanderson. "Here," he writes, "I received a consoling letter from my dear wife." At Northampton and at Bardfield respectively, he sent letters to her. From these the following extracts are taken. They set forth some of the exercises which were his portion while on that foreign shore, viz :—

Northampton, Third Month 20th, 1832.

* * * I have had much close labor in this land, and as much as some could bear who were superficial Quakers; and whose adorning was not that of a meek and quiet spirit, which is in the sight of God of great price. Therefore the simplicity of the truth as it is in Jesus is too strait for them. A desire too much prevails to be called by Christ's name, while they want to eat their own bread and wear their own apparel. Such, wherever they are in meetings, make hard work. But blessed be the great Name of the good Shepherd, He hath abundantly

appeared and given the victory. May my poor soul be humbled before him.

Bardfield, Essex, Fourth Month 4th, 1832.

* * * I feel as though I had plenty of time to get through with all that I have in prospect before the Yearly Meeting in London, without hurrying; and it is a great favor to have, once in a while, a day of rest for my poor body and mind. The exercises of the latter are sometimes almost more than the poor body is able to bear. Yet, blessed be the Lord's holy name, I have been marvellously supported beyond what human reason could suppose. May He forever have the praise, who alone is worthy.

* * * I still continue the prospect of returning in the same vessel in which we came to England—the Algonquin: which will sail, according to advertisement, the 8th of Sixth Month, from Liverpool to Philadelphia. But my dear, all this pleasant prospect must be in submission to the Divine disposal. May our eye be kept single to the Holy Redeemer; looking to Him from whom alone come all our blessings. Thou knowest how He hath blessed us every way; and hath not suffered us to be tried beyond what he has given strength to endure; which has abundantly, I hope, strengthened our faith and confidence in his all-sustaining power. Oh! then may we, my precious one, continue to keep the word of his patience, and no doubt He will keep us in the hour of temptation, which may be permitted to try us yet again. I have been favored since I last wrote, with many large and comfortable meetings. May He alone who is the crown of meetings, have the praise. I have close exercising times amongst my dear friends, yet it is a comfort to me that they very generally receive what I have to communicate,

and appear well satisfied. But a great reformation is wanting in some. May He that raised up our worthy forefathers in this land to bear such precious testimonies, open their eyes to see how they are departing from them. Notwithstanding I have many painful and distressing feelings about some not in the lowest rank, yet my mind is at times comforted that there are some among the youth of both sexes, who do see the danger; as well as many among the elder ones, who are, with my own soul, saying, Lord arise for our help; even thou who didst so clearly manifest thy will to our worthy forefathers, and separated them from a dependence on forms without life; and in a remarkable manner brought them forth to preach in the demonstration of the Spirit and with power, whereby many were added to the church. May such days be known among us again, if it please Thee, our Holy Helper.

The following letter addressed not to Christopher Healy, but to other persons concerning him, gives some insight into the nature of the testimony borne by our friend in England :—

"My Dear Friends :—As we have each had an opportunity of reflecting upon the subjects of discussion with our highly valued friend Christopher Healy, myself for having been the means of their being introduced, and you for the little reprimand which you thought me entitled to for so doing: I feel inclined to cast before you, in the pure freedom and precious feeling of love and unity, some of my thoughts in meditating thereupon. As to myself, considering how we are circumstanced, I count it a privilege to have been made acquainted with his views on the subjects. Perhaps to say that they corre-

spond very much with some of my own original views,
may be almost too presuming. His are so clear, so apos-
tolic and so truly consonant with the practice and usage
of our early Friends, that I cannot but admire them, as
well as delight in the hope that they are in the way of
being revived amongst us, the nation through. Perhaps
there may be many, who with you do not admire, nor
hardly know how to bear his plain dealing with us on the
subject, but 'tis, I verily believe, in the way of his gift;
which I find is exercised among Friends in a conversational, not a ministerial way, out of meetings. And does
not the precious feeling of life and power frequently, yea
for the most part, accompany these his communications.
My impression is that it does, at least wherever I have
been in his company, which has been as much as six or
seven times, or more, both in and out of meetings. Fast
days, the holding the office of special constable, and
attendance of missionary meetings, &c., I have heard
him equally plain upon, and equally convincing to me;
though at the same time condemning some of my own
practices. But what then! We must not rest there. If
our judgment has been warped by the example of others,
or even that we have erred in our own—for the deceiver,
as some of us know by long and very dear-bought experience, hath many ways of transforming himself—even
under the most upright intentions, and in the truest
sincerity of desire, to be dedicated to the service of Him
' whom to know (from the deceit) is life eternal.'

" Therefore, methinks, that all this very plain dealing
of our beloved and honored friend and elder in the
Truth (of which surely he is one among the valiants in
our day) will not hurt or hinder the growth of the
precious lowly plant of renown in us, no not in any of us

old or young. Nay, has it not already been to some of
us like a digging about, in order to clear the spurious
growth from the root? Which I desire may be the case;
and that the root may be watered with the refreshing
streams from Zion's hill, so that we may grow and bring
forth abundant fruit to the praise of the good Husbandman, &c.   Your affectionate friend,

J. W.

"Third Month, 1832."

Alexander Dirkin related that when he was in England, and conversing with the late John Barclay about
Christopher Healy, John remarked, "that Christopher
was the right kind of a man to come there on a religious
visit, for he was not afraid to challenge a Peter or a Paul,
and to say, 'Thou art the man.'"

The following are extracts from letters which were
addressed to Christopher Healy, before he left England,
according to their respective dates:—

"Moyallen, 5th of First Month, 1832.

"We indeed stand in need of help and support in this
place of trial and discouragement. Indeed it abounds
every way, and at times appears as if the flood would not
only overflow the banks, but carry away the ramparts,
and leave little behind. My dear children, intend to add
a little to this letter, so must bid thee farewell in the love
of the gospel, and am with dear love to thee, and thy
companion, thy affectionate friend,

THOS. CHRISTY WAKEFIELD."

"Trumery, Fifth Month 4th, 1832.

"Dear Friend:—I received thy acceptable letter, which
satisfied my desire, for before I got it I was very anxious
to know when thou intended to return to thy native

country, believing it would be the time for me, if liberated
by my Yearly Meeting, to proceed on my prospect of visiting your land; and the way seems now open for me, and
I trust I can be ready, if all is well, to meet thee in Liverpool, the 8th of Sixth Month, as thou proposes. It is a
great comfort to me and my family the prospect of having
thy company across the great deep. When thou wast in
our parts I felt nearly united to thee. I hope thou hast got
comfortably through thy important mission in Europe,
and feels the reward of peace. * * * I hope you may have
as agreeable a Yearly Meeting as we had in Dublin. I believe it might be said in measure, as formerly, the Lord's
power was over all, which is the crown of all religious
assemblies. I trust this may be your experience—that all
crowns may be cast down at his sacred footstool, that He
only and alone may be exalted. There felt to me, when
I was in London last year, a great deal of the worldly
wisdom and head knowledge amongst the members of our
Society, that I was afraid they were not taught in Christ's
self-denying school. I hope thou may not see nor feel
this among you this year. It was very painful to me,
and would be I am sure to thee. With earnest desires
for our preservation in every good word and work, I conclude with dear love to thee, in which my dear wife and
children unite; and am thy affectionate friend,

JACOB GREEN."

Several letters are preserved among Christopher Healy's
papers, from different Friends, expressive of their interest
in his labors in Great Britain, and of unity with the plain
dealing he was drawn into during his visit among them.
At a Monthly Meeting where he was present, he spoke
pretty fully on the dangers which attended Friends join-

ing with persons of other religious denominations in associations for promoting benevolent objects; using such texts as, "Strangers have devoured his strength, and he knoweth it not." The clerk of the Monthly Meeting was a youngish man of great natural abilities. After meeting, he requested an interview with Christopher, saying, their views were not alike on some points. At this interview he proceeded at some length, and with much eloquence to set forth the public benefits and the opportunities of disseminating Friends' doctrines, etc., that would arise from the course some were pursuing.

When he had finished, Christopher asked him a few questions: "Are the views and practices of the Episcopalians the same now as they were in the days of George Fox and our early Friends?" "They are."

"Dost thou believe that George Fox and our early Friends were led out from these things by the Spirit of Truth?" "Yes, I do."

"Dost thou believe the same Spirit of Truth would lead us into that, now, out of which it formerly led us?"

The man's head drooped, and he sat without answering.

They parted pleasantly, and after Christopher Healy's return to this country, he received a letter from the clerk, stating that the few words uttered by him at that interview were the first thing that had opened his eyes, and led to a change in his views.

Diary resumed:—

First-day morning, Fifth Month, 13th.—Attended Grace-Church Street meeting. Afternoon, that of Devonshire house. Second-day, the Yearly Meeting of Ministers and Elders. I informed this meeting that I be-

lieved my labors and services were near a close in this
land; and that my prospect was, if my way continued
to remain open, and with the blessing of heaven, to return to my family and friends soon after the Yearly
Meeting. The meeting thereupon appointed a committee
to produce a certificate for that purpose; which was done.
At this Yearly Meeting, Stephen Grellet, John Wilbur,
Charles Osborne, and myself were in attendance from
America. The meeting was favored, particularly at the
conclusion; and Friends parted in the love of the great
Head of the Church. On the Seventh day of the week,
went to Tottenham. First-day morning attended Friends'
meeting there. In the afternoon rode to Hitchin, twenty-
seven miles from London. Second-day pursued our way
towards Liverpool, the place proposed to embark. Third-
day took stage to Manchester, and thence to Liverpool.
Fourth-day rested. Here I met with my dear friend Jacob
Green, from Ireland, who was going to America on a
religious visit. The thought of having each other's company over the sea was mutually pleasant. Fifth-day
attended meeting at Liverpool. This parting opportunity
was refreshing to many of our minds. The Great Shepherd had cemented many of our hearts together; and
though we now had to part, yet the remembrance of each
other in the Lord, I trust, will not soon be forgotten
by us.

On the morning of the 8th of Sixth Month, 1832, being
the Sixth of the week, we went on board the ship Algonquin, bound for Philadelphia, Thomas Cropper, master.

Christopher Healy and his friend Jacob Green were
the only cabin passengers. They held meetings through
the course of the voyage, to which many of the steerage

passengers came. While on the passage homeward he thus writes :—

My mind is comforted in looking over my visit to England and Ireland; and the prospect is pleasant also in looking towards home, to my dear wife and children, as well as many of my dear friends. Oh may I be humbled in thanksgiving and praise to Him, who rules the winds and on the ocean rides; the only preserver of men.

(Again) :—

First-day, the ship rolled so, that we could not have a meeting. But I humbly trust my mind was preserved in submission to the Divine will. How true is that Holy Scripture testimony, "Thou wilt keep him in perfect peace, whose mind is staid on thee, because he trusteth in thee." Oh may this be my happy case! Then will all things work together for good, and the Lord will have the praise, who alone is worthy.

And again, Sixth Month, 25th :—

The wind increased and the sea rose, tossing the ship very much. 26th.—The wind strong, and the sea very high. Oh the awfulness of the great deep! The sea continuing to increase, a part of the vessel and rigging was carried away. Never did mine eyes behold greater wonders on the rolling, foaming deep, than this day. We got but very little sleep. My trust was in the Lord alone; who could command the winds and the mighty sea that so greatly raged and roared.

Again, Seventh Month, 16th :—

We are now about one hundred and fifty miles from the capes. The weather warm and pleasant. May we be thankful to the Lord for his many favors. Some of our steerage passengers having a longer voyage than they expected, are getting scant of provisions; which must be proving to them. But a hope is entertained that a fair wind will soon spring up, which, with the favor of heaven, may soon bring us to our desired port. But of ourselves we can do nothing. May we, under an humbling sense thereof, look to Him who created the winds and the seas, and rules them at his pleasure.

Our dear friend finally reached his home on the 21st of Seventh Month, 1832, and found his wife and family well, "which," as he records, "was cause of humble thankfulness of soul before the Lord, who had been pleased to put forth, to go before, and to bring again in peace. Taking a retrospective view of my late visit, I feel great peace of mind; though mourning and lamentation were my portion very often while travelling in those foreign lands."

CHAPTER XII.

VISITS MEETINGS IN BUCKS QUARTERLY MEETING, PENN'A;
AND IN NEW JERSEY. VISITS FRIENDS AND OTHERS IN
NEW YORK AND NEW ENGLAND. EXTRACT FROM A LET-
TER TO HIS WIFE. REMARKS ON DIVINE JUDGMENTS TO
BE APPREHENDED FOR THE TREATMENT BY THE WHITES
OF THE INDIAN AND AFRICAN RACES. VISITS MEETINGS
COMPOSING ABINGTON AND HADDONFIELD QUARTERLY
MEETINGS: ALSO, SHREWSBURY AND RAHWAY QUAR-
TERLY MEETING, N. J. VISITS FRIENDS AND OTHERS IN
SEVERAL QUARTERLY MEETINGS IN PENNSYLVANIA.
HOLDS MEETINGS IN NEW JERSEY, WHERE NO FRIENDS
WERE SETTLED. VISITS SOME OF THE TRIBES OF INDIANS
IN THE WEST AND NORTHWEST; AND FRIENDS AND
OTHERS IN MICHIGAN. EXTRACTS FROM LETTERS TO
HIS WIFE. TESTIMONY TO CHRIST INWARDLY REVEAL-
ED AS THE FOUNDATION OF THE FAITH AND PRACTICE
OF FRIENDS.

AFTER his return to America, Christopher Healy's
first religious service from home, was a visit to the meetings composing his own Quarterly Meeting, and subse-
quently the families of the same; and also many of the
meetings in New Jersey; in which, as he writes, he had
to rejoice in the goodness of the Great Shepherd of Israel.
In the visit to the families of Bucks Quarterly Meeting,
he had the company of Abraham Harding, an Elder of
his own Monthly Meeting, and John Comfort, of Sole-
bury. Their company, he writes, was pleasant to him,
and this labor of love satisfactorily accomplished.

His journal again states, that having felt drawn in gospel love to perform a visit to Friends, and those not of
our Society, within the limits of New York and New

England Yearly Meetings, the concurrence of the Monthly and Quarterly Meetings was duly granted; and taking
leave of his dear wife and family, he proceeded thereon
in Tenth Month, 1833, accompanied by Benjamin Cadwallader. The memoranda of this and the few following
journeys, are concise. A few extracts therefrom are as
follow:—

First-day, again attended Coeymans' meeting. A very
large gathering. It seemed as if almost all the neighborhood came together, except those that had separated from
Friends. A more precious season I do not often remember. Blessed be Jehovah's glorious Name. Had a very
favored meeting at Brothertown with a small tribe of Indians. The Indian minister, with some of the most
thoughtful of his tribe, came to Thomas Dean's, who was
the government agent, and where we put up, and dined
with us. They expressed much thankfulness to the Great
Spirit for this favored opportunity. How true it is, that
Christ is given for a light to the Gentiles; that He may
be God's salvation to the ends of the earth.

At Madison, Christopher Healy writes:—

I met with some of my former acquaintance, particularly two men and their wives, who had for years been
associating with the separatists; but hearing at the meeting this afternoon the true faith of our Lord Jesus Christ
opened in a clear manner, they were instructed and comforted; and in the evening came both the men with
their wives to our lodgings, and we had a favored time
together. In a short time they returned to Friends, acknowledging they had been misled. And I have no
doubt there are many more such amongst them. May

the Good Shepherd be near to help these sincere ones, whoever and wherever they are.

While on this visit, he addressed a letter to his wife, from which the following is extracted:—

And now, my dearly beloved wife, be of good cheer; and be filled with joyful hope. I believe if thou continues to cast all thy care on Him who cares for us, and has been our Preserver and Comforter, He will be thy comforter still, in thy husband's absence. I may say without boasting, the Lord is my Shepherd, in whom I trust day and night—this blessed Shepherd of Israel, who was pleased to unite our hearts together, and enables us to resign each other for his blessed cause and testimony.— Neither do I see but that we may be favored to meet again in the sweet embraces of Heavenly love. Benjamin travels cheerfully, and makes a pleasant and very agreeable companion. Give my dear love to his wife. Tell her I hope she may feel the sweet reward of peace for resigning the partner of her joy. He expresses good satisfaction in the journey thus far.

Farewell, my dear wife. Give much love to all the children. Tell them to be good children, and love their dear mother. I hope this may find you all well.

From thy faithful and loving husband,

CHRISTOPHER HEALY.

At Hamburg he had a large meeting. Many of those who attended had gone off from Friends. He writes:—

Here I was led to show the great difference between those who do not believe that our Lord Jesus Christ was anything more than a good man, and we, who as a Society, have always believed as the Saviour himself de-

clared of himself in his intercession to his Father, "And
now, O Father, glorify thou me with thine own self, with
the glory which I had with thee before the world was."—
Again, "I and my Father are one."—And again, to
Philip, "He that hath seen me hath seen the Father, and
how sayest thou, then, Show us the Father?" When our
dear Redeemer said to the unbelieving Jews, "I and my
Father are one," it is written they took stones to stone
him. Jesus said unto them, "Many good works have I
shown you from my Father: For which of those works
do ye stone me?" The Jews answered him, saying: "For
a good work we stone thee not: but for blasphemy; and
because that thou being a man, makest thyself God."—
What is the difference between those of this day who call
our Holy Redeemer but a man, and those unbelieving
Jews that called him a blasphemer because he said "I and
my Father are one?" Oh how mournful is this same
spirit of unbelief! May their eyes be opened to see the
great delusion by which the grand deceiver has ensnared
them.

Upon their return home, he thus writes:—

What added much to the comfort of the journey, my
dear companion was a truly uniting and sympathizing
friend. He travelled cheerfully, though it was a laborious
one as to the flesh. But He who is strength in weakness,
riches in poverty, and a present help in time of need, was
pleased to make bare His Arm for us. Oh may we ever
trust in Him, who never said to the seed of Jacob, seek
ye my face in vain.

Benjamin Cadwallader, in returning his certificate in
the Third Month, 1834, said that Christopher Healy and

himself had visited the greater part of the meetings of
New York Yearly Meeting.

Resuming this religious visit. Christopher Healy, with
Robert Alexander for companion, in the Fifth Month,
1834, attended New York Yearly Meeting; making their
home at his kind friend John Wood's, who, he writes, is
"a precious minister." The memoranda continue:—

Though some seasons during this Yearly Meeting were
trying, there were many deeply exercised minds present,
and some favored testimonies were borne in the life and
power of the gospel; and I trust the meeting closed under
thankful acknowledgments to that Good Hand that first
raised us up to be a people.

He visited during this journey a small tribe of Indians,
with whom he previously had had several meetings. He
writes:—

How thankful they always are; I am scarcely able to
find words to convey my sympathy for these poor afflicted
people. It seems to me the language to us is at the
present day, "Open thy mouth for the dumb, in the
cause of all such as are appointed to destruction! Open
thy mouth, judge righteously, and plead the cause of the
poor and needy." It seems as though the wrath of man
has counted them not fit to live and enjoy themselves in
this world. May we not expect that the Lord will visit
for these things done to this people, and also to the African race. Will not his soul be avenged on such a nation
as we are, unless we repent, and submit to that holy and
just rule of the dear Son of God: "As ye would that
men should do to you, do ye even so to them."

Coming to North Kingston, he says:—

My mind has been drawn to this place several times before; and finding great openness in the people's minds, a precious season it proved. May the Lord sanctify it for good to all present.

He went thence to Greenwich; and next to Providence, where, his journal states,—

I had a very trying meeting in the fore part, but got some relief. After meeting we went home with our dear aged friend Moses Brown, living about a mile from Providence. His conversation was sweet and savory, and the exercise of his spirit helpful. This could be felt as we sat by him. He was then in the ninety-fifth year of his age. He truly seemed like one planted in the house of the Lord, and flourishing in the courts of our God; being green in old age. How edifying and instructive is the company of this dear father in Israel! Oh, saith my soul, may the Lord raise up more such judges and counsellors in his church.

Soon after this, they returned home; and, as he says, "found all well; and we rejoiced in Him of whom I could say, 'The Lord is my Shepherd; I shall not want. He maketh me to lie down in green pastures; he leadeth me beside the still waters.' Oh glory to his holy Name forever!" Their certificates were returned in the Eighth Month, 1834.

His next visit was to Abington and Haddonfield Quarterly Meetings, and the meetings composing them; with that also of Shrewsbury and Rahway, though not the meetings constituting it. As his manner was, in all these he held meetings with those not of our Society. He was favored to accomplish the same to the peace of his own mind. He adds, "Blessed be the Lord who can send help from his sanctuary, and strengthen us out of Zion."

Early in 1836 he was liberated by his Monthly Meeting to pay a religious visit to Friends, and those not in membership with us, within the limits of Philadelphia, Concord, Caln, and Western Quarterly Meetings. Attending the Northern District Monthly Meeting, he writes: "Our friend J. W. kindly offering to bear me company, it was united with, and he set at liberty. We had many public meetings, as well as attended those of Friends, to the strength and encouragement of our minds." Here occurs the following memorandum :—

How clear I am that the profession of the faith and doctrines of our religious Society is a good and holy profession. Oh that *all would live up to them!* then would righteousness indeed cover the earth, as the waters cover the sea; and light and life would reign over death and darkness.

In the latter part of the same year (1836), he obtained the unity of his Friends to hold meetings in some towns and villages, particularly in New Jersey, where no Friends were settled, as Best Wisdom might direct. He writes:—

Being joined by my kind friend Benjamin Cooper, of Newtown, an elder, we visited Newtown, Woodbury, Woodstown, Salem, Bridgeton, Port Elizabeth, and thence down to Egg Harbor; together with many more in that part of Jersey. These meetings were largely attended by those not of our Society. My dear companion, Benjamin Cooper, was a very suitable Friend for such a visit, and very helpful to me herein. Returning towards Evesham, we had a very precious meeting at the Glass-works; and

another at Evesham, also greatly favored. May the good
Shepherd of the sheep have the glory; for to none other
doth any glory belong. Returned home with a peaceful
mind.

Not having completed my prospect in this visit, towards the spring of the following year (1837) I again set
out with my dear friend Benjamin Cadwallader, to the
eastern parts of New Jersey. Had meetings at Plainfield,
Rahway, Mount Holly, and Rancocas, with some public
meetings. In these we felt thankful hearts for favors received from Him, who is the crown of all heavenly meetings. Being enabled to perform this visit, as I believe,
in the love of, and I humbly hope in a measure of the
life of the gospel of Christ Jesus, it brought peace to my
own soul, and to the living members of the church.

The memoranda continue :—

Having felt drawings in my mind for several years to
visit, in gospel love, some of the tribes of Indians in the
western and north-western parts of this continent; with
Friends and those not of our Society in the State of
Michigan; and also to have meetings going and returning; on the 2nd of Fifth Month, 1838, after taking a
solemn leave of my dear wife and family, I set out in
company with Thomas Wistar, Jr., of Abington; a young,
but kind and pleasing companion. We proceeded, having
many public meetings on the way, to a small tribe of
Indians at Brothertown, in the western part of the State of
New York. Whilst I was sitting with these poor afflicted
people, my mind, from the sweet consolation I felt, was
strengthened in believing that my concern originated
from the living truth; and I felt assured that not only
the meetings among the Indian tribes, but many of those

appointed where there were no Indians, were favored in a measure, to feel that the drawing cords of the Heavenly Father's love were round about us to gather us. May it continue and increase with them, saith my soul. We had meetings with five tribes of Indians in the western part of New York State, as well as many more public meetings, to our great comfort.

Whilst on this journey, Christopher Healy addressed two letters to his wife, from which the following extracts are taken :—

Skeneateles, New York, 20th of Fifth Month, 1838.

* * * On leaving Brookfield, we were invited to stop at one of their neighbors, who they thought was dying. We went in and sat down, and in about half an hour the poor man breathed his last. Oh what a solemn time it was! After a precious silence, and a few words of comfort to the family, we proceeded to Brothertown, where the first tribe of Indians on our route reside. On Fifth-day, at three o'clock P. M., the Indians came together, and some white people. The meeting was a good one. They understood our language. Sixth-day came to Oneida, where were about five hundred Indians. Their missionary was a Methodist minister, who was glad to see us. After showing him our certificates, he desired we might have a meeting with them. The Indians being met in Council near by at the time, we went to the Council House, and conferred with a number of their chiefs. These took it on them to give information of the meeting, to be held at three o'clock in the afternoon. The Council House was nearly full. Our guide, the Methodist minister and wife, with ourselves, were all the white people in the meeting. Oh! in looking over this assembly of In-

dians, it seemed to call up just such feelings in my heart, as I had witnessed years before towards these poor people. Under these precious feelings I stood up; and a remarkable season we had together. I thought if I had no other joy in the journey, this would have rewarded for all my privations consequent upon leaving home, with all that is near and dear in this world. Therefore, my dear wife, be not discouraged, but be filled with joyful hope. I believe I am in the line of my duty to our dear Master and Lord, who hath called me to this service; and that the same Good Hand that brought the concern on my mind, will make the way for us. Blessed be his name forever.

Read this letter to our friends who want to hear from us, particularly to Ruth Ely. She loves the poor Indian. She will see what a good meeting we had at Oneida, where her dear father visited them. Give my dear love to her, and all enquiring friends. Farewell. I remain thy loving husband in the unchangeable truth.

CHRISTOPHER HEALY.

Hamburg, 3d of Sixth Month, 1838.

* * * Sixth-day had a meeting with the Cattaraugus Indians, to good satisfaction: though it is hard to speak by an interpreter. Our certificates were read by a young Indian, and interpreted to them. One of their chiefs spoke some time after I had got through, expressing great thankfulness for our visit to them, believing it was from the Great Spirit. They seemed exceedingly glad to hear our certificates in their own language. We parted in a sweet friendship with them. Second-day, attended a meeting of the Buffalo Indians, at their Council House, seven miles from Buffalo. The house was nearly full. One of the young Indian chiefs that I saw in Philadelphia,

was my interpreter. It was a good meeting to the poor Indians, and to the relief of our minds.

The Indians, when we sit in meetings with them, seem just as I used to see them by faith, when my prospect was clear, and thou and I used to talk about these poor children of the wilderness. Yes, my dear, their hearts were made glad: as many of their chiefs and warriors expressed by the interpreters.

Hitherto we have parted in abundance of love and friendship. Oh mayest thou be comforted; for He who is mighty hath done great things for us, and holy is his name.

To my comfort, I received here a good letter from thee, which gave an account of John's narrow escape. Oh may he never forget it! But may he, as well as all the rest of our dear children, remember their father's and their mother's God, now in the days of their youth; before the evil days come, or the years draw nigh, wherein they will say, we have no pleasure in them.

Farewell in the love of the Good Shepherd that made us acquainted with each other, and joined us together in love. CHRISTOPHER HEALY.

Continuing the diary, Christopher Healy writes:—

* * * We then left our horses at Lockport, and taking passage in the steamboat up Lake Erie, came to Toledo; then to Adrian, a settlement of Friends. We wished to reach there in time to attend their Monthly Meeting, but did not arrive until near its close. But we had a precious opportunity together before the meeting separated. May our Divine Master have the praise forever.

Seventh-day, made some enquiry concerning the situation of the Indian tribes in this State, but found to our

14

sorrow the poor creatures much unsettled; the government having made a treaty with them some time before
to give up their homes, and go far west into a more wilderness land; the agents of the United States had just
arrived to bring the Indians word to prepare for remov-
ing.   Finding many of them had left their homes in
order to get something to make them comfortable, the
prospect of having meetings with these poor children of
the wilderness seemed altogether discouraging.   Having
to relinquish this prospect, we proceeded on our visit to
the white people as far as Lake Michigan.   Had a public
meeting at Saint Josephs, which was a favored time.   We
had meetings also at all the meeting places of Friends in
the State, as well as in the houses of those of other societies, to my own comfort and I trust to the edification of
many minds.   A Methodist minister was at a meeting of
Friends, and very kindly offered their house to have a
meeting in; an offer I felt quite willing to accept.   He
took great care to spread information, and attended himself.   It proved to be a good meeting.

Soon after coming into this State, I met at a Friend's
house with a plain looking man, who, in the course of
conversation, asked me some questions, which I answered.
After dinner, a paragraph of our early Friends' views on
the spirituality of the gospel dispensation having been
read, this man also read the 19th and 20th verses, chap-
ter ii. of the Epistle of Paul to the Ephesians.   I asked
him if he read that Scripture in reply to the paragraph?
He said he did.   I asked him if he thought they clashed?
He said he believed that Scripture: and asked me if I did
not?   I told him, yea; I verily did believe that declaration.   I told him that we (Friends) had always held that
true believers in Christ were built, as the apostle testifies,

on the foundation of the apostles and prophets, Jesus
Christ himself being the chief corner-stone. And, our
ancient Friend, George Fox, concerning faith in Christ,
declared: that we believe in that same Jesus that was crucified without the gates of Jerusalem, the same that was the
foundation of all the holy prophets and apostles, and that
He is our foundation; and another can no man lay, than
that which is already laid; even He who tasted death
for every man; shed his blood for all men; and is a pro-
pitiation for our sins, and those also of the whole world.
The more I conversed, the more uneasy I grew, as he appeared to be a man of talents. I told him he was a
stranger to me; and asked him if he was a member of
our Society? He replied shortly, and with a quick tone
of voice, I am; and a minister in good esteem. I told
him he must excuse me, but it was his views of Scripture
that caused me to ask if he was a member of our Society.
I thought I plainly saw that he believed the Scripture
to be the primary rule of faith and practice. I having
another visit to make that afternoon, we parted. A Friend
in the ministry being with me, who was acquainted with
him towards whom I had felt this uneasiness, said he was
glad he had not mentioned the circumstance to me, and
that I had so clearly discovered his unsoundness.

Next day, which was First-day, notice having been
given of our intention of being there at meeting, a very
large company got together. After a solemn silence, I
believed it to be required of me to declare to the meeting,
what foundation true believers have to build upon. That
beloved and experienced Apostle, Paul, did not say, we
are built on the prophets and apostles; but that we are
built upon the *foundation* of the prophets and apostles.
Here we may see that that holy Apostle did not mean to

call himself the foundation of the prophets and apostles,
by no means. But that the foundation they built upon,
was and is Christ; the eternal rock of every age. It
was He who inspired prophets and apostles of old, as we
read holy men were, to write and to speak as they were
moved by the Holy Ghost. And we may likewise see
how the same Apostle gives the honor and glory to God,
in and through Christ Jesus, where he says, " By the grace
of God, I am what I am : and his grace which was bestowed upon me was not in vain ; but I labored more
abundantly than they all ; yet not I, but the grace of God
which was with me."   And our blessed Lord, in speaking
of the Holy Scriptures, saith, " Search the Scriptures ; for
in them ye think ye have eternal life ; and they are they
which testify of me.   And ye will not come to me, *that
ye might have life.*"   Oh how many there are in the present day, who think that in the Scriptures they have all
the knowledge of eternal life.   And thus stopping short,
settle down in a false rest ; and become of those of whom
Christ declared, " ye will not come to me that ye might
have life."   The testimony of Christ in the Scriptures,
and that of those he influenced to write them, is good and
precious, if we receive Christ, by his Holy Spirit in our
hearts, and yield to his holy teaching.   It is then we
build on the foundation that the prophets and apostles
built on.   Then shall Christ Jesus be our Rock and sure
Foundation, against which the gates of hell cannot prevail.

Returning home to his family, he found them all well ;
and acknowledges that the Good Shepherd who had been
with him, had also kept and preserved them.

CHAPTER XIII.

ATTENDS ABINGTON AND HADDONFIELD QUARTERLY MEET-
INGS, AND BALTIMORE YEARLY MEETING. VISITS THE
FAMILIES OF FRIENDS IN BUCKS AND ABINGTON QUAR-
TERLY MEETINGS. HOLDS MEETINGS WITH THE IN-
MATES OF THE COUNTY POOR-HOUSES IN NEW JERSEY;
REMARKS THEREON. VISITS FRIENDS AND OTHERS IN
THE NORTHERN AND WESTERN PARTS OF NEW YORK
YEARLY MEETING, AND IN OHIO. LETTER FROM B. W.
LADD. RELIGIOUS ENGAGEMENTS AT AND NEAR HOME.
INCIDENT CONNECTED WITH A VISIT OF CHRISTOPHER
HEALY TO THE YEARLY MEETING OF WOMEN FRIENDS
IN NEW YORK. LETTER OF JOSEPH EDGERTON.

In the Tenth Month of this year, 1838, Christopher
Healy attended the Quarterly Meetings of Abington and
Haddonfield; and the Yearly Meeting of Baltimore; of
which last he notes, that owing to unsoundness in the
faith and doctrines of our Society in some individuals
present, it was a trying meeting. He attended some
meetings going and returning, and got home with the
penny of peace. The diary resumed :—

In the Twelfth Month of the same year, I felt my mind
drawn to make a visit to the families of Friends belonging to Bucks and Abington Quarterly Meetings. I was
favored to perform this arduous service to the peace of
my own mind; and from what appeared, to the comfort
of the visited. May the Lord have the glory and praise
of his own works! After returning home, my mind was
brought into deep sympathy and tender feeling with the

14*

poor. And as I dwelt under this humbling exercise of
mind, it opened in the Truth that it would be my duty to
make a religious visit to the stewards and inmates of the
county poor-houses in the State of New Jersey. With
my kind friend and elder James Moon, of our Monthly
Meeting, in Sixth Month, 1839, I performed the same to
satisfaction. I am not able to express to the full the feelings which I had in this visit. The spectacle presented
at some of these houses was, I think, more reaching than
the greatest sermon that I ever heard; and my soul was
humbled before the Lord. I often said in my heart, how
many there are who do not rightly prize their blessings,
and perhaps could not until deprived of them! Some of
these poor afflicted ones had no doubt been the means of
their own distress, but who now could not help themselves. How my heart mourned for them. There were
some whose hearts were made glad while sitting in these
meetings. With these we rejoiced together. The language
of such at heart seemed to be, keep me from murmuring
on account of my afflictions. Oh! I did remember many
times in these meetings, the language of David: "Before
I was afflicted, I went astray: but now, [through afflic-
tions], have I kept thy word."

Our dear friend seems not to have been allowed to
remain long at home. He could no doubt adopt the language, in his measure, of the dear Master: "My meat is
to do the will of Him that sent me." Feeling his mind
drawn in gospel love, to visit Friends and those not of
our religious Society in the northern and western parts of
New York Yearly Meeting, and in the State of Ohio, he,
in the Sixth Month, 1840, took leave of his family, having
for companion his dear friend William Hilles, of Frank-

ford; and got the first day to the house of his friend
Joseph Shotwell, at Rahway. The next day, being the
first of the week, and general notice being given, many
not of our Society came together. Christopher Healy
writes : " It was a large and good meeting."

There does not seem to be much to extract from the
account left of this visit, save the following memorandum :—

The man that I discoursed with,* when here on a former visit, came to two of our meetings. He had left the
Society, taking a number of followers with him. It appears by his going to and fro, as though he knew not
what to do, nor where to stay. Such wandering stars
must feel themselves left in darkness. May the Lord have
mercy on them, and bring them into the Garden enclosed,
if consistent with his blessed will. May they thus know
Him as their Shepherd, to lead and feed them, before
they are called from works to rewards.

While Christopher Healy was out on this visit, the following letter from B. W. Ladd, was received by his
wife :—

"Smithfield, Ohio, Eighth Month, 26th, 1840.

" Dear Friend :—We have had with us several days and
nights, the acceptable company of thy dear Christopher,
and his agreeable companion, William Hilles. They left
here yesterday in good health for Stillwater Quarterly
Meeting, which occurs about a week hence ; taking meetings in their way. After that meeting, they have one day
only to travel to Mount Pleasant, until our Yearly Meeting commences. From appearances we are to have with
us an unusually large number of ministering Friends

* See previous visit to New York and Canada.

from other Yearly Meetings, some of whom have already arrived. But it is not numbers we want so much, as those of the right kind.

"It has been a satisfaction and comfort to me, and I doubt not to many other Friends hereaway, to find that thy husband and his companion belong to the old school. I mean, are those who are content with the doctrines of the gospel as they were unfolded by the Light of Truth to our worthy predecessors in religious profession. Well would it have been for us, if we as a Society had endeavored, in the obedience of faith, to mind the same thing and to speak the same language. For want of this, there has of latter years been much shaking and unsettlement within our borders; and some bright instruments, not keeping upon the watch, and relying singly upon Him who declared to his immediate followers, ' Without me, ye can do nothing,' have quite fallen from the good condition which they once happily enjoyed in the church of Christ; and others by listening to the tempter, have come to great loss. Our trials in this way have been very great, and I much fear they are not yet over. Possibly thy dear husband may be instrumental in the Lord's hand, in helping some who once were as bone of our bone, out of their present crippled state. The way to the kingdom was declared by our blessed Lord to be narrow. Our dear forefathers in the truth found it so, when they renounced the ways, worships, customs, and fashions of the world; and the true Quaker, I believe, will ever find it safest to follow their footsteps—in other words to follow them as they in faithfulness and much dedication, endeavored to follow Christ. But this must be in the way of the cross—the only way to the crown.

"It has fallen to my lot to be at several meetings with

thy dear husband, and was pleased to find, after an interval of twenty-two years, that his bow abides in strength—his ministry being in demonstration of the Spirit and of power. I consider it a precious privilege to feel with our brethren and sisters the unity of the Spirit; it is indeed like the precious ointment upon the head, that ran down upon the beard, even Aaron's beard, that went down to the skirts of his garments; as the dew of Hermon, and as the dew that descended upon the mountains of Zion: for there the Lord commanded the blessing, even life for evermore.

"In affectionate love to thee and thine,
                                        BENJ. W. LADD.

"P. S. I might have said something to thee in regard to the great sacrifice which at this, as well as at many other times, thou hast made in yielding up thy dear husband to the Master's service. But thou well knowest, dear friend, where to look for thy reward. I trust in due season, and perhaps before very long, he will be restored to thee with the reward of peace, in which thou wilt be made a rich partaker.   B. W. L."

Returning from Ohio, Christopher Healy says: "I remained at and about home, except attending many of the meetings within the limits of our Yearly Meeting, as well as many appointed ones for those not of our Society; much to the relief of my mind."

The following interesting circumstance was related by Christopher Healy, upon one of his visits to Philadelphia, to a Friend of that city. There may be too much preaching as well as too little; and it is only as the Urim and Thummim of those called to minister in holy things, is

with the Holy One, and they, through the obedience
which is of faith, are made quick of understanding in
His holy fear, that it can be expected they will accept
and carry out in consistent practice, the precept of the
Psalmist: " *Open thou my lips*, and my mouth shall show
forth thy praise." For ever true, and ever to be heeded
by the anointed minister, are the Saviour's gracious words:
" It is not ye that speak, but the Spirit of your Father,
which speaketh in you." The service of Christopher Healy
in means and end was, to say the least, striking; and
is as follows :—

" Upon one of his visits to New York Yearly Meeting,
Christopher laid a concern before the Men's Meeting to
visit that of the Women's, when Willett Hicks and some
others, did not approve of it. But though his prospect
was at first opposed by those persons, the meeting finally
united with it, and James Mott was appointed to accompany him, and they went. After being in the women's
apartment about fifteen minutes, James Mott said ' Time
is precious.' Christopher sat perhaps five minutes longer,
and then rose, saying that a concern had attended his
mind to visit this meeting, without having anything given
him; and now he had nothing in charge for them. As
soon as he sat down, that mother in Israel, —— Willits,
expressed her great satisfaction with his faithfulness in attending to the intimation of duty, and being circumscribed
by it. Some other valuable Friends expressed their unity
with him for keeping within holy limits, till Christopher
said he was afraid they would spoil it all. Next day
Willett Hicks said to him, ' Before thou went in, the
women Friends say, they could do no business for the
quantity of preaching that was going on, but thou
knocked them stone dead, and the meeting afterwards

got on comfortably,' or words to this effect. Christopher
added, that he was never better paid for a visit than he
was for that. What an instructive lesson, to attend to
manifested duty, in simple obedience, and leave results."

The subjoined letter from his friend J. Edgerton, was
received by Christopher Healy in the year 1841:—

"Near Barnesville, Belmont Co., Ohio,
Fourth Month 4th, 1841.

"Dear Friend Christopher Healy:—In near and dear
affection I address thee, and may acknowledge the receipt
of thy very acceptable letter of the Twelfth Month last,
which was instructive; and I can heartily respond to
what thou writes, that the members of the spiritual house
rejoice to hear of each other's walking in the Truth; for
however widely they may be scattered over the earth,
they are brought nigh in the covenant of life, and partake
together not only of the afflictions of the gospel, which
the living members of the body of Christ have to experience, but also those consolations which are at his
right hand. I doubt not that the living, faithful followers of the Lamb in every part of the heritage, travail for
the welfare of Zion, and the enlargement of her borders;
and, notwithstanding many discouragements at times appear, as they keep inward and fervent in spirit, these will
be favored to know what their place and duty are,
whether in silent exercise and prayer, or to be more
actively engaged in this great cause. And we have the
best authority for believing that such a state of mental
breathing unto Him, who is Head over all things unto
His church, will not fail of a due regard.

* * * "I feel much for my dear friends in various
parts, who are deeply tried, and at times may be ready to

cry out, 'The Lord hath forsaken me, and my Lord hath forgotten me.' The subsequent language may, through divine mercy be sweetly applied: 'Can a woman forget her suckling child, that she should not have compassion on her son? yea, they may forget, yet will I not forget thee. Behold, I have graven thee upon the palms of my hands; thy walls are continually before me.' My faith is at this time unshaken in the Arm of Israel's God, that was so wonderfully manifest in the gathering together of this people: as well as, from age to age, to raise up and preserve a remnant upon the same eternal Foundation. And having brought us thus far, He will not leave nor forsake. 'For the mountains shall depart, and the hills be removed; but my kindness shall not depart from thee, neither shall the covenant of my peace be removed, saith the Lord that hath mercy on thee.' * * *

"I conclude; my dear wife uniting with me in love to thee, and thy dear wife and children; and remain, in the fellowship of the Gospel, thy friend,

JOSEPH EDGERTON."

CHAPTER XIV.

ANECDOTES OF THE HAPPY EFFECTS OF FAITHFULNESS
EXPERIENCED BY CHRISTOPHER HEALY IN THE MAIN-
TENANCE OF THE TESTIMONIES OF TRUTH TO PLAIN-
NESS OF ADDRESS, ETC. ANECDOTE OF HIS HUMILITY
IN CONDEMNING A FAULT. OPPOSES THE DOCTRINE OF
PREDESTINATION IN AN INTERVIEW WITH PAUL TODD.

CHRISTOPHER HEALY, though not a member of our Society by birth, seems to have been scrupulously careful to
maintain, from his early introduction into it, what are
called the minor testimonies of the Society of Friends.

Our dear friend believed the testimony of plainness of
speech to be no cunningly devised fable; and hence was
engaged to keep it in the meekness of wisdom; and the
Lord—who looketh on the heart, and who in speaking of
"the weightier matters" in connection with the smaller
"tithes" of our obedience, saith, "These ought ye to have
done, and *not to have left the other undone,*"—honored him
in the eyes of all, even the great of the earth.

This is substantiated by the following narrative:—"At
the Quarterly Meeting of Haddonfield, Christopher Healy
said, in substance, that he did not know why it was, but a
circumstance that had occurred many years ago had been
brought to his remembrance, perhaps for the benefit of
some one present. There was a man in the neighborhood where he then resided, high in civil station, whom
even some members of our Society addressed with titles
of honor. With this man, Christopher said, his brother
had some business to transact connected with his high
station, and desired an introduction from Christopher to

him. As they proceeded towards the residence of this
great man, a deep concern came upon our Friend's spirit
that he might not be found shrinking from the testimonies
of Truth, and the language powerfully arose in his mind,
'Whosoever shall deny me before men, him will I also
deny before my Father which is in heaven.' When he
entered the presence of the visited, the salutation which
he uttered was on this wise, 'Elias, how art thou?' (for
his name was Elias Potter.) They were kindly received
and the business attended to. Some time after, this man
of note told Christopher's brother, 'Some of your people
balk their testimonies by giving titles of honor, but your
brother Christopher is not one of these.' In process of
time, Christopher continued, I had a meeting appointed
there, and Elias Potter did what he could to further it, and
came to it, and behaved very solidly. Christopher Healy
then added some pertinent observations upon Friends in
their associations with others *standing plumb and upright*
for the Truth. 'His lively way of narrating the circumstance,' writes the Friend to whom he afterwards com-
municated it, 'made it deeply interesting; and doubtless it
entered somewhere between the joints and the marrow of
those in the Quarterly Meeting for whom it was designed.'"

The following allusion of Christopher Healy to incidents in his early life, may well cause those who are poor
in this world, to be encouraged to look unto the Lord,
and to seek His favor and direction by a life of faith,
rather than to repine at the situation or circumstances in
which they are placed: knowing that no human reasonings or contrivings, without His blessing, will avail us:
but that "godliness with contentment," is the great gain.

Christopher Healy had been speaking of a Friend, poor
as to this world, in whom he felt much interested, and

who had lately, in the usual course, been acknowledged a minister in our Society; when he thus continues:—

"As poor as —— may be, if he will but keep his place, keep low, and look to the Master, I have no fear for him. The good Master will make a way for him. Haven't I abundant cause to bless his holy name? Was there ever a poorer Quaker than I was? And hasn't the Lord cared for me through many long years, and hasn't He now fixed me in my old age in as comfortable a situation as my heart can wish? Why, yes! I have a comfortable home at which I can welcome and entertain all my friends. Ah! this was the height of my worldly ambition, that I should be able to accommodate my friends; and the Lord has fulfilled the desire of my heart. In my first wife's time I had hard work to keep my head above water; but the Lord strengthened me. My wife was very weakly, and at least half her time so sick she couldn't help: so that with doctor's bills and other expenses, I had to struggle with many difficulties, having no other way to earn a living but by going out at day's works. Many a time after working hard all day at hoeing corn, or other farm labor, I have received my half bushel of corn for my day's work (for the farmers didn't pay us in money), and then after sundown had to carry it on my back a mile or more to mill to get it ground. So I couldn't get it home until long after I ought to have been in bed and asleep, to prepare me for another day's hard work.

"I remember that at one time my doctor's bill was so large, that I had to hire myself out for eighteen months to get money enough to pay it. This reminds me of a circumstance which shows how poor and weak I was, and how easily I was discouraged. I was indeed both outside and in, one of the poorest Quakers that ever was: at least I thought so. My eighteen months were out at Quarterly Meeting time, and my father-in-law brought my wife and two of my children down to the Quarterly Meeting to meet me. When we were going home, father took my wife behind him on horseback, and carried one of my children in his arms, while my wife carried the other in her lap. Of course I had to go afoot, and I had to carry my clothes and some other little matters. We were thirty miles from home. Still I didn't mind the distance, but there was one of the bundles which I couldn't contrive to carry on my back ; it wouldn't stay fixed : so I spoke to a Friend in company, who was one of the overseers of our meeting, and who had a good strong horse under him and no baggage, to know if he wouldn't let me tie that little bundle behind his saddle, telling him I did not like to be a trouble or burden to my friends, but I did not see how I could get it along myself. He looked anything but encouraging and said, ' If this was all the trouble and burden thee was giving Friends, we could more easily put up with it.' Well, I was poor enough in spirit before, but this overset me. I had been bleating out a few words in meeting for some time, and now I thought surely it is all over with me. But the Lord who knew the sincerity of my heart did not suffer me to perish, but hath preserved me, and blessed me even unto this day. That rich overseer came to poverty, and made a bad end ; but the Lord has watched over me for good, given me my life for a prey, and bid me live. It is wonderful how little money we can get along with. When I had concluded to move into New York State, we gathered together all the little property we had in the world, and started. We had a wagon and that was paid for, and in it there was my

wife and six children, and all the rest of our worldly
goods. We had a horse but it wasn't paid for, and when
we landed on the west side of the North River, I had just
one piece of money left, and that was a half dollar.
But I soon got into a school and began to earn something; and am preserved unto this day to praise the
Lord, and to tell of his wondrous works, and of his goodness to the children of men."

These remarks of Christopher, writes the Friend who
heard and who penned this account, are very striking in
themselves, but they had an additional force to those who
heard them, from the animation of manner, and lively
energy in the delivery. He sat and rocked on his chair
as he spoke, and at times his voice would mellow away to
a solemn melody, especially when he was speaking of the
Lord's mercies to him. A feeling of thankfulness seemed
very much the constant clothing of his mind, and he loved
to tell others of the riches of the mercy and providential
care of the Lord Jesus, towards and over his dependent
little ones. A very short time before he was taken sick
with his last illness, coming to his home, perhaps after a
chilly ride, and finding everything comfortably prepared
for him in his little sitting room, and a good fire blazing
on the hearth, he sat down and seemed overcome by the
thankful emotions of his heart. He could not forbear to
speak of the Lord's mercies to him, of the promise made
him in early life of future earthly blessings, if he would
be faithful, and of the sweet fulfilment he then experienced.

The anecdotes that follow are instructive. Christopher
said :—

"I remember when I was in England, I had one day
15*

eaten something which gave me severe pain; and while I
was suffering therefrom I was betrayed into irritability of
temper, by not keeping so close a watch over my spirit as
I ought to have done; and in consequence I said two or
three words, for which my conscience smote me. I do
not remember what I said, but I recollect very well that I
soon found the sting in my conscience harder to bear than
my bodily pain. I think there were twenty or more
Friends in the room, eating dinner; but as I could not eat,
I sat in my rocking-chair, rocking backwards and for-
wards, as long as I could; and then I spake right out
and said: 'Friends, I cannot bear this any longer, for I
feel that I did very wrong in saying those few words just
now; but I hope I shall be forgiven for it, for I am truly
sorry for having said them; and I cannot hope to have
my peace of mind restored, until I acknowledge my fault
and express my sorrow for it, which I now do in the
presence of all of you who heard me.' One of the company immediately said, he did not see that I had said
anything out of the way, that I need express or feel any
sorrow for; and so divers others expressed themselves.
But there was a plain and simple-looking woman Friend
present, who I think was a minister, who said, 'I am
truly glad that our dear friend, Christopher Healy, has
been made willing to own his fault thus publicly, and
that he hath been strengthened to condemn it at once, in
so decided a manner. I, like other Friends, did not at
the time perceive any evil in the words he uttered, but I
now see that he has taught us a lesson, and given us an
example, which I hope we shall all try to profit by; for I
see we are not so watchful over our spirits, and over our
words, as we ought to be; and I hope we will all endeavor
to get low and humble enough to imitate our tender-

spirited friend, in acknowledging and condemning our faults, whenever we are betrayed through unwatchfulness, into the commission of them. It has been, I must say, a very instructive lesson to me, and I hope it will be so to all of us.' "

Christopher said : " The Friend's remarks had a very reaching effect upon the whole company, and I felt myself healed at once: so that I was enabled to go that afternoon to an appointed meeting, which proved indeed a very satisfactory one, and the gospel message flowed through me, as I scarcely remember it to have done before. And, (he added) I do believe that I should not have been able to have opened my mouth that day in the way of the ministry, if I had not been faithful in condemning my fault before all the company, who had heard me commit it. I know that I lost nothing in the estimation of these Friends by doing so, but on the contrary, I am fully persuaded that they thought all the better of me. And my heavenly Father was also well pleased with the sacrifice which I made of self on the altar of humility and truth. Indeed *there is no other way* to true honor but *by the road of humility and self-abasement.*"

" I once had an appointed meeting at ——, in the State of New York, in which I was led to speak of the pernicious doctrine of election and reprobation, as many persons believe in it, and are thereby led to take up a false rest, very far from the true rest which remains for the people of God ; and which has a tendency to foster in them that pharisaical spirit which can thank God that they are not like other men are, and make them look down upon those whom they in their spiritual pride, call publicans and sinners.

" There was one of the great men of this world at

meeting that day, who was a judge, and, as I understood, a brigadier-general also. This man did not relish the doctrine I had to deliver; and at last he stood up and interrupted me in my discourse; and I, in my freedom, answered him as well as I was able. After meeting, he kindly invited me—indeed he did more than that, for he pressed me very earnestly—to go home with him to dine. I felt something more than a mere willingness to go with the man, and told my companion that if he was free to go along, that I thought it might be right for me to go. As my companion was willing to bear me company, I went, and was kindly treated and hospitably entertained. After dinner, he said, I desire to have some conversation with you, sir, in relation to the doctrine you preached this morning. I told him that I was at present not very well in health, and that I was at best but a poor weak man, and no great hand at an argument, as I could not say anything of myself, and if Master would not help me, I could do nothing.

"But as he insisted that I should defend the doctrine I had delivered, I consented to hear him, but told him that there were a few preliminaries, which I would like to have settled before he began his argument.—*As I cannot give flattering titles to men*, [see Job xxxii. 21, 22], I want to know thy name and to have full liberty to call thee by it, desiring that thou wilt take no offence by my so doing, for it is not out of disrespect, but as a matter of conscience that I so speak. My name is Christopher Healy, and I would much prefer thou wouldst call me by my name. And my name, said he, is Paul Todd, and I have no objection to be called by my name.

"There is another proposition (said Christopher) which I wish to make, and that is, if I should say anything, which thou shouldst think to be too hard, about principles and doctrines, I hope thou wilt not take it to thyself, so as to make a personal matter of it, and get offended with me; for it is principles and not persons, I trust, that we are going to discourse about. And I consent to let thee say as hard things about my doctrines and principles, as thou may see fit, promising thee not to be offended thereat. To all which he gave his assent, saying it would be very weak in either of us to get affronted."

After the Judge had stated a few of his objections against Friends' doctrines, Christopher said :—

"Now, Paul Todd, from what thou saidst in meeting this morning, and from what thou sayest now, I think I understand precisely where thou art ; I presume that thou art a Presbyterian." To this he assented. "I suppose, too, that thou hast 'got religion,' as your people express it." "Yes," he said, "I got religion thirty years ago ; and when our minister is absent, I sometimes exhort the brethren myself." "No doubt, then, thou art fully persuaded in thy own mind that every thing which happens, past, present and to come, does so in accordance with, and in conformity to, the fixed and unalterable decree of God ; and that nothing ever did, or ever can come to pass, but in exact conformity with His will—fore-ordained and determined before the foundations of the world were laid." "Yes," he said, "these are my views and belief, and they are, in my apprehension, in strict accordance with the Bible." "Now," continued Christopher, "let me put one simple case to thee. Thou art a judge, and as such, thou hast, no doubt, tried many criminals. We will suppose that some wicked man— and the wickeder he is, the better for my purpose—comes, and, in the secrecy and darkness of midnight, murders thy innocent neighbor, or thy dearest friend ; and he is tried before thee, and his guilt proved in the most positive and unquestionable manner : what wouldst thou do with him ?" "Condemn him to be hanged, most certainly." "But thou hast said that there is no act done, but in strict conformity with the will of God. Therefore, if God foreordained this man to commit this very murder, who art thou, that darest to punish him for doing the will of his great Creator? According to thy belief, he could not in any way, or by any possible means, escape from the necessity of killing this man; and must he be punished for it? Why, this horrible doctrine makes God himself the author of all the wickedness that is in the world! Is it not blasphemy? Now, Paul Todd, I want thee seriously to consider this matter, and decide what thou oughtest to do with criminals, if the truth be as thou hast believed it to be."

The Judge said, "this subject has been placed before my mind in a new light. I never so contemplated it before. I do not know what I ought to do." "But I," said Christopher, "do know what thou ought to do; and that is, give up, renounce, and utterly forsake, all such false doctrines, which are derogatory to the character of our heavenly Father, who wills all men to be saved, and to come to the knowledge of the truth. But they limit the offices of Christ, and detract from the merits of that most holy sacrifice, which the dear Son of God made of himself, when He shed his blood on the cross for all men ; and they quench the Holy Spirit in the hearts of many ; for a manifestation thereof is given to every man to profit withal. Our heavenly Father long ago declared, ' For I have no pleasure in the death of him that dieth, saith the Lord God, wherefore turn yourselves and live.' And shall we, worms of the dust, limit the Holy One of Israel, either in his power or his mercy, or his loving kindness to the children of men; who sent not his Son into the world to condemn the world, but that the world, through Him, might be saved? And my advice to thee, Paul Todd, is, that thou shouldst not trust to anything which thou mayest have received thirty years ago; for unless thou receive a renewal of the Holy Spirit from day to day, and hast fresh and heavenly nourishment ministered more often than the returning morning, to enable thee to resist temptations, thou wilt die in thy sins, notwithstanding all the experiences in which thou hast entrenched thyself. Yea, destruction shall suddenly come upon thee, and thou shalt be cut in sunder, and have thy portion in that eternal misery into which, as a judge, thou wouldst send the poor wretches who have committed what are called capital crimes."

"The judge received my close dealing without offence. He appeared somewhat affected, and we parted friendly. But before my return home from that journey, Paul Todd was no more. Whilst walking in his garden one day, he fell down and expired."

CHAPTER XV.

VISITS FRIENDS AND OTHERS IN THE LIMITS OF INDIANA
YEARLY MEETING; AND SOME OF THE INDIAN TRIBES
IN WISCONSIN TERRITORY. LETTER TO HIS WIFE. RE-
MARKABLE RELIGIOUS OPPORTUNITIES WITH INDIANS
OF THE BROTHERTOWN AND STOCKBRIDGE TRIBES. LET-
TER OF JOSEPH GIBBONS. LETTER OF CUTTING MARSH.
VISITS MEETINGS IN IOWA. EXTRACTS FROM LETTERS
TO HIS WIFE. ATTENDS MEETINGS IN INDIANA. LET-
TER OF SARAH KEESE. NOTICE OF RELIGIOUS ENGAGE-
MENTS IN PENNSYLVANIA, NEW JERSEY, AND NEW
YORK.

Though Christopher Healy, subsequent to the period
now reached, was engaged in several more religious visits
abroad, the one we are about to record is the last, so far
as his memoranda show, of which he himself has left us
any account. He was now nearing that point of life—
his three score and ten years—when the shadows of the
evening were being fast lengthened out, and the time not
very distant when this dedicated servant was to rest from
his labors in the church militant, and to join the church
triumphant, in the ceaseless anthem of glory and praise
to the Lord God, and the Lamb that was slain, forever
and ever. In reference to this visit he writes:—

I felt my mind drawn in gospel love, to visit Friends
and others within the limits of Indiana Yearly Meeting;
and some of the Indian tribes in Wisconsin territory.
Obtaining the unity of Friends, I took an affectionate
leave of my dear wife and family, and on the 6th day of
Fifth Month, 1842, left home in company with my friend

John S. Comfort. On the 17th of the same month we got to Benjamin Ladd's, in Smithfield, Ohio.

Christopher Healy and companion, proceeded to Canada, and visited the settlements of Friends there. Of a meeting at Norwich he says: "Next day, which was First-day, attended meeting there; others being informed, it was a very large meeting, and to good satisfaction; many were comforted, and my own soul rejoiced." The diary adds:—

On First-day we had an appointed meeting at Adrian, Michigan, in a Baptist meeting-house. Many people attended, and a number of Friends came also. A precious meeting it proved, and some expressed their comfort with thankfulness of heart. May the praise be given to Him to whom it is due.

At Adrian they were joined by their friend Joseph Gibbons, of whom mention is made in the following letter from Christopher to his wife, written at this place:—

Adrian, State of Michigan, 13th of Sixth Month, 1842.

My very dear Wife: * * * We left Smithfield after attending their Select Preparative Meeting, and a public meeting on Fifth-day, which was large and favored. Sixth-day went to Mount Pleasant, and attended their Select Quarterly Meeting. On Seventh-day their Quarterly Meeting. First-day we were at a public meeting, to the comfort of many. Second-day set out for Alum Creek. That night lodged at Benjamin Hoyle's, where Joseph Edgerton spent the evening with us, to our comfort. Next morning Benjamin accompanied us seven miles to the turnpike. That night got to Zanesville, on the Muskingum river, and were kindly entertained at

16

J. D.'s. Fourth-day got to Robert Comfort's, distant from
Benjamin Hoyle's a hundred and four miles. Fifth-day,
rode to Alum Creek Monthly Meeting, where we met with
Jacob Healy, brother Joseph's son: a kind and religious
young man. He was our guide back to Greenwich,
where his father lived. Robert Comfort went with us to
Alum Creek, on horseback, though in his seventy-ninth or
eightieth year; the distance being about eighteen miles.
Sixth-day; returned to Robert Comfort's, and had a public
meeting at Owl Creek, at three o'clock in the afternoon.
Next morning, with Jacob Healy for our guide, we got to
my brother Joseph's, at Greenwich. They were exceedingly
glad to see us. First-day, had a large and crowded meeting at that place. The house could not hold the people,
and seats were placed out of doors. Many minds were
witnesses of the presence of our good Master, to the melting and contriting of our hearts together. Blessed be His
holy name. Third-day, at Sandusky, at ten o'clock.
Fourth-day, at Mount Gilead, where was a marriage;
and general notice having been spread, the house could
not contain the people by more than three hundred; but
convenient seats being put up at the door, the meeting
was a remarkably quiet and instructive season to many
minds. Many came from the village of Mount Gilead.

(After stopping at a few more places, and visiting some
meetings, they at length reached Adrian; and were kindly
received by Joseph Gibbons. The letter continues):—

Since we have got to Adrian, our dear friend Joseph
Gibbons, who was once at our house, has concluded to go
with us amongst the Indians. This arrangement suits me
well, he having already been through that country. More-

over, many Friends of Adrian Monthly Meeting, which was held yesterday, having felt and expressed a very near and dear unity and sympathy with us in our arduous undertaking, drew together after meeting, and encouraged and assisted Joseph Gibbons to accompany us, and I think he will be likely to go on, after leaving the Indians, to Iowa. This makes the way seem much more pleasant.

I write this account that thou, my dear wife, may be comforted in my journey, and with thy husband bless that good Hand and holy unslumbering Shepherd of Israel, who has thus far been my blessed Helper in temporals and spirituals: being also mouth and wisdom. Blessed be his glorious Name forever. We expect to leave Adrian to-morrow morning for the Indian settlement. We are in good faith, humbly desiring our blessed Shepherd and heavenly Guide may be pleased to go before us, and keep us in the right way; and give us to "drink of the brook in the way," so that we may be enabled to do whatsoever He requires at our hands.

And now may we both thank our dear Master, and take fresh courage. I am more and more confirmed that this great undertaking is required at my hands. Dear John is exceedingly kind and travels very cheerfully. We have been remarkably favored with our health. It is thought to be about five hundred miles to the Indian settlement.

Taking my leave, I bid thee farewell in the truth; and remain thy loving husband,

                              CHRISTOPHER HEALY.

He attended and appointed a number of meetings on the way, till they came to Chicago, the 22d of Sixth Month. Pursuing a northwesterly course from here, they at length got to their friend Andrew Schofield's, ninety miles from Chicago. They left their horses at this Friend's, he kindly joining them and taking his. The journal proceeds :—

We are now four in company—cheerful travellers in this good cause. Arriving at Brothertown, the first Indian settlement, on Fourth-day the 29th, we were received by the natives, it might be said, with open arms. We put up with one of the Indians belonging to this tribe, where we were kindly and very comfortably cared for. The next day had a meeting for these poor children of the wilderness, which was crowned with the living presence of our holy Redeemer, to the tendering of many of their minds. Sixth-day went see the Stockbridge tribe, six miles distant. Here we had a meeting on Seventh-day. Nearly all the tribe were present ; and a tendering time it proved, to the rejoicing of many of their hearts."

The diary of Christopher Healy next gives a short account of their visit to an old Indian woman, named Gracey Tocus, as follows :—" First-Day had a meeting at an Indian woman's house by the name of Gracey Tocus, which was a time of favor. This Indian woman was raised up to speak in this meeting in the life and power of Truth, to the comfort of many present. I trust it will not soon be forgotten by us." This religious opportunity is spoken of by Christopher Healy's companion, John S. Comfort, in a journal kept by him, and in a letter of Joseph Gibbons. The journal of John S. Comfort thus introduces it :—"Fifth-day, Sixth Month 30th, 1842. After a walk of about a mile from our place of tarriance, upon returning we found a woman seventy-four years of age, whose name was Hannah Dick. She remembered Christopher when he visited their tribe in New York State, before they emigrated hither. She appeared like a thoughtful, well-meaning woman. In allusion to a paralysis which had affected her speech, she said, placing her hand on her heart, 'I have lost nothing here. I feel concerned for myself, and my conduct; for my children, and the whole human family.'"

"On our way here Christopher had spoken of an Indian woman of this tribe that expressed a few words, lively and pertinent, at the close of a meeting which he had with them in the State of New York, before their removal from thence; but whose name he could not recollect. He had frequently wondered whether she was living, and whether he should ever meet with her again. Querying of this Hannah Dick in reference to the circumstance, she could not remember anything about it; and thought it must be herself. But Christopher did not find in this woman what he expected in the one alluded to. Here the matter rested, till after a meeting held for the Indians wherein our friend Christopher Healy was much favored in testimony and supplication, when we were invited to go and see a sick woman. Upon arriving at her house, we found her to be the very one after whom Christopher's inquiries had been. Her name was Gracey Tocus. She knew Christopher, and seemed rejoiced to see him, exclaiming, 'Is it true that my eyes once more see my old friend? I remember when you told me, away off yonder at Brothertown, that you thought of coming here; and I have been looking for you many times: and when I have thought of it, and you did not come, I concluded you had been called home.' There were some now with us who had not been at our previous meeting, and several that had, having borne us company. Christopher's certificate being read, we all dropped into silence; when he had

16*

considerable to say very encouragingly. After which
Gracey Tocus stood up, and in a truly feeling manner
said: 'I believe it will be right for me to say a few
words, not that I think myself anything; I am a poor
worm of the dust, not worthy to open my mouth before
the Lord's servants; and I feel it a great cross to appear
in this way, but I feel it my duty to say, that through
the mercy of the Lord, when I first heard this dear
ancient minister and servant of the Most High, away
down in Brothertown, his words sent conviction to my
heart, and it has remained with me ever since; and I can
bear my testimony, that it is the eternal Truth of God that
he has told us; it is that that will do to live by, and that
that will do to die by; and I feel thankful in my heart
and bless my Heavenly Father for this opportunity; and
that He has sent his dear servant into this far country,
that I might hear him once more before I die. I have
but a little longer to stay, and this dear ancient servant
of the Lord, and minister of the Gospel, is also nearly
done his work; and I feel glad to see all these dear
friends here, and pray that the Lord may bless His work
in your hands, and that you will remember me in times of
favor, when the Lord permits you to approach near unto
him. And although I am a poor unworthy creature, and
it is a great cross for me to speak before the Lord's servants, and before the others that are present; yet my
heart rejoices with joy unspeakable and full of glory, and
I feel to encourage all, and bless the Lord for this opportunity.'"

Christopher, in a letter to his wife, describes this opportunity :—

We arrived amongst the Indians on Fourth-day afternoon; went first to an Indian's house, who kept a tavern,
and put up with him. On Fifth-day, had a meeting at
4 o'clock in the afternoon, a meeting to be remembered
by all present who had come to religious sensibility.
Some of the tribe not being present, they were desirous
of another meeting. This tribe is called the Brothertown
tribe. After meeting some of these dear Indians wishing us to make a visit to an Indian woman, who was not
able to get out, at about half a mile from the meeting-
place, we went with them, and in an opportunity in her
family (her husband being blind), it was an unusual time
of Divine favor. After I expressed what was on my
mind the dear old woman spake in a most remarkable
manner, which made deep impressions on us all not soon
to be forgotten: this opportunity closed under a precious
covering of the Blessed Truth.

Seventh-day.—Had a meeting among the Stockbridge
tribe, about six miles distant. They are not so much
civilized, but a large and favored meeting it proved, both
to us and them. Two of their chiefs being present, were
very much tendered. We parted from them in gospel
love which had spread over us in the meeting.

After this meeting we returned to the missionary home,
where we had some satisfactory conversation with a young
man who made great profession of religion. He pleaded
that Christians might defend themselves by the sword, but
the missionary did not join him, but seemed to favor our
views, and related some remarkable instances of the pro-
tecting hand of Providence in saving those who had not
resisted evil, but had put their whole confidence and trust
in the Lord. Our conversation seemed to silence the
young man, and from the respect he showed, and the mis-

sionary also, to us, we believed our labor was not in vain with them. First-day morning we had a tendering opportunity in this family, and left them in a tender frame of mind. This afternoon went to the house where the blind Indian lived whose wife had spoken so remarkably before. They, with some other Indians, had been in the practice of sitting down together, and, as they said, if they felt anything on their minds, to speak as the Spirit gave them utterance. We sat down with them, and a favored opportunity it proved: most of them were much tendered.

In the afternoon attended the meeting at their meeting-place, appointed for us at five o'clock. The house could not contain them by many. A remarkable season it proved; my poor soul was humbled under the flowings of gospel love, and the plain doctrines thereof, which was acknowledged by their ministers, and joyfully received by many of these dear children of the wilderness. Oh may it be as the dew that lieth long on the tender grass, causing the plant of the Father's right hand planting to grow and bring forth fruit to his own glory and praise.

The following are extracts from the letter of Joseph Gibbons to Sarah Healy, to which allusion has been made :—

"Stockbridge, Wisconsin Territory,
                    Seventh Month, 2nd, 1842.
"Dear Friend Sarah Healy :—Not only at the request of thy dear husband, but from feelings that accompany my own mind (for I remember with great satisfaction the very pleasant visit I had at your house a little more than a year since), I am willing to try to give thee a little information in relation to the visit so long in prospect, and so much dreaded, not only by Christopher himself,

but by many of his friends on his account. But we read
in the Good Book that "hard things shall be made easy;"
and truly we have to a great degree experienced this to
be the case in our journey to this far-off land. We have
been agreeably disappointed in several respects: in the
first place, we have all enjoyed the great favor of pretty
good health; and Christopher has for the most part
seemed to feel very comfortable, and to press forward
with good courage, believing himself to be in his proper
allotment. In the second place, we have found the roads
altogether better than we expected; so that we could
come comfortably all the way in a carriage; while even
the distance was not quite so great as was anticipated
Now, also, that we are really among the Indians, we find
them living very much like ourselves; dressing like ourselves; speaking like ourselves; and almost looking like
ourselves; and we have hardly found more comfortable
fare as to eating, drinking, and lodging anywhere on our
journey, than since we have been among the Indians.
And last of all, though not least, we find an open door to
receive us and our doctrines; and Christopher has seemed
much exercised, and unusually favored with 'mouth and
wisdom, tongue and utterance,' since we have been amongst
them. For although he has only as yet had one public
meeting, yet in several family opportunities we have been
made truly glad; so that we might perhaps adopt the
language, repeated by a poor Indian woman in a family
sitting the day before yesterday, viz: 'My heart rejoices
with joy unspeakable and full of glory.' But before I
say much more in relation to our visit here, let me return a
little and trace our progress since the date of Christopher's
letter to thee at Andrew Schofield's. A meeting was appointed there at nine o'clock on First-day morning last,

which was well attended by persons of different persuasions; and, to our surprise by (as we were told after meeting) twenty-two members of our Society (including ourselves). The meeting was so greatly favored that I told Christopher, after it was over, that it seemed almost worth our while to have come all the way here, if it was but to attend this one meeting.

" In the afternoon we had another meeting at Mequane-go, about six miles distant. But there seemed to be something present that obstructed a full, free flow of gospel ministry. After meeting, we thought we could discover, in part, what it was. There were two or three dark spirits present, who professed to be Mormon preachers, and had made some converts to their faith in that place. They fell into an argument with Christopher after meeting, but we did not think gained much credit by it. Next morning, Second-day, Andrew Schofield harnessed two of his horses and came on with us; leaving ours to rest until we return. We found a very good road through an open prairie country, with the exception of perhaps about twenty miles, so that in a little less than three days we reached the Brothertown Indians, and put up at a very comfortable place among them.

" The next day we had a good open time in a meeting appointed at four o'clock in the afternoon. After meeting, went to see Grace Tocus, an Indian woman who had seen Christopher before, and well remembered him, but was not able on account of ill-health, to attend the meeting. Christopher had a sweet flow of tender counsel and encouragement for them, and after he closed, and we had sat some time in silence, Grace rose, and in a very weighty, solemn manner, spoke nearly as follows : [His version of the communication is omitted, being very similar to that already given.] I do not remember ever to have felt more sympathy, or nearer unity of feeling, or evidence of divine favor, towards any collection of Friends or others in my life, than in this poor Indian's family. I do not think there was a dry eye present after this opportunity. Christopher and myself went home with an Indian, William Dick, and his wife, who seemed very glad to see us. She said travelling Friends had often put up at their house when they lived in the State of New York. They treated us with great kindness, even putting us into large separate beds, with clean sheets and pillow-cases: saying they wished us to rest well, while they had a bed on the floor for themselves to sleep on. In the morning we had a remarkably favored opportunity with this family. Christopher spoke until he seemed almost exhausted with the length and intensity of his exercise. We had one or more favored opportunities yesterday, and then came to this place, which is among the Stockbridge Indians, where a meeting is appointed for them at two o'clock this afternoon.

"Evening. — The meeting this afternoon was large. Most of the tribe were present, and a more favored meeting I think I never was in anywhere in my life. I never heard Christopher when I thought him more, if as much favored, in a full, free, and lucid manner of explaining and laying home gospel truths. He seemed anointed to lay open and impress upon the minds of these poor Indians the doctrines and principles of the religion of our Lord and Saviour Jesus Christ, in all their simplicity and purity; and with such divine authority attending, that I could see the tears rolling down the swarthy cheeks before me. I am very much of the mind that many of them will never forget the opportunity. Some of them could scarcely bid us farewell for their emotion.

"Thus, my dear friend, I have attempted to give thee a very little and imperfect sketch of this part of our journey. Please remember me affectionately to B. Cadwallader's family, and to all other friends there who enquire for me; and also accept my kind remembrance for thyself and family.

JOSEPH GIBBONS."

We now return to the diary of Christopher Healy, viz:

Had another meeting at their (Indians) usual place of holding them. The house was full, and all could not get in. A very solid and blessed season it proved to us altogether. May He who is glorious in holiness, fearful in praises, doing wonders, have all the honor; to whom it doth belong forever. We had also many precious family visits, wherein the principles and doctrines of the blessed gospel were opened to this poor, afflicted, and despised part of the human family; yet for whom Christ died, as well as for us. These favored seasons caused their hearts to rejoice; and many of them expressed it in great thankfulness of soul.

While among the Stockbridge Indians they frequently met, it seems, with a minister or missionary named Cutting Marsh, who resided there. He was by profession a Presbyterian. The following letter from him to Sarah Healy, is not without interest, as confirming the acceptableness of our dear friend's labors among these far distant and sadly oppressed and persecuted children of our western wilds:—

"Stockbridge, near Green Bay, Wis. Ter.,
July 5th, 1842.

" To Mrs. Sarah Healy:

"Madam :—Your dear aged husband, with three other Friends, came here on the 1st instant, and paid us a Christian visit. On the 2nd he preached to the Stockbridge Indians, amongst whom I am laboring as a missionary. Be assured, Madam, that his visit, together with his company, was very acceptable both to myself and family, and to the Indians also. Some of them feel under great obligations to the Friends, as they have kindly educated some of their children.

"Although I am a Presbyterian by profession, yet I can cheerfully extend the hand of Christian fellowship to other denominations also, where I perceive the image of the Saviour. Yes, all who have been born of the Spirit, have a common Lord, and it is their delightful privilege to love one another with a pure heart fervently, and greet them wherever they meet them, as fellow-travellers to the same heavenly rest.

"I love to dwell upon those pure principles of the holy religion of Jesus Christ which the Friends are so zealously disseminating ; and my ardent desire and prayer is, that these may continue to extend wider and wider, until the song which the shepherds on the plains of Bethlehem heard the heavenly host sing, shall be the song of every people and nation upon the habitable earth.

"I hope your dear husband may still be spared to accomplish great good in the Master's blessed cause. I know you will be glad to hear from a stranger that his health and spirits at his advanced age, appeared to be as good and buoyant as my own, although I am but little turned of forty.

" He made lively mention of your cheerfully consenting to tarry at home, and guide your numerous family, and bear all alone the heavy burden of it, so that he might travel, and teach the unsearchable riches of the gospel. This excited in my own mind a lively and tender interest in your welfare, and that of your dear family. May you also be sustained in your numerous trials and cares in so important, laborious, and responsible duties as you must meet with and perform. So that when he mentioned about writing you, I felt that I could do it with great cheerfulness, for I know it will encourage, and do you and your family good to hear from him by strangers, and to know that his religious visits are kindly and affectionately received. I saw that my Indians were deeply interested in his preaching, and would have been highly gratified if he had felt it his duty to preach again. But at the close of his discourse he said that he felt satisfied, and should then take his leave of them. One of the old men inquired of me, with tears in his eyes, if your husband was not going to preach again. But I told him, no. These poor Indians seem at once to love those who take a deep interest in them ; and the counsel of your husband, in his discourse to them, was exceedingly kind and affectionate ; this pleased them, and they therefore listened with deep interest ; and I have no doubt with profit also.

" These Indians are the remnant of a once powerful and warlike tribe. But long since they have given up this savage practice, and many of them give evidence of being true Christians ; but they are very poor, in consequence of having to remove so often, as they have in time past, but especially on account of their former intemperate habits. For a number of years past, great efforts have been made to promote the cause of temperance amongst them, and with happy success; so that few drink at the present time. In proportion as they become temperate, they become industrious; and manifest a desire to take care of themselves, and provide for their families.

"I have forgotten to mention that your husband left here on the third instant, to go to a settlement, a few miles south of the Brothertown Indians, where he expected to hold a meeting on that evening. May the Lord guide and support you; and bless your family also abundantly, and make them all children of his grace.

"With great regard for yourself and yours, I subscribe myself your Christian friend,

CUTTING MARSH."

From the journal of Christopher Healy, it appears that they left the Indian settlements on Second-day, the fourth of Seventh Month; and on the following Fourth-day got to Andrew Schofield's again, where they were kindly received. The next Sixth-day, taking their departure thence, and holding some meetings on their way, they arrived at Salem, Iowa, distant about two hundred and fifty miles, the 16th of the same month. They were hospitably entertained by their friend Jacob Pickering and his family. From here Christopher addressed a letter to his wife; in which he says, in allusion to these religious opportunities with the Indians, * * * "these meetings bring my concern fresh to my mind; and while standing exercised in them, it fastens on me and on them as a nail in a sure place; and my soul is rewarded an hundred fold for yielding up to perform this journey. May thy heart also be made joyful with that of thy husband."

From the diary of John S. Comfort the following is

selected, referring to the subject of a part of Christopher Healy's more condensed letters :—

"Learning there were some Indians that met at Gracey Tocus' twice a week, to hold meetings somewhat after the manner of the Society of Friends, we made enquiry concerning them ; and whether they had any one to act as a regular officiating preacher. The answer was, they had not. But if any believe themselves called thereto, they thought it right to speak as the Spirit gave utterance. We concluded to go and sit with them. Christopher had a good deal to say ; after which, Gracey Tocus arose and again spoke, to the admiration and edification of all present."

The first part of this communication, though not so lively, is somewhat similar to the foregoing one. We therefore insert only the conclusion of it here, more particularly because of its having application to every one of us who profess to be followers of the meek and lowly Jesus, yet Sovereign and impartial Lord of all. It is as follows :—

"I wish to ask one favor of you ; that when you return to your friends and brethren at home, you would give them my best love, in the fellowship of this gospel we have had preached this day ; and tell them a poor unworthy Indian sister wishes and prays for their prosperity and advancement in the Truth, and that they may be obedient and faithful to their Master, in whatsoever He makes known to them, and requires at their hands ; and that in their seasons of divine favor, they would remember this poor despised part of the land."

Another fact of interest is recorded by John S. Comfort, which is not mentioned by Christopher Healy ; viz :—

"After meeting yesterday, many of the Indians came

and shook hands with us; and among the rest our kind landlord, O. D. Fowler, from Brothertown, came to bid us farewell, as he said, for the last time; but he could hardly speak, he was so affected. He appears to be a sober, thoughtful man. When we left his house yesterday, we offered and pressed to pay him for our board and horse feed; but he refused, and said he knew it cost us a great deal; but we told him we had wherewith, and expected and would rather pay than not; but he refused, and said, in a manner that showed that he looked upon all that he had as a gift of heaven: '*I know where I get it from,* and I am not willing to take anything.' I thought it would have been a lesson to many in more favored circumstances in our Society, as it was to me, if they could have heard him."

Christopher Healy, continuing his memoranda, writes :—

We were at the Preparative meeting of Ministers and Elders (Salem, Iowa,) to a good degree of satisfaction. On First-day, general notice being given, the meeting was large, and owned by the great Shepherd of Israel. During the same week we attended all the meetings belonging to Salem Monthly Meeting, except one; and on Seventh-day the Monthly Meeting. The abundance of business caused them to adjourn to the Second-day following. First-day we had a very large meeting, and a memorable season it proved. The house would not hold the people; a shed was fitted up on the north side, and many sat under it.

This is all that our dear Friend says of the meeting; but his companion, more in detail, has recorded the subjoined. viz:—

　"Christopher had a good deal to say, and after sitting

17*

down, he got up the second time, and stated to the meeting our belief in the Scriptures of truth. Although there had been nothing in what he had previously said to call it forth, or to require any explanation or confirmation of our belief in the Bible; yet it seemed, the second time he was on his feet, his whole business was to show the value our Society set upon the Scriptures. I afterwards learned, that there was a man the day before, who was pretending to set forth Friends' principles to a large company; who, among other things, affirmed that Friends did not believe the Bible. The man and his hearers were at the meeting. Christopher, I am persuaded, knew nothing of the circumstance of the man's disparaging story for several days after." John S. Comfort adds the following:— "In the afternoon, Joseph Gibbons left us for his own home. We have travelled in near unity and fellowship, being of one heart and one mind."

Christopher's memoranda resumed :—

Second-day, the adjourned Monthly Meeting convened; and after several hours of solid deliberation, it concluded to the comfort of many minds. Fifth-day, Eighth Month, 4th, got to Uriah McMullin's; he and his wife are choice Friends. Next morning rode to Hopewell, and had a meeting there under the shade of the trees, the house not being sufficiently large to contain the gathering. I scarcely remember a more precious season of Divine favor. From this place we went to Vermilion, and attended a preparative meeting of Ministers and Elders. Seventh-day sat with them in their Monthly Meeting, wherein I had good service. First-day we were at Elwood, which was a crowded meeting; many could not get in. The people of the neighborhood were generally gathered together; they seemed prepared to hear the doctrines of the blessed Truth. May it fasten as a nail in a sure place.

They then held or attended meetings at Pine Creek, Flint, and Bloomington; and from thence went to the Quarterly Meeting called the Western Branch, held the 14th of Eighth Month, 1842. On First-day they were at the same place. The diary records :—

Here the blessed effects of the sufferings and death of Christ, experienced through obedience to His inward appearance in the heart, with the necessity of our receiving Him, and following Him there, were dwelt upon as *that* which brings redemption and salvation to us. Oh the necessity of receiving with meekness the engrafted Word, which is able to save the soul. May this ever be the constant concern of our minds.

They next had meetings at Rocky Run, Rush Creek, and Poplar Grove. "These," Christopher Healy writes, " were all largely attended by Friends, and those not of our religious Society; and blessed be the name of Israel's Shepherd, He was pleased in an eminent manner to be with us. May all praise be given to His ever glorious and holy Name, forever." He next attended some Quarterly and other meetings, respecting which he makes but little or no comment.

The following are extracts from a letter to his wife, which was written near this time :—

Bloomfield, Indiana, 14th of Eighth Month, 1842.

My very dear Wife :—Yesterday was the Quarterly Meeting at this place, wherein I had good service; and it ended to the comfort of many. We are getting along to our satisfaction among Friends, and the public meetings are remarkably large, and according to Friends' judgment, favored seasons. I have been careful not to have more than one meeting a day, except sometimes on First-day. Meetings in this part of the land are near together, and Friends are many. A goodly number of them appear to be concerned for the good cause. To-day, which is First-day, general notice for a meeting is given at this place.

We seem now to be turning our faces homeward, though I expect we shall not get home until after the Yearly Meeting (Indiana). Our Divine Master has abundantly made way for us wherever our lot has been cast on this journey, in a remarkable manner. May the praise and glory be given to Him, and to Him alone.

I received thy second letter, day before yesterday, to my comfort, having waited long therefor. I was sorry to hear thou had gotten but one from me, as this is the fifth I have written or sent. I received one from William and Sarah. It was truly comforting to find they remembered their dear father. Give my dear love to them, with all our children, and tell them I love them in the truth. Read this letter to them. My time is so much occupied with travelling and meetings, that my dear children will excuse me, I trust, from writing to them. It is not because I am unmindful of them, for they are daily in my mind, even every one of them. May the Great Shepherd that has been their dear father's helper in every time of need, be their leader and guide; and He will be so to them, if they receive with meekness his engrafted word. Give my dear love to all that enquire after me. Let them know my love was never stronger for the blessed cause of Truth than now; and this love being shed abroad in mine heart, keeps my soul alive in Him that is true, in Him who was dead and is alive again, and liveth forevermore. Oh, my dear, He is the desire of our souls! He is the Head of the church; and if we keep our love chaste and pure to Him, He will be our present helper in every needful time.

Afternoon, we attended the First-day meeting here, which was very large; and in a remarkable manner owned by the Head of the Church. May we be humbled in the dust before Him.

I suppose the time may seem long before we may meet again, but I believe if it is His good pleasure that we enjoy each other again, the blessed Shepherd will be our consolation. We know, my dear bosom friend, in whom we do believe; and as we yield each other up for our Divine Master's sake, He will never leave nor forsake us; neither withhold any good thing from those that love Him.

Farewell in the blessed Truth. I remain thy dear and tender husband,

CHRISTOPHER HEALY.

The annexed letter from Christopher Healy to his wife, or rather extracts from it, is the last epistolary communication from his own pen, preserved in these memoranda:—

Henry County, Indiana, 15th of Ninth Month, 1842.

My very dear Wife:—We have attended five Quarterly Meetings in Indiana, and many other appointed meetings. With the exception of one of the Quarterly Meetings, which was a trying season, they were favored times. At New Garden we saw a colored man, a member of our Society, one hundred and six years old. He is nearly blind; but got to the Quarterly Meeting, and seemed rejoiced to shake hands with me. Friends are very thickly settled in this part of Indiana, and the meetings are generally large. Two weeks from yesterday (Second-day), the Meeting for Sufferings will be held. Third-day, the Meeting for Ministers and Elders. Fourth-day, the public meeting. Fifth-day, which will be the 29th of the month, the Yearly Meeting for discipline will be opened, which commonly ends on the Third-day following; which will be the 4th of Tenth Month. After that we expect to leave for home if we are well; and hope that by the 25th of Tenth Month, if our Divine Master should prosper our way, we may be favored to see each other again. And now, my dear wife, be of good cheer. The same good Hand that has always been with us is still mindful of us, and as we keep near to Him, He will be very near to do us good. I was comforted in hearing thee say, that thou wast in the good practice of reading a portion of Holy Scripture in our family. I hope thou wilt continue to do this. I believe it to be a help to the children, and a satisfaction to thyself, as it is to thy absent husband.

I lately received a precious letter from Samuel B. Morris; giving an account of a good visit he had with thee and our children; also of our son Mark's visit to him, with the letters thou sent him from Joseph Gibbons and the missionary; which were, as he says, highly interesting. With regard to this visit I may say, I never had a more encouraging one thus far. How the remainder may prove we know not, but hope that He who first put forth, will continue to go before, and to show forth His praise, that so fruits may be brought forth by which our Divine Master may be glorified, who alone is worthy forever.

Friends are exceedingly kind in this land; and very many precious meetings we have had. Many of those not of our Society, seem much comforted. Oh! may He who calls for the labor, be sure to fasten it as a nail in a sure place; that so the praise may be given to Him who is glorious in holiness, fearful in praises, doing wonders. I think I never travelled anywhere where the people of other societies were more attentive to hear the Truth as it is in Christ. Oh! may they be willing to *do* it! Then will they be able to build on that Rock, against which no storms can prevail, nor anything lay waste. And Oh! my dear, may we continue to look unto the Rock from whence we were hewn, and the hole of the pit whence we were digged. And may we remember, too, good old Abraham our father, who resigned his beloved son Isaac to the Lord. Upon which, said the Lord: Because thou hast not withheld thy son, thine only son, in blessing I will bless thee, and in multiplying I will multiply thy seed as the stars of the Heaven, and as the sand which is on the sea-shore. This is the faith, with works, that pleases the living God, who alone is able to save.

Give my dear love to all that enquire after me. Tell them I love the Truth; and that it never was more precious to me than at this time, and sweet is the fellowship I have with them that walk therein. In that love that many waters cannot quench, nor floods drown, farewell, saith thy husband,

CHRISTOPHER HEALY.

After this Christopher Healy attended meetings at Elm Grove, Carthage, Blue River, Walnut Ridge, Knightstown and a few other places. About this time the following epistle from Sarah Keese to Christopher Healy was received. It alludes to one she had gotten from him, wherein he seemed to have been instrumental in stirring up the pure mind in her; and, obeying the injunction to "comfort them that mourn," to have soothed and refreshed her drooping spirit. The letter is as follows:—

"Weston, Ninth Month 19th, 1842.

"Dear and valued Friend:—It is under a deep sense of obligation that I acknowledge the reception of thy favor of Eighth Month, 17th. It did, indeed, afford us great satisfaction to find that we were still remembered by thee; and we were much interested also in hearing through thy own pen of thy welfare and preservation every way. Tender solicitude on thy account has been felt, in thy very arduous and important engagement—still bearing the burden and heat of the day, under the infirmities of advanced age. But I doubt not that amidst all, Divine support hath been abundantly experienced to be near, producing the acknowledgement that 'hitherto *Thou* hast helped me.' Oh! what an attainment and a favor, that the poor mind thus knows its own home, the place of its rest. That after it hath been called forth into deep and laborious exercises, even when this too may seem to be almost labor in vain, or as bread upon the waters, that it can breathe the grateful language, 'Return, then, Oh my soul, to the place of thy rest, for the Lord hath dealt bountifully with thee.'

"I hope when Friends return from the Yearly Meeting, we shall receive further accounts from thee. It would be a gratification to learn more of thy future prospects! Where next? and whether thou hast any view of our Quarterly at thy return? In these inquiries I would not burden thee with the task of communicating particulars.

"My health has improved considerably, so that I have

walked to our little meeting several times. And since receiving thy letter, I have visited my friends in the neighborhood of Alum Creek. As thou desired thy remembrance to Friends, I took it with me, and quite a number shared in the satisfaction.

"Thy visit to us, and particularly to me in my then weak state of health, is remembered with gratitude; the savor of which at times rests sweetly upon our spirits.

"I feel interested in the proceedings of the ensuing Yearly Meeting, and according to my measure, feel with the true burden-bearers. Oh that wisdom may be dwelt in; remembering that help is laid upon One that is mighty. I am aware to whom I am writing, and would not exceed my bounds, feeling myself as a child, and thou a father.

"Should I fail in writing to thy dear wife before thy return, please present her with my sympathetic and affectionate regards, with the hope that when thou returns from thy present field of labor, laden with sheaves of peace, she too may be entitled to share with thee. I cannot fail to be interested with any account from thee at any time; and when thou returns to thy far distant home, and should be writing to thy friends at Greenwich, a remembrance in that way, if it is not asking too much, would be grateful to one who feels that she hath the constant need of the help and prayers of the faithful. My husband unites in the expression of love and sympathy to thee. Affectionately thy friend.

SARAH KEESE."

The diary resumed :—

Fourth-day, Ninth Month, 21st, we got to the house of our friend John Poole, at Richmond. Here we rested till

18

First-day, when we attended their usual meeting. Second-day met with the Meeting for Sufferings of Indiana Yearly Meeting. Third-day went to the Yearly Meeting of Ministers and Elders. Fifth-day the Yearly Meeting commenced, which continued by adjournments until Third-day, 4th of Tenth Month. Though some trying circumstances took place, yet the Yearly Meeting was owned by the Divine presence, whereby the church was edified. The next day we set out for home, by the way of Springborough, Zanesville, Mount Pleasant, Sewickly, &c. The following Fourth-day week we got to Isaac Evans'. Fifth-day to our friend William Rhoads'; and the next day, at evening, Tenth Month, 21st, I was favored to reach home, and was gladly received by my dear wife and family; and felt a thankful heart to Him, who had called me forth, and brought again in peace. May He have all the honor. Blessed forever be His holy Name.

This closes Christopher Healy's diary of his various labors in the love of the Gospel, prolonged beyond the time allotted to most.

He returned his certificate in the same month, with the information that the visit had been greatly to the peace of his mind. He brought with him also divers testimonials of unity with his company and religious services, from Monthly and Quarterly Meetings which he had attended, and also from Indiana Yearly Meeting.

After his last-mentioned visit to Indiana, and to some of the Indian tribes in Wisconsin Territory, in 1842, Christopher Healy, as appears by the minutes of his Monthly Meeting, paid religious visits, but without leaving any record of them, to the meetings composing Abington Quarter, with liberty also to appoint some meetings with those thereaway, not in religious profession with us. This certificate he returned in the Fourth Month of 1843. The Seventh Month of the same year he procured a minute to attend some of the meetings of Friends in New Jersey, and to appoint some in places where none of our members reside. And in the Eighth Month, one to attend Shrewsbury and Rahway Quarterly Meeting, and to appoint a few meetings within its limits. In the First Month of 1844, he obtained a minute to appoint a few public meetings within the compass of Bucks and Abington Quarterly Meetings. In the Eighth Month of the same, he procured a minute to hold public meetings within the limits of Concord, Western, Salem and Shrewsbury and Rahway Quarterly Meetings.

In the Fourth Month of 1845, he obtained the approbation of his Monthly Meeting to pay a religious visit to Friends and others within the limits of New York Yearly Meeting. In the First Month, 1846, he visited some of the meetings constituting Salem and Concord Quarterly Meetings, and appointed some meetings within their limits. In the Sixth Month of the same year, he paid family visits to the Friends composing Abington Quarter, liberty also being granted to appoint meetings, if way should open for it, in some of the towns within the borders of the same. In the Sixth Month of 1847, a minute was granted him to visit Friends, with those not in connection with us, in Salem, Haddonfield, Shrewsbury and Rahway Quarters; and if way should open, to the same class in Concord, Caln, and the Western Quarterly Meetings; with a few meetings east of the Susquehanna River, belonging to Baltimore Yearly Meeting. In the Sixth Month, 1849, he asked and obtained liberty to visit Friends of Haddonfield Quarterly Meeting, and to appoint some public meetings in that and Salem Quarter. In Ninth Month, 1849, a minute was granted him to visit Friends, and those not of our religious profession, in Concord, Caln, and Western Quarterly Meetings; likewise the meetings composing Nottingham and Little Britain Monthly Meetings.

CHAPTER XVI.

APPOINTS PUBLIC MEETINGS IN SEVERAL OF THE NEW ENGLAND STATES.

At a Monthly Meeting, held Fifth Month, 1850, Christopher Healy expressed a concern, and received its full concurrence and encouragement to appoint some public meetings with those not of our religious Society in several of the New England States.

This concluding engagement seemed like the evening sacrifice. In the course of it he had forty-seven meetings, many of them being held in places for worship belonging to Methodists, Baptists and other denominations; and his gospel labors were said to have been remarkably owned by his gracious Master. These visits are all represented as being to the satisfaction and peace of his own mind.— And divers testimonials were also given him of the sweet unity and fellowship, and encouragement of Friends, where his lot had been cast.

In the performance of this visit, Christopher was accompanied by his wife Sarah M. Healy, an elder, and also by George W. Brown, a Friend of his own neighborhood, from whose memoranda the following account has been taken; both had certificates, suitable to the occasion, from the Monthly Meeting of which they were members.

In the progress of this religious visit, Christopher attended forty-seven meetings, to all of which public invitatation had been extended. He also had considerable service in a more private way, in companies, in families, with individuals, in conversations; and received much kindness and favor from the people generally amongst whom his lot was cast.

They left home on the morning of the 20th of Sixth Month, 1850, and were received at New York city by one of Christopher's nephews, who conducted them to his own dwelling, where Christopher met with two of his children, a son and daughter by his former marriage.

At five o'clock in the afternoon, went aboard a steamer bound for Stonington, a hundred and fifteen miles distant. The evening was spent in one of the spacious rooms of the steamer; and it proved to be an interesting season. Christopher entered into a conversation with a man from Boston, and as they proceeded, others gathered around them, until the number amounted to a large proportion of the numerous passengers. About five at times took part in the subjects introduced, and our dear friend was favored to answer their inquiries and suggestions discreetly, and to address suitable counsel and admonition to the company collectively. The feelings of the people were evidently enlisted, and expressions of satisfaction and approbation were heard from several individuals. This opportunity lasted about two hours, and was a further evidence of the religious solicitude which Christopher had so long manifested for the best welfare of those not of our Society, of the peculiar grasp which he secured upon the

18*

minds of many of these, and of his extraordinary faculty
for interesting their thoughts and feelings.

Sixth Month, 21st.—Took passage by railway for Westerly, and found kind friends and hospitable entertainment
there. At this place Christopher met with John Wilbur,
one of his ancient and life-long friends. The greeting
between the two aged patriarchs was cordial. They had
been friends in early life, and that friendship had been
cemented by long years of gospel labor and fellowship,
and both were now tottering over the grave. A meeting
at Christopher's request was appointed to be held the next
afternoon at four o'clock.

Sixth Month, 22nd.—The appointed meeting proved to
be a favored time, being largely attended.

Sixth Month, 23rd.—First-day; attended meeting at
Hopkinton; the morning was wet, and the meeting perhaps smaller in consequence; but a considerable number
attended. A meeting had been appointed to be held in a
school-house, one and a-half miles distant, in the State of
Connecticut, at five o'clock in the afternoon. This building stands on the opposite side of the road from the site
of the old one (now demolished), where Christopher
received school instruction in his youthful days, and had
taught school for several years. His company arrived
before the conclusion of the meeting of Seventh-Day
Baptists, there assembled, and remained on the outside of
the house until the breaking up of the congregation,
when, after a short respite, the people again took their
seats, and several others coming in, a large meeting
assembled. A solemnity soon spread over them, and
Christopher was moved to administer word and doctrine,
exhortation and reproof, in the demonstration of the
Spirit and with power. He stood at least one and three-

quarter hours, and taking into consideration the length of time most of the audience had been sitting previous to the commencement of our meeting, it was admirable to see the quiet and order that prevailed. The interest and solemnity continued throughout, and the opportunity closed comfortably. Several of Christopher's scholars and old acquaintances came around him after meeting, and gave him the hand of friendship, as did also the two Baptist ministers in attendance.

Sixth Month, 24th.—Arrangements had been perfected to hold an appointed meeting in the vestry of a Calvin Baptist meeting-house, and information was spread accordingly through the factories and schools. This place of worship is located at Bushville, between two manufacturing villages, each half a mile distant. Thither the company repaired at the hour appointed, accompanied by some of their friends, but not a solitary individual had arrived, and the door of the house was locked. At length the key was produced, and information that way did not open to suspend operations in the factories until the usual time, which was after sunset; but that the people would convene as soon as possible afterwards. The door was unlocked, and about half-past eight o'clock a large company assembled, entering the room in an orderly manner, and sitting very quietly. A solemnity soon spread over them, and Christopher was drawn forth in testimony and counsel, which continued about one and a-half hours. It was not so much a doctrinal sermon as a persuasive exhortation, and particularly adapted to those young in years. This opportunity was manifestly owned by Israel's Shepherd, gospel love and power distilled as the dew, and as the gentle rain upon the tender plant, and was apparently received and relished with much cordiality. The meeting was appointed to be held at seven, and it closed about ten o'clock. One of the company proposed paying for the lights, but the answer was, " No, you have nothing to pay: we are thankful for the meeting." Doubtless, there were hearts clothed with reverent gratitude for the peculiar favors vouchsafed this day.

Several appointed meetings were held to satisfaction in the neighborhood of East Greenwich, Rhode Island, where Christopher Healy was well known to the inhabitants.

One of these, held Sixth Month 30th, was at a Baptist place of worship, where Christopher had formerly held several favored meetings, and to which he appeared to feel an unusual drawing at this time. The gathering proved large. Quiet prevailed, and a solemnity soon spread as a canopy over them; under which precious covering Christopher arose and handed forth doctrine, reproof, instruction in righteousness and encouragement. The hearts of the people were contrited and solemnized together, and somewhat of the baptism of the Spirit was felt amongst them.

A meeting was appointed Seventh Month, 2nd, to be held at the Methodist place of worship, in Fiskville, at three o'clock in the afternoon. After the meeting they stopped at the house of an aged physician, an old acquaintance of Christopher's. He was feeble, chiefly confined to his bed, and appeared to be drawing near the close of life. He was sensible of his situation, and looked forward to his dissolution with composure, testifying that the Lord was gracious to him. As the company sat by his bedside, he asked that they might have a religious opportunity together, and those present gathered into stillness. After a time of silent waiting, Christopher was drawn forth in exercise of soul on his account, which, doubtless, was comforting to the aged sufferer. It proved a heart tendering season, and the baptizing influence of heavenly love and power was felt amongst them.

On their northward journey they passed, near Providence, the residence of the late venerable Moses Brown, a Friend of great possessions and large benevolence, yet his dwelling was neither large nor ostentatious. They also passed the plantation where that eminent minister, Job Scott resided, previous to his embarkation for England; and reached Fall River, Massachusetts, on the 5th of Seventh Month. Here, on First-day morning, Seventh Month 7th, they attended Friends' meeting. An invitation to the public had been extensively spread, many attended, and through the condescending goodness of the Head of the Church, who promised to be with those gathered together in his name, it proved a solemnizing season—something like the baptism of the one spirit into the one body. Words flowed freely, accompanied with gospel life and power, and he that sowed, and some that reaped, rejoiced together. The afternoon meeting at three o'clock, was larger than that in the morning. In it Christopher labored in the authority of truth. It was a memorable season, and one not soon to be forgotten by some present.

Seventh Month 10th.—At North Berwick, Maine, attended a meeting appointed to be held in the Baptist meeting-house; it proved large and favored. Christopher labored honestly, and some plain truths were spoken, especially in reference to forms and ceremonies, and qualification for the ministry. A part of his testimony was somewhat sharp; but apparently it was well received, and many expressed satisfaction with the meeting.

Seventh Month 11th.—Attended Friends' meeting at North Berwick, and Christopher had considerable service by way of exhortation and counsel. Toward the conclusion he again arose, and, in sympathy with this little company, who had passed through many tribulations and anxieties in endeavoring to guard the ancient faith of the Society, and in sustaining its order and discipline; extended comfort and encouragement to those who truly mourn in Zion.

Seventh Month 12th.—Left North Berwick this morning, rode thirteen miles over a pleasant, undulating country to the village of Kennebunk, and received kind entertainment in a family of Friends. A meeting had been appointed to be held at their dwelling, at three o clock in the afternoon, and the usual invitation had been spread. At the time appointed a considerable number of the neighboring people assembled. Christopher was led to distribute doctrine, reproof and instruction in righteousness, and as his testimony was continued, an increasing solemnity spread over the company—oil was poured into wounds, the sincere-hearted encouraged, and the meeting ended under the solemnizing and cementing influence of heavenly love. In the evening, several beside their own little company being present, Christopher was very interesting in conversation; and as the hour of parting for the night drew on, he testified that he then realized some of the prospects which had attended his mind before he left his own home. The Friends assembled were tenderly affected, and somewhat of that unity of spirit and bond of peace, which is not of man, nor of the will of man, but by Divine grace and power, was felt, binding the hearts of some of the company together in a measure of that life in which those of true and living faith are sometimes permitted to know and greet each other. Doubtless, some were present who were enabled to thank their Heavenly helper for his many favors, and to take courage.

After some further labor in Maine, the travellers journeyed southward, holding several meetings, and having acceptable religious service in the families they visited. It was with much interest they noted at Boston, the spot where William Leddra and others of our early Friends laid down their lives for their faithful obedience to their Lord and Saviour, departing from this world with the glorious assurance of a happy immortality. As they passed the meeting-house where Comfort Collins attended meeting many years ago, the remembrance of this faithful minister was brought freshly before them, as an instructive instance of the efficacy of Divine grace. She had been faithful in her day and generation, and lived to a great age. Her mental faculties became so far impaired that she did not even recollect that she ever had a husband, but was still mercifully permitted to retain the savor of spiritual life, and even when near the end of her lengthened pilgrimage upon earth, was qualified to speak of her many mercies, and to exhort her friends in living, impressive and instructive testimony.

Seventh Month 21st.—First-day. Attended Friends' meeting at Nantucket, where a large assemblage collected; under a precious covering Christopher arose, and delivered that which was given him for the people, and it is trusted that many minds were instructed, and many hearts comforted. The afternoon meeting was held at five o'clock, and it was estimated that over six hundred were in attendance. Stillness soon prevailed throughout this large assembly, and it was believed that many were truly gathered into the silence of all flesh, and felt the precious influence of the Heavenly Father's love to extend to them, solemnizing their feelings and increasing their faith. Our dear friend was raised upon his feet, and delivered a large testimony in gospel life and authority; the mourners in Zion were comforted; the fearful in heart were encouraged; the unfaithful were warned; the lukewarm were aroused; and the wanderers were invited to return. His testimony was somewhat close against those who take up carnal weapons, and against those who preach for hire and divine for money; but the power of truth reigned over all opposition, and the meeting closed under the prevalence of solemn and contrited feelings, to the praise of the great Master of assemblies, who evidently had owned it and magnified himself therein.

After leaving Nantucket, Christopher Healy held a number of meetings in New Bedford, Fall River, Newport and other places in that section of country. In these his testimony was often close and plain, clearly pointing out their withered condition to those who wandered from the fold of Christ; yet being delivered in the authority and with the love of the gospel, and mingled with encouragement for those whose faces were turned Zionwards, they were generally acceptable. At one of these meetings, held in a Methodist meeting-house, where Christopher had been led to criticise some of the practices of other professors of Christianity, the minister who usually officiated at the place remarked, that he would be glad if their house could often be occupied in that way. Near the conclusion of his account of this visit, his companion observed, after alluding to the Christian boldness which had marked the public labors of our friend, "Apparently his gospel labors have been very generally, and perhaps universally, well received, much satisfaction therewith has been expressed, and we do not find that he offended any. He has been divinely assisted in his goings forth, and we, his companions, have been comforted in bearing him company."

The last of the meetings held on this journey was held at Westerly, Rhode Island, Eighth Month 18th. The house was crowded, but the audience was quiet and attentive. Christopher was again clothed with gospel life and power, and handed forth that which was given him to distribute in right authority. Several ministers of other denominations were present, and although some plain and close testimony respecting hireling ministry, and to the call to the ministry, went forth to all those whom it might concern, yet it apparently was well received, and may, in the cool of the day, have been remembered, to the instruction in righteousness of some who were present on the interesting occasion.

Eighth Month 20th.—They arrived safely at their own homes. Two months had been occupied in the performance of the visit, and thirteen hundred miles had been traversed. Christopher Healy brought home with him several certificates of the unity of Friends with his labors during this visit.

After Christopher Healy returned from his religious visit to New England, the last distant field of his gospel labors, bringing sheaves of peace with him, and appreciating the favor of a safe return to his comfortable home, he continued diligent in the attendance of the religious meetings for worship and discipline of which he was a member. He visited a neighboring Quarterly Meeting, received his friends cordially at his own dwelling, and made several social visits.

Christopher Healy, as these minutes, with the whole of

19

his memoranda, show, was called to labor extensively in
the cause of his dear Master, whom he ever delighted to
honor: his meat and his drink being—in the expressive
language of conduct—to follow in the obedience which is
of faith, the undeceiving Light of Life. And for others,
the great desire of his heart appeared to be, to bring them
to Christ Jesus,—the ever-living and redeeming power—
the inexhaustible fountain of eternal excellency—the
foundation of many generations.

In his ministry, and in his conversation—in principle
and practice—he was engaged to uphold with faithfulness,
simplicity and zeal, the primitive doctrines of our beloved
Society, which he had early espoused for their purity,
and because of his love to their divine original. He
often dwelt upon our fallen and lost condition as children
of the first Adam, with the gradual and severe, yet indis-
pensable cleansing operation of that baptism which is
declared to be with the Holy Ghost and with fire; as
being that alone which can purify the soul from every
defilement, and restore it to a state of reconciliation and
peace with God. This inward work—the leavening and
thoroughly changing power of Christ's Holy Spirit received and co-operated with in the heart—was much the
theme of his exhortations and ministry. So that truly
may it be said of him, that in his gospel labors both in
public and in the more private circle, he preached not
himself, but Christ Jesus the Lord. Thus Sarah (Lynes)
Grubb, in one of her letters " to a young Friend," writes:
"Just now I recall to mind that Christopher Healy, from
America, told us in the Select Yearly Meeting (London),
in a very impressive manner, to '*let nothing move us from
our steadfastness in Christ Jesus.*'"

An outline of another discourse of his follows, as re-

ported by a Friend in attendance, at an appointed meeting
at Germantown, Seventh Month, 12th, 1846. He arose,
with expressing his thankfulness that he knew and valued
the Holy Scriptures, which were "profitable for doctrine,
for reproof, for correction, for instruction in righteousness: that the man of God may be perfect, thoroughly
furnished unto all good works;" but adverted to the great
necessity there was that we should read them aright and
understandingly. He said he had the account of the
transfiguration of the blessed Saviour brought to his remembrance this afternoon; and he repeated the interesting incidents of the account as given by the apostle:—
when Peter said, "It is good for us to be here," and "let
us build three tabernacles," &c. Christopher thought he
was influenced by the Holy Spirit, but he did not himself
know *why* he thus spoke; saying, "Oh! how beautiful the
instruction conveyed." On the different portions of the
account he very interestingly commented, in his peculiar
and striking manner: Moses, representing the Law; Elias,
whom our Saviour himself declared to be John the
Baptist, the forerunner, typifying the preparatory dispensation with the elementary baptism; and Christ the
Promise—were here together on the Mount, and a bright
cloud overshadowed them. The voice was heard from
the cloud; not, hear *them*—Moses and Elias—but, "*This
is my beloved Son, hear ye him.*" When the disciples
heard it, they fell on their faces and were sore afraid.
And when they lifted up their eyes, they saw no man
save Jesus only. The representatives of the preceding
dispensations were gone, with their rituals and observ-
ances; and Christ only remained. The purer dispensation to which the others led, was brought in.

He showed how, under the Law, it was said, "Thou

shalt love thy neighbor, and hate thine enemy:" but
Christ declared, "I say unto you, love your enemies."—
See, friends, what a change! The very root of wars and
fightings was to be destroyed. Here Christopher briefly
showed the incompatibility of war with Christianity, either
offensive or defensive. Some might say, why if you don't
fight, the enemy might come and overpower us. The
Jews opposed the spread of right things upon the same
ground, saying: "If we let this man alone, all men will
believe on him, and the Romans will come and take away
both our place and nation."

He commented upon the offices of John the Baptist,
"the voice of one crying in the wilderness," and his elementary baptism. He said he thought some people did
not rightly understand the Saviour's words, where he
said, "Among them that are born of women, there hath
not arisen a greater than John the Baptist; notwithstanding, he that is least in the kingdom of heaven is greater
than he." He did not mean to shut him out as a saint
from the kingdom. His work is accomplished, and he
has entered into rest. But the least child in the kingdom
was greater than he. John saw the fading of the legal
dispensation, and warned the Jews no more to say, "We
have Abraham to our father!" and he saw Christ's office
and proclaimed, "Behold the Lamb of God." "I indeed
baptize you with water, but there standeth one among
you, whom ye know not: He shall baptize you with
the Holy Ghost and fire." Ah! they did not know
Christ; they would not receive him! How many are
there now in the same case! Christopher then said he did
not know that there were any here who thought water
baptism necessary to salvation. But what was given him,
he had to speak.

He proceeded to show the insufficiency of putting away the filth of the flesh, and to testify concerning the baptism of the Holy Ghost and its purifying, heart-changing effects, which were necessary to conversion and salvation. Here he quoted the language, "He that believeth and is baptized shall be saved." This was not an historical belief—a mere confession of the name of Christ—but an operative one, having the answer of a good conscience.—The text did not say, *has* believed and *has* been baptized, but it is in the present tense, "*believeth* and *is* baptized." They might have known better, and then fallen away.—He knew there were many, up and down, who held, "once in grace, always in grace," but this was totally at variance with our blessed Saviour's parable of the vine and the branches. "As the branch cannot bear fruit of itself, except it abide in the vine, no more can ye, except ye abide in me. I am the Vine, ye are the branches; he that abideth in me, and I in him, the same bringeth forth much fruit; for without me ye can do nothing. If a man abide not in me, he is cast forth as a branch, and is withered; and men gather them, and cast them into the fire, and they are burned!" Now mark, friends, they had been engrafted into the vine, Christ Jesus, and drew nourishment from it—had been in grace—but they had become withered, fallen away, and fruitless—lost their state of grace. The same effect follows unfaithfulness now. When those who have known something of the Truth, fall away from it, the men of this world gather them unto its associations, and its mixtures, and confusions, and sad is their condition—even that of the unfruitful branches. A feeling address was here briefly made to some who had known better days; upon whom dryness and withering had crept; that they might en-

19*

deavor to know the holy circulation of the sap of life renewed.

He referred to the so-called "ordinances" the bread and wine, &c., and quoted the passages, "The bread of God is He which cometh down from heaven, and giveth life unto the world." "I am the bread of life," &c., and showed that this was no outward bread, and that down to this very day his true disciples feed on him; He was their meat, their sustenance; and He was also their drink, their refreshment. You remember, most of you, what he said to the woman of Samaria, at Jacob's well. Have not most of you read the account? (Though I do fear you don't read the Scriptures as much as you ought to.) And He is still in his faithful followers, a well of water springing up into everlasting life.

He addressed parents, particularly those in younger life, with many little children around them, desiring them to come to Christ themselves, that they might have something to give their dear children. He giveth liberally and upbraideth not.

CHAPTER XVII.

NOTICE OF SOME OF HIS RELIGIOUS COMMUNICATIONS,
AND INCIDENTS RELATED BY HIM.

THE following short extracts of communications by
Christopher Healy, at his own meeting at several different
times, were taken by a Friend present, who informs that
they were all delivered either in or subsequent to the
year 1842.

The first communication by our friend, recorded here,
was in supplication. His sister in the truth, and with
whom he had doubtless often taken sweet counsel, Elizabeth Pitfield, was also present; who, after exhorting those
young in years not to trifle with Omnipotence in rejecting
his offers of grace and mercy, but to be faithful to all of
his requirings; reminding them of the many prayers and
tears that had been offered for the children of godly
parents, was followed by Christopher Healy on the bended
knee; who supplicated on behalf of the same class, as too
ready to take wing and fly away; being loath to give up
the ways of the world. He interceded that the hearts of
these might be opened, and that all might turn unto the
Lord, that so they who sow, and they who reap, might
rejoice together.

The discourses to which allusion has been more particularly made, follow :—

"In our meeting to-day, our beloved friend Christopher
Healy was led to hold forth persuasive counsel, reciting
the words of the Psalmist: 'Oh, my soul, look thou unto
the Lord, for my expectation is from Him!' He brought
to view the necessity of this being the prevailing tendency

of our desires; an   without which we shall never know the excellency of silent waiting. That there is a vast difference between those who feel poor, and weak, and unworthy, and whose expectation is from the Lord; and those who endeavor to worship him in their own will and wisdom, and whose expectation is much from the poor instrument. It is only the humble, dependent, waiting ones, that will come to know the excellency of silent waiting.

"In the meeting for business, our dear friend extended encouragement to us, especially to those young Friends who came a good way to meeting. He thought that they would never repent the sacrifices they make for the sake of attending our religious gatherings; and the more they give up thereto, the more they would love to attend. Stating it as his belief, that whether poverty or sweet peace be their portion when assembled, they would find it good for them that they had been there."

"To-day our dear friend preached a very impressive sermon, and among much instructive testimony, said, 'The righteous shall have tribulations, but the Lord will deliver out of them all.' Holding up to view the necessity of having living faith in the Divine promises, and then tribulations would be borne patiently, and our faith will increase with our trials. There is, he said, but one sure foundation; but one foundation that will stand when all things else fail. And unless we build rightly thereon we cannot be saved. He spoke of the necessity of having faith in that Almighty Power, which a servant of old described in this language: 'The sea saw it and fled. Jordan was driven back. The mountains skipped like rams, and the little hills like lambs. What ailed thee, O thou sea, that thou fleddest? thou Jordan, that thou wast driven back? ye mountains, that ye skipped like rams? and ye little hills, like lambs?' This was the power that gathered our Society from the maxims and customs of the world—from the forms and ceremonies of a lifeless profession—from all will-worship, and from an hireling priesthood. And though many may fall on the right hand and on the left, yet the faithful will be preserved; and he believed that if all our members walked answerable to our high profession, there would be an hundred come unto us, to where there is one now; and we should indeed be as a city set upon a hill, that could not be hid. Our conduct would then speak louder than words; and many would be invited by our example, to come look upon Zion; and to behold Jerusalem a quiet habitation, with none of its stakes broken, nor cords loosed."

"Our meeting just held was an interesting season. Our beloved friend Christopher Healy was favored to hand forth an instructive testimony, in demonstration of the Spirit and of power; quoting the language: 'Remember now thy Creator in the days of thy youth, while the evil days come not, nor the years draw nigh, when thou shalt say, I have no pleasure in them,' and bringing to view the blessed effects of obedience to the Divine will, and the danger of putting off the day of visitation. That we all have need of a mightier power than our own to guide us safely to the realms of peace. He believed that some whose faces had been turned Zionward, felt a little discouraged because their troubles were greater now, than when more careless about spiritual things; but he told us this was nothing new. For while we are pursuing self-gratification, and walking in the way that Satan would have us to go, he troubles us not, but endeavors to make the way smooth and easy. But when we take a stand against him, and turn our faces toward Zion, 'tis then he is aroused to vigorous action, with his assaults, temptations and insinuations, in order to hinder and to turn us from the way that leads to salvation. This keeps us in a state of continual warfare against our soul's enemy. But it is good for us. The watch and the warfare must be maintained, and with weapons that are not carnal, but mighty through God to the pulling down of the strongholds—the strongholds of sin and Satan. He had stood by the bedside of one who acknowledged that he had despised the counsel of the Lord, and had served Satan in almost every respect; and he thought it was the most awful sight he had ever beheld! The soul struggling under the just judgments of the Lord, seemed to be in torment while yet in the body. The poor victim had no hope of pardon and redemption, and ended his days much in this awful condition. Our beloved friend seemed much affected in the contemplation of this lamentable state of human existence; and held it up to view as a solemn warning to us. He upheld the necessity of seeking the Lord while He may be found, and making preparation for the solemn close before the evil days come or the years draw nigh when we shall say, we have no pleasure in them. The Lord will not say to the sincere wrestling seed of Jacob, 'Seek ye my face in vain.' Oh do not any of you despise counsel. He also intimated that there was danger of some falling away who had made a good beginning, and would, unless they were obedient to Divine requirings. Our dear friend also spoke of his own experience, how he had been assailed by the enemy, and had fled to the Lord Jesus for refuge; who pointed him to the strait and narrow way; and as he endeavored to walk therein, had raised him up out of the miry clay, and set his feet upon that rock, which he could declare was the Rock of Ages, even Christ Jesus."

"After a time of solemn silence, our valued friend Christopher Healy arose and stated, that his mind had been exercised almost from his first sitting down in the meeting, in a way comparable to our Saviour's answer to those who spake of the Temple, how it was adorned with goodly stones and gifts. The reply was: 'As for these things which ye behold, the days will come, in the which there shall not be left one stone upon another, that shall not be thrown down.' Now, Friends, these things must be fulfilled spiritually in us, as much as they were fulfilled outwardly: the glory of this world must be stained in our view; our delight in the riches, the fashions, the customs, and whatever is worldly must be thrown down.

"There is too much of a disposition in us to shun the cross. We want to come to the Saviour, and at the same time hold fast to the things of the world. We are convinced that there is no better profession, than the profession of the Society of Friends; and we would love to become religious members, and walk answerably to our high profession, but the cross is in the way. We are not willing to suffer for the Saviour's sake, who himself was a man of sorrows and acquainted with grief. He had met with many while travelling up and down through the land, who were willing to acknowledge that Daniel's God was the only true God; that there is no better profession than ours; and yet they would not live up thereto.

"When the light of the Divine countenance shines upon us, we are almost or quite persuaded to be Christians, and resolve to live in obedience to the Divine will; but when the light is a little obscured, we stumble at the cross and turn away. He queried of some present what was the cause of these things? The cross must be borne, though it may lead us into singularity, and to be despised and rejected by the worldly wise. He did not mean to insinuate that we should make ourselves disagreeable in the eyes of the world, further than to live in obedience to Divine requirings. He had felt it, as plain as he had ever felt any thing outwardly with his hands, that there were those present who had sustained great loss by going on from year to year, and not sufficiently confessing their Saviour before men; and if there had been more faithfulness to their Divine Master's will, there would have been more fathers and mothers in our Israel raised up amongst us, to encourage others to come look upon Zion, the city of our solemnities, not one of its stakes broken, nor cords loosed; and they would have found Him indeed to be their Counsellor; the mighty God; the everlasting Father; the Prince of Peace.

"In allusion to the unalterable necessity of self-denial and the daily cross, he said, he should not marvel so much that so few are disposed to take up the cross, and follow the Captain of their salvation, if their real enjoyments were abridged thereby. But on the contrary the way of the cross is the only way to lasting peace, and the only way in which true enjoyment is to be found even here."

Christopher Healy paid a visit to Friends in the neighborhood of Gwynedd, in the summer of 1847. A family sitting during that visit is thus described by Hannah Williams, late of Plymouth, Pennsylvania, to Jacob and Phebe Roberts, Seventh Month 17th, 1847:—

"He commenced with supposing we all believed that every good gift was from God; that we had nothing but what we had received; that we were entirely dependent; we could save neither 'body nor soul;' that faith was His gift; if we believed there was a way to be saved, it was His gift. So He stripped us of all things, and we saw ourselves standing naked and alone before the great all-seeing Eye. Here he brought in the omniscience of our great Care-taker. His compassion for our helplessness, as we with sincere hearts looked toward him; and when we fell short and did evil, and repented and humbled ourselves, how, oh how He would make the dry ground of the heart springs of water; that instead of the 'thorn' should come up the 'fir tree,' and instead of the 'briar' shall come up the 'myrtle tree:' and it shall be to the Lord for a name, for an everlasting sign that shall not be cut off.'

"The diligent and right attendance of all our religious meetings he encouraged; said that though we might sometimes feel poor and low, yet He would not send empty away those who waited for him in singleness of heart. On the subject of unfaithfulness he said, a little unfaithfulness, and very little too, how quickly it weighs down the scale against the little good we might have done; concluding with, 'Oh Friends, be encouraged! be faithful!'

During the same visit in another opportunity in the same family, Christopher Healy spoke of faith which he seemed to think we had found to be as an anchor, staying the mind in seasons of trials. He then proceeded to describe a ship anchored firmly with the watch on board in a storm; that the watch needed, in an especial manner, to mind the cable, which was fastened to the ship and to the anchor, and held all safe. If that parted, the poor ship would be driven hither and thither at the mercy of the winds and the waves. He dwelt on the importance of the watch having an eye to the cable, to see

20

that it did not part. Christ Jesus was He in whom our anchor, *faith*, was firmly stayed. The other part of the figure it was easy to apply; the ship would ride out all the storms of time safely, only let the 'watch' mind the 'cable.'"

Allusion has heretofore been made in these sketches, to Christopher Healy's conversational talent. This, when with his friends in the private circle, he often exercised to their entertainment and instruction. It is said, Richard Jordan, that wise Israelite, who was also remarkable for this talent, has stated that he felt himself as much under the Divine anointing when pressing religious truths in a conversational or anecdotal way, as when engaged in his public ministrations from the gallery. Christopher Healy also often pressed close home in a lively manner, solid and pertinent truths in his familiar and easy method of communication. He seemed in this as well as other things, to let his "light shine" by giving diligent heed to the precept of the Apostle: "Whether ye eat or drink, or *whatsoever ye do*, do all to the glory of God."

The following incidents, related by him at different times in companies where he was, are inserted here, viz:—

"Upon Christopher's visit to the Southern States, in the year 1824, he found that Elias Hicks had commenced disseminating his unsound views, and that a few in those parts had imbibed them. At one place our friend attended a small Select Meeting. There were not more than about ten present. Christopher said something came over him that he could not get rid of, and so he quoted the expression of the prophet: 'Shut the door, and hold him fast at the door; is not the sound of his master's feet behind him.' When any one believes that there is no devil, no evil spirit other than the natural inclinations of the human heart, whether he is a Friend, or belongs to another denomination, he is ready to deny the divinity of our Saviour. Christ was tempted of the devil, and he could not have been tempted by his own nature, it must have been by an evil spirit. Through this door [of denying the existence of a devil] all infidel principles can come in, even till a man comes, with the fool, to say in his heart, there is no God.'

"After the meeting had dispersed, his companion told him that he had heard one of the Friends present state his opinion in these very words, that there was no devil other than the natural inclinations of the heart. Nothing had been said to Christopher about it, and at the time he felt the impression, he was not aware that any present held such views."

"Fourth Month 15th, 1849.—At the house of a friend, Christopher said, 'I suppose that there are few members of our religious Society now living, who have passed through sorer trials of their faith, or have been plunged into deeper baptisms of suffering than I have been; but,' he added, 'I can now see that it has all been for the best, and that they have been permitted, or perhaps I may say appointed, to purify me more effectually from defilement, and to wean me from the perishing things of this world, and to induce me to seek for consolation where alone it can be truly found. And lastly, that I may sympathize with, and comfort those who are under suffering, with a little of that comfort wherewith I myself have been comforted of God. And I do believe that it is not only my privilege, but my duty also, to do what I can to comfort and encourage my Friends who are under trials and afflictions, by telling them how good Master has been to me, not only in sustaining and supporting me under my many and varied provings and besetments, but in bringing me out from under them in His own appointed time; and when He has seen that it was enough, permitting me and enabling me to sing His praises on the banks of deliverance. Glory be to his ever worthy name therefor!

"I just now remember a time when I was plunged into as deep distress as perhaps I was ever in; and I am willing to tell thee of it, (addressing an individual present) for thy consolation and encouragement. I had been speaking a little in meetings from time to time, as thou hast been, and not without doubts and reasonings from within, and opposing spirits from without, as I suppose thou hast had to encounter. But the cause of my then great trouble was on account of some debts which I had left behind me unpaid, in Rhode Island. I knew that they ought to have been paid long before, but I had never been able to do it, though I had worked early and late, and denied myself almost the necessaries of life in order to do so; yet I had not been able to procure the means. The consideration of these things troubled me very much, for I feared that my creditors would believe that I was dishonest, and that I intended to cheat them out of their just dues, by refusing to pay what I owed. Indeed, I was so much troubled about it, and got so worked up in my mind, that I felt almost confident that a complaint would be sent to our Monthly Meeting against me, and I was really afraid to go to Monthly Meeting lest I should there hear myself charged with being a dishonest man.

"One evening in particular I was brought very low in my mind. I seemed to have got to the very lowest spot that a poor mortal could be plunged into. My wife had gone to bed, and was asleep, but I was afraid to go to bed, and there I sat, or walked about, reduced almost to despair. After a while I thought I would get my Bible, and see if I could not find some comfort in it; or at least if I could not divert my mind from its very distressing thoughts, by reading in that good book. The first passage I read did but increase my distress. I have forgotten what it was, but it plunged me still deeper into misery; and the further I read on, the worse I got, so that I thought I would go distracted if I did not shut up the book. It was then after midnight. I put my Bible away, and concluded to go to bed, expecting nothing else than I would toss and tumble about without sleep till morning. But I think I was not in bed five minutes before I fell asleep; and I seemed to awake as suddenly. I stared around me, and it was broad day, and the sun was shining full in my face.

"We lived then in a log cabin, at the east end of which there was a window of six lights, through which the sun was shining bright and clear as I ever beheld it. I looked round the room. There lay my wife sleeping sweetly by my side, and I could see every thing in the room, looking as natural and in its place as usual. I looked out of the window, and everything there seemed bright and beautiful: the glorious sun seemed to be half way up the sky, shining with its accustomed splendor; and there I lay in bed debating with myself whether it was really day, with the sun half way up to the meridian, or whether it was a vision of light that encompassed me. But whilst I was considering this question, the light faded from my view, and I found myself lying in my bed with the darkness of midnight around me. I then knew that it was either a dream, or else a vision of light from the Lord to comfort my heart, and to bring me out of my sore distress. And blessed be His holy name, who thus did comfort me, and gave me at once faith to believe that He would make bare His holy Arm for my help, and bring me out of my great and sore troubles. Yea, the Sun of righteousness did already shine into my heart, as the sun of this vision of light shone into my face, and lighted up the flame of hope, giving me to believe that He would enlighten my path, and enable me to see of the travail of my soul, and be satisfied therewith. Being thus refreshed and comforted, I fell asleep and slept soundly till morning.

"Next day I wrote to a Friend in Rhode Island, and told him how distressed I had been about my debts, assuring him that I was desirous and anxious to pay them, but that hitherto I had been unable to do so; and I requested him to inform my creditors, that I was striving to earn the means of paying them, and I would send it to them as soon as I could get it, which I hoped to do before long. I soon after received an answer, saying that I might make myself easy about my debts, as all my creditors knew that I was an honest man, and they were willing to wait for the money, until I was able to pay it without distressing myself. Times soon changed for the better with me. I had a pretty good crop of wheat, which I sold, and I parted with some other things: so that I collected a pretty considerable sum of money for me, though not quite enough to pay all I owed; but I sent it to my friend C., desiring him to divide it among my creditors. I soon after received a letter from him, enclosing receipts in full from all my creditors.

"So the Lord helped me out of that difficulty, as I trust He will help thee out of thine; for I know that He will help all his poor distressed children and servants out of their difficulties and trials, if they will but trust in Him, and not cast themselves down as I did, and as the devil tried to tempt the blessed Jesus to do, when the old deceiver quoted Scripture to accomplish his wicked purposes. It is wrong to cast ourselves down, and it is nearly as bad to stay down in the cellar a moment longer than we can help it. A cellar is a cold, damp, and sickly place, and it is equally unwholesome for body or mind. Come up out of it as soon as thou canst, and hold fast the shield of faith; don't cast it away, as though it had never been anointed with oil; for if thou hold on, the Master will bring thee up out of the horrible pit, and out of the miry clay, and set thy feet upon a rock, and establish thy goings; yea, He will put a new song into thy mouth, even praises to our God: yea, He will enable thee to sing a song of deliverance, even one of the holy songs of Zion, to his praise."

"A missionary among the Stockbridge Indians was sadly given to the practice of using compliments. Upon a certain occasion, when Christopher was surrounded by a good many Indians, the missionary indulged himself even more than usual with him, in this way. As Christopher felt his mind drawn to administer a little reproof, he quietly asked him, 'what he would think of a Bible, if he should buy one that had in it Mr. Paul and Mr. Peter, instead of simply Peter or Paul, as our common Bibles call them? Wouldst thou not say, away with it; this is a cheat and a counterfeit: I'll have none of it, because it is not genuine; for I know the Holy Ghost never taught men to write so? Now if holy men of God spake as they were moved by the Holy Ghost in old time, as the Apostle Peter says they did, does the same holy and heavenly Teacher lead thee and others to speak a different language now?'

"The missionary seemed to be very much disconcerted,

but made no reply; and the Indians nodded from one to another an assent to the justice of the rebuke which had been administered."

"After the Second Month Quarterly Meeting (Bucks), Christopher Healy visited his ancient friend Ruth Ely. At the time of parting he took her hand, and said, 'Farewell: Perhaps we may meet again in mutability, and perhaps we may not.' 'It seems lively with me,' said Ruth, 'to say to thee what two valuable Friends said at parting: one said, "We may see each other again;" to which the other replied: "No: when thou comest this way again, I shall be in heaven."' Ruth added, 'I believe I am waiting. I had thought I must go out again; but I believe I am waiting.' Christopher said, after a pause, 'I must tell thee what I once heard a good old Presbyterian say to one who thought he was waiting: "There is no waiting state until the work is done!"' 'Then,' said Ruth, with great solemnity, 'I must see what remains for me to do yet. This has been a very pleasant visit to me. The unity that has always been between us, is not to be broken; neither heights nor depths, nor anything in this world can separate us.'

"After this interview, Ruth Ely paid several visits that were upon her mind, to her own comfort, as well as to that of the visited. She also got out once more to meeting. When, the work being done and the waiting state attained, she was suddenly called home to the joy of her Lord, on the 18th of Third Month, 1851, in the eighty-third year of her age.

"The next time Christopher went that way was to attend her funeral, at which time he intimated he should soon follow her; and about three weeks after, he was taken sick."

CHAPTER XVIII.

LAST ILLNESS AND DEATH.

THE following account is extracted from memoranda kept of his last illness and death:—

"The 8th of Fourth Month, 1851, our dear friend Christopher Healy was taken alarmingly ill; upon which he intimated that it might be his last sickness; and wished it understood that he felt no condemnation, but experienced that scripture verified: 'There is, therefore, now no condemnation to them that are in Christ Jesus, who walk not after the flesh, but after the Spirit.'

"11th.—He said, 'I feel very poorly; but tell all my friends that if I go now, I go well. I feel nothing but peace. All is peace!'

"He manifested solicitude on account of a Friend who called to see him; and exhorted him to be careful that he did not get into the spirit of the world, to the neglect of his religious duties; as some had sorrowfully done.

"A thankful spirit was eminently his; and he appreciated the outward comforts with which he was surrounded; and contrasted them with the destitution of many of his fellow-creatures: repeating the little verse,

'While some poor creatures scarce can tell,' &c.

He said that the accumulation of wealth might have been a snare to him; but that he never sought after great things; and what he had asked for had been abundantly granted. His mind seemed clothed with contentment and gratitude.

"19th.—In the afternoon his articulation became much

obstructed, so that but little could be clearly gathered;
but the following expressions were distinctly understood:
'Our poor shattered Society! But I have done what I
could.' 'All is peace! all is peace!' 'The righteous
shall have living comfort.' 'The living praise the Lord;
the dead cannot praise Him. They may praise him in
the letter; but they cannot praise Him in the Spirit.'
'They that live in the Spirit, must walk in the Spirit.'
'I have a hope, an everlasting hope of being gathered
"where the wicked cease from troubling, and the weary
are at rest." My secret help, my hope, and my salvation
is Christ.'

"20th.—To his wife he said, 'We have lived together
many years in great harmony and unity. I believe that
the time is drawing near when we shall have to part; and
I hope that we shall be favored to meet in a better country. I trust that if I have missed it, it is forgiven me. I
feel no condemnation. I have sometimes felt a desire to
live to see our Society in a better state than it now is; but
I still believe that there will be a remnant preserved, that
will uphold our ancient doctrines, and that without equivocation. There is a disposition in many who profess our
ancient doctrines, to equivocate; and wherever there is
equivocation there will be a going off. I think the number
will be small that will stand; but after that there will be
a gathering.'

"To a Friend who called to see him, he said in substance, 'I am glad thou hast come; and I hope thou wilt be
careful to do what thou findest it thy duty to do. I have
labored a long time in our poor Society, but my labor
has nearly come to a close, and I can say as the apostle
said: "My speech and my preaching were not in the
enticing words of man's wisdom, but in demonstration

of the Spirit and of power."' The Friend, being about
to leave, inquiring what he should tell his friends, he replied, 'Tell them, I love all that love the Truth, and walk
in it; but I cannot have fellowship with those who forsake it.'

"22nd.—'I do not think that I see anything in my way.
All seems well. What a favor to be an inhabitant of
that city that needeth not the light of the sun, nor the
moon to shine in it, for the glory of the Lord doth
lighten it, and the Lamb is the light thereof! Oh! if I
could quietly pass away to that blessed inheritance, how
glad I should be! I hope there is nothing in the way!
"My soul thirsteth for God, for the living God; when
shall I come and appear before him!" "As the hart
panteth after the water-brooks, so panteth my soul after
thee, O God."'

" About noon to-day the accumulation of phlegm in
the throat seemed as though it must produce strangula-
tion; and his friends were apprehensive that the period
of his release had nearly come. In his struggles for life
he said: 'I cannot stand it. I must go! Oh be honest!
Oh be faithful! Joy forevermore appears great!'

"24th.—To-day he remarked: '"Christ knoweth his
own sheep, and his sheep hear his voice, and he leadeth
them out, and goeth before them; and a stranger they
will not follow, but will flee from him, for they know not
the voice of strangers." Poor and unworthy as I am, I
see nothing in my way; and I hope I shall be patient
until it shall please my Divine Master to cut short the
thread of my life—to cut short the work in righteousness.'

" A beloved friend sitting by his bedside, he said, ' We
love each other in the Lord; we have both known the
Truth, and the Truth hath made us free; and if Christ

hath made us free, then are we free indeed!' He
spoke much of the necessity of standing firm in the day
of trial; of standing upon both feet [being firmly planted]
and of the danger of falling if standing but upon one
foot, and said, 'I have borne my testimony faithfully
against unsoundness and innovation, and have never
turned my back in the day of battle.'

"25th.—One of his daughters coming to see him, he expressed his hope that his children would tread in the footsteps of their father; who had been made willing to take
up the cross in early life, which had preserved him from
many snares and temptations. 'Oh! Truth is Truth; it
cannot be divided! As regards our poor Society, I believe there will be a suffering time for the true seed, before
it can reign. Then it may be said: "Therefore I will
allure her, and bring her into the wilderness, and speak
comfortably unto her. And I will give her her vineyards
from thence, and the valley of Achor for a door of hope;
and she shall sing there, as in the days of her youth
and as in the day when she came up out of the land of
Egypt."' He also quoted as the fruit of this: '"Look upon
Zion, the city of our solemnities: thine eyes shall see
Jerusalem a quiet habitation, a tabernacle that shall not
be taken down; not one of the stakes thereof shall ever
be removed, neither shall any of the cords thereof be
broken. But there the glorious Lord will be unto us a
place of broad rivers and streams; wherein shall go no
galley with oars, neither shall gallant ship pass thereby.
For the Lord is our judge, the Lord is our Lawgiver, the
Lord is our king: he will save us."'

"'Oh! if I could now settle away, and go to sleep in
the arms of my beloved Saviour, how glad I should be!
But it is not time yet. His time is the best time, and the

right time. He has brought me through all my trials and temptations, and landed me safe in a well-grounded hope of a happy eternity! What a consolation it is to me; and how glad I am, that I can say at such a time as this, that I feel no condemnation. Everything looks pleasant. Yes, as clear and bright as the light. I have that hope which is as an anchor to the soul both sure and steadfast; and enters into that within the veil, whither our Forerunner hath gone.'

" 'I have no wish to survive the morning. I am ready to leave this troublesome world, to pass through the valley and shadow of death to that city whose inhabitants "shall hunger no more, neither thirst any more, for the Lamb which is in the midst of the throne shall feed them, and lead them unto living fountains of waters, and God shall wipe away all tears from their eyes." As said the apostle, "We have not followed cunningly devised fables, when we made known unto you the coming of our Lord Jesus Christ." I have this to comfort me, that I have always believed the truths of the gospel: that the true gospel is the power of God unto salvation to all them that believe. The angel flew through the midst of heaven having the everlasting gospel to preach. That everlasting gospel was not a book; it was the power of God unto salvation. The angel had no book, but he said with a loud voice, "Fear God, and give glory to Him, and worship Him who made heaven and earth, the sea, and the fountains of waters." The outward account of the gospel is not the gospel.'

" 'I now say as I have often said, Friends speak often one to another; and if we speak right, the Lord will hearken and hear. I don't mean that we should speak often one to another in common conversation, or *about the things of the world,* but about heavenly things; and encourage one another; and endeavor to get into that state in which we will say no evil; and the Lord will hearken and hear; and a book of remembrance will be written for those that fear Him, and that think upon his great and glorious Name.'

" 28th.—His outward sight was very much gone, but in allusion to his inward feelings, he said, ' What a pleasant morning! It is a morning without clouds! Is it so out of doors?' Being answered that it was a bright morning, he responded, ' All seems bright and pleasant with me; and if I could now pass away to the realms of bliss, how glad I should be!'

" Upon taking some water, he remarked, ' It will be but little more water that I shall need *here;* but I believe that I shall shortly partake freely of the waters of life: " He maketh me to lie down in green pastures; He leadeth me beside the still waters." "Though I walk through the valley of the shadow of death, I will fear no evil: for Thou art with me: thy rod and thy staff they comfort me. Thou preparest a table before me in the presence of mine enemies; thou anointest my head with oil; my cup runneth over." '

" He placed a high value upon that unity which subsists between true brethren, baptized by the one Spirit into the one body; and in reference to such unity, repeated the 133d Psalm: ' Behold how good and how pleasant it is for brethren to dwell together in unity; it is like the precious ointment upon the head, that ran down upon the beard, even Aaron's beard; that went down to the skirts of his garments; as the dew of Hermon, and as the dew that descended upon the mountains of

Zion; for there the Lord commanded the blessing, even life forevermore.'

"To a friend who visited him, he said, 'I am glad thou hast come to see me. We are poor things of ourselves; but what an unspeakable mercy if we can only feel that we have no condemnation—that we are in Christ Jesus—the only safe abiding place. The old enemy is a deceiver and murderer; and would discourage us and try to make us believe that there is no such thing as perfection.' 'Oh that our Divine Master would bow the heavens and come down, and put darkness under our feet, and make a way for his travailing seed.'

"Fifth Month, 2nd.—He said: 'I feel the guardian angel of His holy presence to be round about me, to guard and comfort me through the valley and shadow of death. I have done my day's work; and would be glad if I could now pass quietly away to my everlasting inheritance—to the realms of peace, 'where the weary are at rest.'"

"When under great bodily suffering he ejaculated, 'O Lord! be pleased to give me patience to endure unto the end. My pain is very great; and may'st thou be pleased to bless my dear wife, and dear children.' Then addressing these he said: 'But your loss will be my eternal gain; and I hope you will feel it so. My Lord endured great sufferings. He was a man of sorrows and acquainted with grief. You will have to pass through this last dispensation—and oh! be prepared!'

"3rd.—Some Friends from a distance calling to see him, he said, he had been much comforted, and had sweet peace of mind in visiting their part of the vineyard; believing that there were many there that preferred Jerusalem to their chiefest joy; adding, 'and may their num-her increase! Oh, dear Friends, speak often one to another of the good things of the world to come! Keep in the unity! and a blessing will attend you. Give my love to all Friends in that part of the land.' •

"'I have been led much among those not of our Society, and the language has often been sounded in my ear: 'Other sheep I have which are not of this fold; them also I must bring, and they shall hear my voice; and there shall be one fold, and one Shepherd.'"

"4th.—After having been in much bodily distress, he uttered the encouraging language: 'The Lord will bless Zion. He will sanctify Jerusalem. He will make her walls salvation, and her gates praise. The Lord will bless Zion. When he pleases, he will fortify her walls, he will set up her gates! O Lord! the mighty One of Israel! I feel thy comfort, and I rejoice, and sing thy name and thy praises in the land of the living!' 'Unto you that fear my name, shall the Sun of righteousness arise with healing in his wings.' 'This is a great and blessed Supper.'

"Alluding to some who seemed to be departing from our ancient faith, he said: 'I have no unity with those who go in this way. I can only unite with those, and walk with those, that go in the way that the Lord opens and preserves in.' Being dipped into sympathy with the oppressed and struggling seed, he said: 'What will become of the poor little precious flock and family! May their heads be a little anointed with oil. He will anoint their heads with oil!' 'Inquire after the good old ways, and the ancient paths, and shun the paths that lead to evil."

"5th.—Being in great pain, he passed a suffering night, and obtained but little alleviation this morning. But through his protracted sufferings, his soul seemed to be centred on heavenly things, and clothed with devotion, spending much of the night in earnest intercession at the Throne of Grace. His mind was unusually exercised. He prayed fervently for the best interests of his wife, his children, his friends, and all the church of Christ; and, notwithstanding the decay of nature, was, at times, remarkably strengthened with might in the inner man; manifesting abundant evidence that they who have fixed their habitations on the unchangeable Truth, are not forsaken in the time of need, but are supported and sustained in the hour of sore trial and deep distress, when vain is the help of man; and are even enabled to rejoice in tribulation, and sing praises unto their Creator; and that while they are thus established, no divination or enchantment will be suffered to prevail against them, to destroy their holy confidence and well-grounded hope of the attainment of an inheritance, incorruptible, that fadeth not away. The faith of these is no cunningly devised fable, but a sustaining and substantial truth, that is as an anchor to the soul both sure and steadfast; and their light shineth more and more unto the perfect day, until the purified soul is swallowed up in immortality!

"Towards noon his mind seemed to be carried back to the days of his youth, and he expressed his gladness that he had come out from the forms and ceremonies of a lifeless profession, and had been brought into a more spiritual way. He spoke of the great importance of bearing a faithful testimony to the faith once delivered to the saints—to the faith once delivered to our forefathers: of the necessity of great watchfulness, lest hurtful things should take root amongst us, and weaken our faith in the precious doctrines and testimonies that had been given us as a people to bear: 'for,' said he 'it was while men slept that the enemy sowed tares. The good wheat had been sown amongst us, but the enemy also had sowed tares.' He seemed to be much impressed with the great importance of preserving the clean seed unmixed; and rejoiced in the belief, that there were those preserved amongst us, who do bear a faithful testimony against those things which may be compared to the tares.

" He travailed greatly in spirit for the prosperity of Zion. The welfare of our Society seemed almost constantly to be mingled with his best feelings; and his fervent intercessions often arose to the Father of mercies, that it might be preserved upon its ancient foundation; and that He would spare His people, and give not his heritage to reproach.

" Though abundantly favored with an evidence that the Divine Presence is round about him, to sustain and comfort this soul, and with a holy assurance that as he puts off the tabernacle of clay, there will be prepared for him a building of God, a house not made with hands, eternal in the heavens, yet (writeth the author of these notes) it has been with him as with most Zionward travellers, some seasons of poverty of soul have been his allotted portion, doubtless for the further trial of his faith, but not sufficient to shake his confidence in that never-failing Arm of Power that has hitherto sustained him; and which he believed would continue to support him through all his remaining trials, yet sufficient at times to afflict his spirit; and expressions of this kind occasionally were heard: 'My soul is exceeding sorrowful.' 'They have taken away my Lord, and I know not where they have laid him.' 'Pray for me.' But it has seldom been that these feelings have been permitted to cloud his triumphant spirit, and they have soon passed away, and left his mind calm and peaceful in the enjoyment of renewed faith and holy hope and confidence, even as a morning without clouds.

"6th.—He said that his day's work was done, and his peace made; and without manifesting any impatience on account of the protracted period of his earthly pilgrimage, he queried why it was that he was kept here so long, evincing a longing desire to depart when it should please his Divine Master to take him hence; evidently waiting, with holy confidence, for the gracious invitation, 'Enter thou into the joy of thy Lord.'

"He ejaculated: 'O Lord, thou art good and kind to thy truly exercised children! Thou hast been my stay and my staff through my pilgrimage. Be pleased to continue to be to the latest period of my life.' Again: 'O Lord, be pleased to remember thy disobedient and gainsaying children. Make them to know that thou art God; and that they must appear before thy judgment seat to receive the reward of their deeds, let them be good or evil. Every one that will not bow in mercy, must in judgment. Dear friends, fear God and keep his commandments, for this is the whole duty of man. For God shall bring every work into judgment, with every secret thing, whether it be good or whether it be evil.'

"He was often much exercised on account of the low state of our once favored Society; and said it was his unshaken belief, that the testimonies that were given our forefathers to bear, would not be suffered to fall to the ground: but that there would be standard bearers raised up, and watchmen to proclaim the day of the Lord: as said the Prophet formerly, 'I will turn my hand upon thee, and purge away thy dross; and I will restore thy judges as at the first, and thy counsellors as at the beginning:' afterwards, 'Thou shalt be called the City of Righteousness.' Then the song will be, 'Lo, the winter is past, the rain is over and gone, the flowers appear on the earth, the time of the singing of birds is come, and the voice of the turtle is heard in our land.'

"11th.—A disinterested love and living desire for salvation of all souls, it is believed has seldom been more prominent in the experience of any of Zion's children, than in that of our departed Friend. When health and liberty permitted, his labors in the line of religious duty were abundant, beyond the pale of our Society; and as the energies of the outward man became prostrated, and the termination of his earthly existence apparently drew near, still that universal love of souls came up before him, and he supplicated fervently for this generation—for this untoward generation.

"12th.—To a friend who called to see him, he said, 'I love to meet my friends; it generally brings tenderness with it.'

"He spent much of the night in supplication and exercise of soul, but owing to great exhaustion and feebleness of articulation, but little could be gathered, except the frequent naming of his Maker, and a few detached sentences, such as, 'How good'—'how comfortable'—'how sweet'—'His glorious presence'—'I love my friends.'

"16th.—This day about eleven o'clock, our dear friend departed this life. An easy passage was mercifully granted him, his close being calm and peaceful; and his last words, 'Peace, peace!'"

He was in the seventy-eighth year of his age, having been a minister about fifty years.

A concern had long rested on the mind of our beloved

friend to have his remains enclosed in a coffin of very plain and simple appearance; and as his illness progressed, and the solemn period of his departure appeared to be drawing near, the subject revived with increasing weight; and he solemnly enjoined upon his friends the faithful performance of his wishes in this respect: which request was strictly complied with: "Have my coffin made of white pine boards, without stain or color, brass hinges or lining; and have it flat on the top; and let it be laid in the earth without any outside coffin or box." Though the fulfilment of this concern might present to some minds the aspect of needless singularity, yet it evidently felt to our dear friend to be a testimony of very grave importance, which he was conscientiously bound to sustain. He had long mourned over a growing propensity among Friends to exhibit a vain display at funerals; which he believed was gradually leading us away from the becoming simplicity of our forefathers, and introducing us more and more into conformity to the world and its spirit; and he felt religiously engaged that neither his example nor precepts should tend to the promotion of such ends. He also believed that it was not consistent with the will of an all-wise Creator, that there should be any decoration or adorning about the corruptible part, which, in the return of "dust to dust" was to lose all its comeliness; but that strict simplicity was far more becoming the solemn occasion. Considerations such as these, we believe, under the influence of heavenly light, operated upon his mind, and produced a powerful conviction, that there was a necessity laid upon him to bear a faithful testimony against all appearance of pride or ostentation in the preparation of the poor body for the grave.

On the 19th, his remains were interred in Friends'

burying ground at Fallsington, Bucks County, Pennsylvania, attended by a very large collection of Friends and others: after which a solemn meeting was held, and many public testimonies borne to the Christian virtues of the deceased; and to the undoubted assurance that his spirit had been gathered into the fold of everlasting rest.

"Mark the perfect man, and behold the upright, for the end of that man is peace."

INDEX.

PAGE.

www.ingramcontent.com/pod-product-compliance
Lightning Source LLC
Chambersburg PA
CBHW031401020726
47499CB00005B/1469